PENGUIN BOOKS

SUMMER'S LEASE

John Mortimer is a playwright, novelist, and former practicing barrister. During the Second World War he worked with the Crown Film Unit and published several novels before turning to theater. He has written many film scripts as well as stage, radio, and television plays, including *A Voyage Round My Father*, the Rumpole plays—which won him the British Academy of the Year award—and the adaptation of Evelyn Waugh's *Brideshead Revisited*. He is the author of ten collections of Rumpole stories, and two volumes of autobiography, *Clinging to the Wreckage* and *Murderers and Other Friends*. His novels *Summer's Lease*, *Paradise Postponed*, and its sequel, *Titmuss Regained*, have been successful television series. His latest novel is *Dunster*. John Mortimer lives with his wife and two daughters in Oxfordshire, England.

JOHN MORTIMER

Summer's Lease

PENGUIN BOOKS

PENGUIN BOOKS
Published by the Penguin Group
Penguin Books USA Inc.,
375 Hudson Street, New York, New York 10014, U.S.A.
Penguin Books Ltd, 27 Wrights Lane,
London W8 5TZ, England
Penguin Books Australia Ltd, Ringwood,
Victoria, Australia
Penguin Books Canada Ltd, 10 Alcorn Avenue,
Toronto, Ontario, Canada M4V 3B2
Penguin Books (N.Z.) Ltd, 182–190 Wairau Road,
Auckland 10, New Zealand

Penguin Books Ltd, Registered Offices:
Harmondsworth, Middlesex, England

First published in Great Britain by Penguin Books Ltd 1988
Published in the United States of America by
Viking Penguin, a division of Penguin Books USA Inc., 1988
Published in Penguin Books 1989
This edition published in Penguin Books 1991

9   10

A signed first U.S. edition of this book has been privately
printed by The Franklin Library.

LIBRARY OF CONGRESS CATALOGING IN PUBLICATION DATA
Mortimer, John Clifford, 1923–
Summer's lease/John Mortimer.
p.   cm.
ISBN 0 14 01.5827 8
1. Title.
PR6025.07552S8   1989
823'.914—dc19   88-32417

Printed in the United States of America
Set in Ehrhardt

For Judy Astor and Jim Wolfe
who came on the trail to Urbino

And summer's lease hath all too short a date

Shakespeare, Sonnet XVIII

Preparations

CHAPTER ONE

The woman walked round the corner of the house and saw a snake consuming a large Tuscan toad.

The victim was motionless, looking about it only slightly puzzled, blinking, whilst the snake attacked its leg. The toad had the appearance of a fat businessman being done some sexual service by a hard-faced girl on the make and doing his best not to notice. The snake, with its sleek, shiny head and curled body, was long and smartly patterned in grey and black.

The woman, wishing to put an end to this outrage and feeling involved on the side of the toad, picked up a stick. But as she straightened, armed, the nervous snake abandoned its prey and slithered away into the shadows under a fig tree. There it was lost among the wild flowers and in the spring grass. The toad sat on, unafraid, bleeding slightly and blinking into the sun. The woman dropped her stick and stood looking at it, bewildered.

'Mrs Pargeter.' A man came up behind her and she turned towards him. He was dressed in a blue blazer and white trousers as though for some pre-war cruise. The sunlight behind him penetrated the thinness of his ginger hair and polished his scalp. 'Is there anything more I can show you?'

'No, thanks. Nothing more.'

She looked back towards the fig tree and saw that the toad had lumbered off into the tangled garden, perhaps to rejoin its tormentor. 'Do you honestly think,' she asked, standing in front of the stone walls and cool archways of the villa, 'that it'll be suitable?'

'Suitable for what?'

'For children, of course.'

'My dear Mrs Pargeter. You've read the advertisement?'

Read it? She had learnt it by heart. *Villa to let near small Tuscan town. Suit couple, early forties, with three children (females preferred). Recently installed swimming-pool may compensate for sometimes impassable road. Owner suggests preliminary viewing to prevent disappointment or future misunderstandings.*

'Doesn't it say, *Suit couple . . . with three children?*'

'It says that.' She had noticed it particularly.

'I should've thought that was pretty plain.' The man smiled as though that were quite enough on the subject of children. 'I'll be around in the summer to show you the ropes, depend upon it. You'll want to know a source of Gordon's gin, angostura bitters, streaky bacon. All life's little essentials. I can even find potted shrimps when the wind's in the right direction. The *Financial Times* may be a bit of a problem. Hard to come by in Mondano-in-Chianti. I happen to know of a supply in Siena but I'd rather you kept it dark. It's not the sort of knowledge one likes to have spread around.'

'Don't bother.' There was sunshine on her face, an unusual sensation in March, and she felt light-hearted now that the snake and its co-operative victim had withdrawn. 'The *Financial Times* is probably the least of our worries.' And then she added, as casually as possible, 'Grey with sort of black markings. Would that be a grass snake?'

'I don't know. I've never seen one.'

'No grass snakes around here at all?'

'No snakes of any kind,' he said firmly. 'Not as far as I'm concerned. And don't worry, Mrs Pargeter. No scorpions getting into your slippers at night either. Seen all you want to see, have you?'

She looked for the last time. The doves gave up strutting and whitening the old ping-pong table and set off, flapping busily towards the purple hillside. However, their flight was soon aborted and they settled back on the table.

'Yes.' She had seen all she wanted to see.

'Then perhaps you'll run me into Mondano?'

The seat in the rented Fiat was warm under her skirt. The man sat beside her and, after asking her permission, lit one of the thin Havana cigars he happened to know where to come by. His features were regular but he had a distinct cast in one eye, so that he couldn't stare straight at her without looking somewhere else. Apart from that he was rather a handsome man, she thought, if you happened to like that type of thing.

Molly Pargeter's drive down the long, rutted track across the hills to Mondano was part of a journey that had started in her childhood and only reached its present stage when, in the middle of a freezing London January, she read the advertisement in the *Daily Telegraph*: *Villa to let near small Tuscan town.* She had always had, as she would say with that breathless half of a nervous laugh with which she met anyone's emotions including her own, this sort of a 'thing' about Italy. Her father had wanted her to turn out to be something exotic, an actress perhaps, or even, in the camera-obsessed sixties, a model, and he couldn't conceal his disappointment at the growth of a big-boned daughter who seemed without ambition. Her mother spent most of her afternoons resting and Molly's was a lonely childhood. She would kneel on the floor behind the sofa and pull out the tall books of art reproductions. Avoiding those which formed part of her father's collection of naked Indian or Japanese bodies locked together in unusually gymnastic postures, she had, throughout her childhood, stuck to the Italian schools of painting. So she gazed and her finger traced the outlines of nymphs – thinner, higher cheek-boned than she could ever hope to be, garlanded with flowers, stepping barefoot through the forest; and sometimes she saw an exhausted Venus, a hand below her belly, lying in a countryside where oxen were driven and ships set sail on uncharted seas. She had looked seriously at soft-eyed young men, pierced, as often as not, by arrows. At the chilly boarding-school to which her parents sent her in the mistaken belief that she would be less lonely among girls of her own age, the prizes for mathematics – a subject which she didn't particularly care for but which came easily to her – were framed reproductions of the works of Italian painters. Duccios and Signorellis and Martinis hung by her bedside at a time when other girls pinned up Elvis and Cliff or even Paul Anka. Such pictures she always found calming to her nerves and she had no need of the large net which was hung at the top of the staircase, to catch those distracted adolescents who attempted suicide in the converted country house where she received her education.

Villa to let near small Tuscan town Suit couple, early forties, with three children (females preferred).

When she was sixteen, in the age of Gucci shoes and Lambrettas, and being taken by her father on birthday treats to his favourite trattoria in the King's Road (white lavatory tiles and low-slung lights, waiters singing 'O Sole Mio' and her father embarrassingly ordering *'due cannelloni, per favore*, and *molto formaggio* for my daughter'), Molly was conscious of becoming attracted to men with a lot of black hair round the bracelets of their wrist-watches.

She went on a school trip to Tuscany and saw many of the pictures she had known for so long. At first they seemed brighter, smaller and cruder than she had been led to expect by the polite reproductions. Her friend, Rosie Fortinbras, always getting lost between the Pinacoteca and the Duomo in Siena, boasted of having kissed her way round all the waiters in the restaurant in the Piazza del Campo, saving for the last, like a favourite soft creamy centre, little Vittorio with the face of a page-boy in the corner of an Adoration of the Magi. 'Kiss? You can call it kiss if you like. It's a quite different word in Italian.' Rosie whispered *'scopare'* to her as they sat beside each other at a concert in a dark and chilly palace behind the square. 'What's that mean?' 'It means "he ground himself into me", as it says in the book I bought at the airport.' Rosie's further explanation was lost in a burst of Vivaldi and Molly didn't believe her. All the same, the holiday had excited and disturbed her. She never forgot the sound of Italy, brutal as the sunshine on the hard pavements, and the nightly passage of crowds in the Piazza. Sharing a single ice-cream, she and Rosie watched an ever-circulating stage army of lovers arm in arm, young and old, walking very fast as though to give the illusion of purpose. Among them, young men with shining, pointed shoes astride snarling Vespas shouted, '*Ciao, bellissima,*' but usually to someone else. As the years passed, the sights and sounds became less alarming in her memory and she came to think of Italy as the place where she had been happy.

'*Three children*. Why *females preferred*? It sounds a bit fishy.'
'Perhaps they think girls do less damage.'
'Damage?'
'To the furniture.'
'I'm not sure I like the sound of it.' Molly's husband frowned. He looked, as always at the prospect of a new departure, an undertaking likely to cost money, desperate for ways of escape. Although he had no dark hairs growing round his wrist-watch, Hugh Pargeter had, in his youth, the regular features and slightly curled hair of young men who model knitting patterns. He had gone into his father's firm of solicitors where his looks endeared him to wives in divorce cases, although his extreme reluctance to take decisions prevented them obtaining the best results. As a rule he would wait for others – judges, opponents, even his wife – to decide matters of importance. If things turned out well he would quietly take the credit. If not, his brown eyes wore an expression as helpless and martyred as those of Saint Sebastian in the paintings Molly had always admired.

'What do we know of these people? We know nothing of them.' As a lawyer, he had learnt that the safest course was inactivity; if you don't do things, you can't usually be blamed for them. Now he hoped he had found a fatal flaw in his wife's plans and they could, as usual, spend the summer holiday with his mother in Dorset.

'Nothing, until I write to the box number. Of course, I shall get full details.'

Hugh sighed. Once she had written, another decision would have been taken, and he would tell them in the office that they were having a stab at Italy this year, he'd managed to track down a villa in Tuscany. So much of their lives, each of the three children, the house in Kensington Park Road and now, it seemed, their summer holiday, followed inexorably after Molly had made a decision.

It was not only the prospect of Tuscany that had captivated Molly, it was the strange provision about three children, females preferred. Her husband had found this fishy, and perhaps for that reason it filled her with intense curiosity. Her life had not been particularly adventurous and at school, where her friend Rosie Fortinbras courted adventure, she had been regarded as a dull girl and a plodding worker. At night, however, or during the long school holidays, she read detective stories, earning the contempt of her father who told her that his answer to the question 'Who dunnit?' was invariably 'Who cares?' But, indulging a passion more secret than her love for Italian painting, Molly had early gone off with Holmes and Watson in a cab through the pea-souper, or sat on the edge of her chair while Poirot summoned the guests to assemble in the library after tea. She read with great attention, few clues escaped her, and it was with a suppressed little scream of excitement and fear that this large, lonely girl would guess the murderer three or four chapters before the end. She disposed quickly of red herrings, usually sought out the least probable suspect and rarely failed.

So why should anyone advertise their house as being specially suitable for a couple in their *early forties*, *with three children* (*females preferred*)? The fact that she and Hugh happened to fit the bill seemed to give her every opportunity for finding out.

Accumulating the evidence would be an occupation to keep her going whilst she organized her children's lives with Mrs O'Keefe, who came in each day to look after them. Some of it arrived about two weeks after she had written to the box number, in the shape of three typewritten pages. There were also several coloured photographs of the villa 'La Felicità'; all taken from a low angle, so that it seemed to tower against the sky; a place where the owners might appear on the battlements to a flourish of trumpets and a cry of heralds. The swimming-pool, also shot from ground-level, might have been a sizeable lake, only the distant, slightly blurred figure of a man betrayed the scale. There was a photograph of the bedroom in which the bed appeared gargantuan, with a great carved wooden headboard and foot, neatly made, although somebody's sunglasses had been left on the patchwork quilt. There was a picture of the terrace on which meals were taken 'except during thunderstorms' and several of the garden, but none of the kitchen or of the children's accommodation. Each photograph had stamped upon the back the words PRIVATE PROPERTY.

She turned next to the typewritten pages. The work was divided into various sections, the first being headed *General remarks: The villa 'La Felicità' can only be enjoyed by the observance of strict rules and a certain discipline. Most of these rules will be obvious. The wasteful use of the bathrooms, for instance, can turn a summer holiday into a time of intense anxiety and the purchase of water by the lorry load may strain the budget of even the best-heeled family. None of the following devices should, on any account, be switched on at the same time: the immersion heater in the master bathroom, the swimming-pool filter or the dishwashing machine. If a hair-drier is in use, it's generally wise to temporarily disconnect the refrigerator. More detailed instructions will be found taped on the walls over the appliances concerned. Above all, avoid flushing the lavatory next to the small sitting-room more than once in any given half hour or serious results may follow.*

Whose was this voice which Molly found to be both bossy and

patronizing? She turned to the end of the document and saw a signature S. KETTERING over the address of the villa, LA FELICITÀ, MONDANO-IN-CHIANTI, SIENA, ITALY. Probably a Sam and not a Selina Kettering, she thought, and the signs of an absentee male landlord's domination became more pronounced in the final paragraph.

In conclusion, 'La Felicità' has a certain atmosphere and is used to special treatment which we ask you to respect. The house is unaccustomed to the sound of transistor radios or record-players by the pool. There is adequate equipment to play music on the lowest shelf of the bookcase in the small sitting-room. We would also ask you to observe the tradition of dinner on the terrace taking place by candlelight. Those alarmed by insect life should consider holidaying in Skegness.

S. Kettering had gone too far. Why should the children be consumed by mosquitoes and confined to three or four scratched LPs? 'Frank Sinatra Goes down Memory Lane' she imagined or 'The Magic Flute of James Galway', tucked into their disintegrating sleeves on the bottom shelf. And then she read *The villa will appeal in particular to devotees of Italian painting. It makes a perfect centre for the study of the Sienese school. More importantly, perhaps, the work of Piero della Francesca can be followed from the frescos in Arezzo to the pregnant Madonna in the small chapel at Monterchi. Enthusiasts can take the trail to Sansepolcro and on, across the Mountains of the Moon, to see the sublime 'Flagellation' in the Ducal Palace at Urbino, undoubtedly the greatest small picture in the world. Those making this journey should ensure that the stopcock is closed and all electrical appliances switched off before departure. The pleasures of art tend to be diminished by returning to a complete absence of hot bath water.*

Now, in spite of the unsympathetic tone of his letter, S. Kettering had won her. Molly could put up with the mysterious fallibility of the electric devices; she would overcome her husband's reluctance at the prospect of any sort of adventure. She was going, at some time that summer, to follow the Piero della Francesca trail across the Mountains of the Moon to undoubtedly the world's greatest small picture. And if the shadowy Mr Kettering's requirements had some secret explanation, as she suspected, she was going to find it out.

So she wrote to the box number and suggested a date for a preliminary viewing to avoid disappointment or misunderstandings. Everything was working out more easily than she could have hoped.

Leave the Florence–Siena raccordo and follow signs to Conterchi. In Conterchi take the concealed right-turning between the church and the supermercato, then left under the bridge, following signs to S. Pietro in Crespi. In S. Pietro, turn right by the fountain and immediately left, just past the posto di polizia. After two kilometres you will cross a bridge and see a large ilex tree on your right. You are best advised to turn left down the dirt road which provides a short cut (known only to the Kettering family) to Mondano-in-Chianti. In Mondano, turn left again by Signora Fantoni's alimentari (best mozzarella cheese in the district) and immediately double back to the right down a single-track road which will bring you out behind the Castello Crocetto (most reliable source of Chianti). From then on the unmade road (beware of pot-holes) will take you straight to 'La Felicità'.

Further orders, typed and duplicated, lay beside Molly on the empty passenger-seat. In front of her the motorway shimmered in the sun like the sands of a desert. She was in a mood of high excitement, flicking on her indicator light and passing thundering lorries and bucketing Fiats, overloaded with Italian families, with unexpected expertise. She was elated by a further message, not typed this time, but written, apparently in haste, on paper printed with the villa's address. *Will be at the house between two and three on the afternoon of the 12th, getting things ready for the children's holidays. Look forward to meeting you then.* The last document was signed, as always Ś. KETTERING.

This almost welcoming message kept her going down the *raccordo* to Siena. After she'd turned off, she became tired and nervous. She drove slowly in Conterchi so as not to miss the turning and Italians hooted at her or raised their fingers in gestures she knew to be obscene. Once, knowing she couldn't be heard, she shouted back and was conscious of looking like a pinkish, fair-haired and flustered fish with its mouth moving silently behind glass. Her hands sweated and soaked the steering-wheel. In San Pietro she drove fast to avoid abuse, missed the road by the police station and had to do a U-turn to obey her directions. As her anxiety grew the small towns and villages looked grey and inhospitable. Steel shutters barricaded most of the shops and those that were open displayed only a few boxes of tired vegetables and strings of plastic toys. In Mondano-in-Chianti three old men, busily engaged in sitting on a wall beside the petrol pumps, seemed to jeer at her and a child threw a small stone which rattled against her car bonnet.

She had doubts about the road but then found herself driving along the grey fortress walls of what she hoped might be the Castello Crocetto. At its gates a tall woman leading a Borzoi dog viewed her passing with disdain. And then she dived and rattled down the dirt-track which seemed to go on for ever across an empty hillside. As the insects met a sticky death on her windscreen and brambles and gorse bushes clawed at the bright sides of her hired Fiat, she wondered if she should have stayed at home and if she would ever, in fact, see 'La Felicità'.

Suddenly she did. The track had climbed, twisted, rocked her in its pot-holes and then swept down in a flurry of loose stones and flying dust, to a house gradually lit, theatrically, as the sun returned from behind a stray afternoon cloud. Her first thought was that the photographs hadn't lied. The place looked fortified, not as a grim walled castle but impregnable all the same, with thick walls and, in the centre of the square, unornamented two-storey building, a stocky tower from which arrows or muskets might have been shot or red-hot ploughshares hurled down on invaders. The iron-studded door in the central archway looked impervious to battering-rams, but above it, behind a line of similar arches, was the big open terrace on which S. Kettering expected the family to dine – an instruction, Molly thought, which it would be no particular hardship to follow. Three great stone pots contained geraniums which trailed down to the walls beneath them, softening the stern appearance of the house.

In the centre of a pavement leading to the front door was a well head with an ornate ironwork structure over it. She had no idea of the age of 'La Felicità' but such houses had stood on the white furrowed hillsides in the pictures she knew by heart. She felt then that S. Kettering's almost military orders were appropriate and added to the feeling of security about the place.

She parked under a straw-covered shelter and got out slowly, still vibrating. The silence was underlined by the drumming of grasshoppers and she noticed that there was no other car which might have brought S. Kettering. The door she tried was unyielding; the bell she pulled echoed inside some shuttered hallway but nobody answered. Her confidence, which had returned on her first view of the house, once more ebbed. She wanted to pee and she walked round the house in search of a bush.

It was there that she saw the man lying on the plastic strips of an off-white metal reclining chair beside the pool, which was undoubtedly smaller than it had looked in the photograph. His straw hat was balanced on his forehead, his jacket lay folded on the concrete beside him, and she noticed that he wore balding suede shoes and some form of club or regimental tie.

'You've arrived.' He opened one eye and said, 'You must be a practical sort of person.'

'The directions were brilliant, actually.' She knew she sounded effusive but she remembered the lordliness of S. Kettering's style and wished to propitiate him.

'Some people,' he told her, 'get horribly lost in Conterchi.'

'Poor them!' She wanted to assure him that she wasn't that kind of idiot.

'So you drove here straight from Pisa?'

'Yes.' All the bushes she could see were small and scrubby and

she couldn't find an excuse to leave S. Kettering and double back
to the front of the house.

'Then you'll want to use the facilities.' He stood up smartly
and she followed him with gratitude as he took from his pocket a
large bunch of keys, from each of which dangled a carefully written
label.

*The chain requires one sharp downward pull. Don't be tentative or
give repeated tugs which achieve nothing.* So read the notice in the
particular facility to which he led her. She pulled sharply and was
rewarded. She rejoined the man, embarrassed by the sound of the
cascade behind her.

'Managed it first go.' He smiled at her. 'Unusually masterful.'

'This' – she held the fluttering pages of description in her
hand – 'must be the small sitting-room.' The room was lit by a
shaft of sunlight from the single open shutter. The furniture
seemed large and dark, pieces designed for a grander room.
'What's this used for?'

'For anything, I imagine, that you have a mind to. The big
sitting-room's downstairs. Converted from the cowsheds. You
could do anything in there. Get up a musical comedy.'

'Is that what you do?'

'Good heavens, no.' He looked at her as though it was she who
had made the unusual suggestion. 'That's not my style of thing at
all.'

'And the children's bedrooms?'

'Top floor, I should think. I haven't much personal experience.
Not of where children sleep.'

'I should like to see them, please.'

'I suppose, if you're really keen on it.'

'I've come all this way . . .' she smiled.

'And so you have. I'm here to help you. Absolutely all I can.'
He led her quickly up a staircase which began by being broad and
stone and went on up to twist woodenly to the top of the tower.
She followed the short-back-and-sides hair-cut of this curious S.
Kettering, who, apparently, never said good-night to his
children.

'How many have you got?' The rooms he opened for her had few signs of childish occupation. There were some rows of books, bright bed-covers and cushions, some reproductions such as she had once had of Italian paintings. There were no photographs, posters, record-players, piles of clothing from Oxfam shops, drawings pinned to the wall – nothing much to indicate children at all.

'Myself, absolutely none,' the man told her. 'It's been the experience of my chums that offspring break up marriages. Mother gets wrapped up in the kids and the poor old husband gets left on his ownio.'

'But you said you'd be here getting things ready for the children's holidays : . .'

'Checking up, yes. Seeing that nothing's drowned in the pool recently.' The man looked at her with sudden amusement as a penny dropped. 'You hadn't taken me for Kettering?' He laughed at her confusion. 'I'm not Kettering, or anywhere near it. The name's Fosdyke. William Fosdyke. I'm cursed with living in Mondano all the year round, all through the rains of January and Feb. So I do things for chaps from the U.K. Keep an eye on their properties. And the like.'

Of course, she told herself, she should have known at once that he wasn't Kettering. Kettering would have been a less accessible and more commanding presence.

'No, I'm certainly not him,' Fosdyke went on, garrulous after her mistake had been discovered. 'Wish I were sometimes. Lucky fellow, Kettering. He's got 'La Felicità', of course. And his marriage; that's something I miss. Mrs K. thinks the world of Kettering. One hundred per cent devotion. Kettering, not to put too fine a point on it, is the apple of her eye.' They stood in the single child's bedroom and Molly joined in a short, silent tribute to the Kettering's marriage, whilst some large, blundering insect bumped against a window that had been long closed.

'I lost my wife,' Fosdyke told her. 'Many years ago.'

'I'm sorry.'

'Oh, that's all right. I mean literally lost her. We went shopping in Brighton. We arranged to meet at twelve-thirty under the clock. She never showed up. Missing, believed to have scarpered with the manager of Boots. Women are curious creatures. Nothing personal, Mrs Pargeter.'

She did her best to become businesslike. 'I think this will do splendidly for our three.' She crossed to the window and looked down to where the pool sparkled in the early sunshine.

'Got snaps of them, have you?' Mr Fosdyke asked her.

'What?'

'I'll bet you carry snaps of your young. I know Mrs Kettering does. I'd feel very privileged if you'd let me see them.'

So she opened her handbag and produced for the man with the scarpered wife a selection, some faded a little and creased with age. Although mistrusting children, he showed an absorbed interest as he took the photographs and gazed at Henrietta (fourteen), Samantha (just ten) and the baby Jacqueline (now three and born after a long period during which Hugh had displayed a lack of interest in physical contact). As soon as Fosdyke had taken the pictures, she felt that she had shown him too much of her private life and put out her hand to receive them back.

'Fine little family,' he said, releasing them. 'They look as though they'd fit in jolly well at "La Felicità".'

'I think,' Molly said firmly, 'I'd like to have one more look round. By myself this time.'

'Of course. Be my guest. Or rather' – he stood with one hand in his blazer pocket, squinting only a little – 'the guest of Mr Kettering.'

When she looked round the house on her own, it seemed more impressive. The big downstairs room might have been a converted cowshed, but when she opened the tall shutters and the sunlight poured in, it looked more like a state apartment. At one end there was a platform with a piano on it, so Fosdyke might, for all she knew, have been right about the musical comedies. The kitchen was a huge stone cavern with an open fireplace, the size of a small room, beside which logs were piled so that she could see herself (but certainly not Hugh) barbecueing thick steaks on an iron grill, turning them over with tongs the size of a medieval weapon. In the bedroom cupboard, scented with lavender, a man's shirt and a woman's white skirt swung among the empty coat-hangers. None of the drawers was locked; all of them were empty. Looking around the bedroom, she saw that it was almost exactly as it had been in the photograph, although now there was a book open and face downwards on the patchwork quilt. She wondered who had been reading so recently on the carefully made bed, or if this fat book, which she now saw to be a collection of Sherlock Holmes stories, were a relic of the past summer, and the maid, or whoever cleared the house, was devotedly keeping her employer's place. She also left the book undisturbed but felt, as soon as she saw the title, a further fellow feeling with S. Kettering.

Her inspection of the bedroom finished, she walked down the staircase into the coolness of the stone-flagged hallway. A large collection of sun-hats hung on pegs in the entrance hall, bowls were filled with dried lavender and a huge pottery jar was crammed with walking-sticks, some of which had ornate silver handles. By the time she reached the front door the house, she knew, had to be hers for the summer. If it had a secret she would do her best to discover it and she was not going to miss the trail across the Mountains of the Moon to what was undoubtedly the greatest small picture in the world.

Molly Pargeter, a woman of forty, whose hair was kept in place with difficulty, might have looked like one of the larger Graces in the paintings she admired had not her size caused her such embarrassment that she lowered her head and stooped a little as she walked. She was a woman of mixed awkwardness and determination. Now dressed in striped cotton with sensible shoes and a cardigan, she stepped into the sunshine and walked round the corner of the house. And there she caught a snake consuming a large Tuscan toad.

As she drove William Fosdyke back to Mondano he assured

her that he would be always at her disposal and could guarantee to make her family holiday a success. 'You know what the Brits in this part of Tuscany call me?' he asked her. 'Signor Fixit. They know they can rely on me, you see. And I must say that gives me a great pleasure.'

She left him in front of a café and as she drove away to follow the complex instructions back to the *raccordo* she saw him in her mirror, standing with his hand still raised in the sort of military salute with which he'd taken his leave of her.

'You really liked the place?'

'Of course. I loved it.'

'Can we afford it?'

'I can afford it,' she assured him. A legacy from a great-aunt had bought their house and provided her with a small income. She was free to dream of paintings and detective stories.

'No drawbacks?' Hugh's voice betrayed his disappointment.

'Absolutely no drawbacks whatever. Of course, we must be careful to see that the children wear shoes.'

'Shoes?' He sounded more hopeful. 'Why shoes?'

'Prickles in the grass. Things like that. It's really all very wild. But beautiful.'

She didn't tell him about the snake. Had she done so, he might have had a reason to object to the holiday and a great deal of trouble would have been saved.

CHAPTER TWO

'I hear you're going to take that house in Italy.' The elderly voice, half a challenge and half a tease, came down the telephone to Molly as she was in the middle of giving Jacqueline her supper. She popped a toast soldier into her own mouth to give herself the strength to deal with her father.

'I called you earlier. Sam answered, she seemed to be alone in the house . . .'

'She wasn't alone. Mrs O'Keefe was here.'

'"And Gamps," Sam said. "You'll never guess. We rented this unbelievable posh villa." How pleasant it is to have money, heigh ho! Of course, I could never have your patience and study the stock exchange prices, Molly Coddle. I'd far rather do something exciting, like sit here and watch my fingernails grow.'

Not for the first time she wondered how on earth her father had persuaded the children to call him 'Gamps' and decided that he had done it for the sole purpose of driving her mad. With the same end in view, no doubt, he called her 'Molly Coddle' – a name he had never thought to use when she was a child – and he insisted on changing the sex of his grandchildren so that Henrietta became Henry or Hal, Samantha was naturally Sam, and the three-year-old Jacqueline 'Jack the Lad'. So far as her father was concerned, Molly didn't know what to call him. She had never responded to his embarrassing invitation, made to her during the permissive sixties, to use 'Haverford', his Christian name. Now that he was in his mid-seventies he signed his rare letters to her

'Daddy' or even 'Pops'. When they spoke she did her best to avoid calling him anything.

'That was my toast soldier and you took it,' said Jacqueline.

'I've been brushing up on my Italian,' Molly's father went on, 'with the aid of an extremely sexy-sounding signorina I got on a tape from the Fulham Public Library. We have spent some passionate evenings together changing traveller's cheques and looking for medicine to cure stomach disorders. Each night I try to memorize a spot of Dante. I have it in English down one side of the page and in Italian on the other.'

'It was mine!' The child's voice rose in righteous indignation as Molly bit desperately into another toast soldier.

'Oh, shut up,' Molly said, 'and don't be so selfish.'

'Selfish?' Her father's voice protested. 'I haven't said a single word about joining you in Italy.'

'I was talking to Jacqueline.' She restrained herself from pinching another soldier. She always found the supper she cooked for the children irresistible and when she gave them bacon and baked beans she would swoop down on their plates like a vulture on a battlefield. She didn't like herself for it. 'I wasn't talking to you, of course.'

'As a matter of fact, I had taken it for granted that you wouldn't want a boring old fart like me trailing after you round Siena.'

'I never said that. You know I never did.' She resented the guilt she felt because the thought had crossed her mind.

'Believe it or not, Molly Coddle, I rang up quite simply to wish you *arrivederci*.'

'It's not until August. We shan't be going until then.'

'And where shall I be in August? Set out on the Great Package Tour of the Skies.' It was her father's habit to refer to his approaching death as a sort of cosmic joke. 'I suppose I might have liked one last lunch in the Piazza del Campo.'

'Don't do that, please!' Mollie shouted. Jacqueline, starved of toast soldiers, had slid from her chair and, having circled the table, was starting to de-gut the loaf of bread.

'Don't do what?' the old voice crackled down the telephone. 'I suppose you're accusing me of trying to manipulate you.'

'I never said that.'

'I'm not manipulating you at all. I'm merely stating facts. I shall not be with you much longer and I may well not see Italy again.'

'I told you. I'm busy. It's Jacky's tea-time.'

'What a full, rich life you lead! Could you just look in your diary. Let me know when it's not bath-night and you can have a few minutes chat with your aged Pops.'

'I've got to go now.' She meant it.

'Don't sound so *serious*. You know me better than that, don't you? I was only teasing. Only having that quaint old thing, a *joke*. So out of fashion nowadays. I shall be perfectly happy at home this summer, having a very meaningful relationship with Signorina Berlitz. You know old Nancy Leadbetter lives the spit of an olive stone from Mondano? Remind me to kit you out with a letter of introduction . . .'

'Please! Leave the bread alone!'

'Of course, if I were with you, Nancy would have us all over to dinner.'

He rang off then, before she had a chance to reply. As Molly put down the telephone, she saw Jacqueline, her mouth full of dough, staring at her with the large, accusing eyes of an Oxfam poster.

Molly's father awoke the next morning with a start, a dry mouth and an erection for which he had no need. His first feeling as he emerged from the short but deep sleep which came to him at the end of every restless night, was that he was bloody glad to be alive. But then why, as he lay there pink and rested in his striped Viyella pyjamas feeling no older and certainly very little wiser than he had when he used to open his eyes in his prep school dormitory over sixty-five years ago, should he not be alive and kicking? The answer came in a sudden cramp in his left leg which caused him to roll out of bed yelling as though the flat were on fire and stamp away to the bathroom as the bones and muscles slowly settled into a position to cause him only moderate discomfort. What had he to look forward to during the day ahead? What girls could he telephone? What gossip might he learn in the old Nell Gwyn pub down the end of the King's Road? Above all, what mischief might he get up to? He considered the matter as he might have done when he was only half a century old in what he still called the 'swinging' sixties, when lunch for two might be had at Alvaro's for a five pound note and his column 'Jottings' by Haverford Downs in the weekly *Informer* had been described on the wireless as 'Max Beerbohm with a social conscience'. This was an assessment with which Haverford, in all humility, felt bound to agree. It might not be a bad day. He could call in at the *Informer* office in Chancery Lane and use the telephone to arrange a suitably stimulating lunch. And then he caught sight in the bathroom mirror of the collapsed features, the swollen neck and ragged grey hair of the old man upon whom he still looked as a stranger. He also remembered with a sense of humiliation and disgust that the pages of the *Informer* were now given over to articles on gay rights, the 'politics of feminism' and peer pressure towards glue-sniffing in the inner cities. 'Jottings' had not quite been pushed overboard; it was clinging by its fingernails to the edge of the raft, to be found, often seriously cut, between the competition and the personal column at the back of the paper.

The feeling of gloom persisted as he bathed and dressed slowly, having particular difficulty with his socks. He made many a false attempt, standing on one leg tottering like an overweight stork before he could trap a dangling foot and pull the wool over it. And then, when both feet were clothed and he sank into a chair exhausted, he suddenly remembered Italy and felt cheered. In the end Molly would have to take him. She owed that to him at least for having been, over the years, such a disappointment to her father. And if he could put up with humourless Hugh for three weeks in the sun, the family, who couldn't have many jokes to look forward to, would be glad of a running commentary on their holiday by the well-known author of 'Jottings'.

It was not that he had never loved his only child. She was a girl, which greatly predisposed him towards her. When she was two years old she had seemed to be of a cheerful disposition and laughed obediently when he made a witch out of his knotted handkerchief or cast a swan's shadow against her bedroom wall with his fingers. Molly's mother, married for her beauty, had turned out to be a solemn and conventional woman, alternately angry and exhausted. He and his daughter, he imagined, would form an alliance based on shared jokes and secret indulgences against a lonely and often disapproving wife. But then Molly grew up to be serious and, what was worse, she grew up to be big. As some girls suddenly look too tall to be ballet dancers, she became too large for her father's devotion, for Haverford always preferred smallish women with what he had once described in one of his more personal 'Jottings' as the 'tip-tilted noses of impertinent page-boys.' And then, as a schoolgirl, Molly had further distanced herself from him by being good at mathematics. After he had separated from her mother and when she was away at boarding-school, he would drive down to visit her, often accompanied by some rather mature page-boy in jeans or a mini-skirt and Molly would sit with them in silence at an endless tea in the local Trusthouse Forte. 'The young have become so puritanical,' Haverford would explain to his companion on the way home. 'I get to feel more and more like some splendid Regency buck surviving sadly into the horrible reign of Prince Albert the Good.'

To do Haverford justice, he wasn't altogether happy about his lack of rapport with his daughter; at times he came as near as he ever could to feeling guilty about it. He had therefore decided to be as charming as possible to her during the summer holiday in Italy – as soon as he had managed to persuade her to let him join the family there. Meanwhile, he shuffled off towards the tube station and Chancery Lane.

The girl behind the desk in the untidy and cluttered reception area of the *Informer*, sitting below a poster protesting about Eskimo rights and an original cartoon showing the American President as an ageing cowboy astride a Cruise missile, had certain page-boy qualities, although her tip-tilted nose supported a pair of granny glasses and she was working hard at her chewing-gum. Haverford Downs, dressed now in a tweed jacket, grey flannels and a white polo-necked sweater, holding an ivory-topped walking-stick in a plump hand on which a single green-stoned ring – alleged by him in his wilder moments to have been worn by Aubrey Beardsley – winked malevolently, gave her his full septuagenarian charm.

'How are you, darling?'

'Was you wanting something?'

'Only to lay my "Jottings" on you, my dear.' He reverently produced two folded typewritten pages from an inside pocket. 'I deal this week with the innate puritanism of the young. Although you look far too pretty to suffer from the present malaise, you might find it means something to your generation.'

'What was the name again?'

'You're joking!'

'I'm meant to ask all the names like.' The girl, on a youth training scheme, was waiting sullenly for an opening in a hair-dresser's.

'Haverford Downs, my dear. And I think you might remember that my "Jottings" have been in the paper since long before your grandmother had her first G.I. in the War. I'll take it through to the Editor.'

'I think he's just slipped out,' the girl said, as she had been instructed to do if ever Mr Downs presented himself. At which moment, the Editor, a young man from Glasgow, who seemed to bear on his narrow shoulders guilt for all the sins of the Western world, emerged from his office and was off to lunch with a left-wing Labour M.P. in the Gay Hussar. He moved towards the door with his head down but Haverford laid an ancient mariner's hand on his arm and detained him.

'The "Jottings", Stuart. I have an idea for the "Jottings".'

'Oh, yes?' said Stuart, the Editor. 'We'll have to give the future of your column some thought. Considerations of space, you know, and the advertising ratio . . .' In fact, he would have elbowed the 'Jottings' long ago had not the Chairman of his Board reminded him that Nye Bevan had once found them 'bloody civilized'.

'How would you like, my dear boy' – Haverford appeared to be offering his Editor a unique opportunity – ' "Jottings" from Italy this summer?'

'Random thoughts on Botticelli? Not for us, I'm afraid.'

'The hell with Botticelli.' Haverford, moving forward in a conspiratorial manner, almost had to stand on tip-toes to reach the ear of the pale Scot. 'I thought more of pieces on the lines of "Whither Euro-Communism?", "The Scandal of the Vatican Banks", "The Common Market and the Black Economy", "Child Prostitution" . . . He ended hopefully – "On the Appian Way"?'

Haverford was not entirely a fool. He knew his market and the Editor appeared partially hooked. 'We couldn't possibly pay your travelling expenses though.'

'Of course you won't have to. Have no fear.' Haverford reached up and put a hand on the young man's shoulder. 'It won't cost you a penny, you dear old thing. Except, of course, for my usual modest fee.'

Before he was allowed to escape, the Editor had muttered his agreement, and his heartfelt wish to supplant the 'Jottings' with a regular feature on ethnic cooking, written by his live-in companion, was once again postponed.

'We're trying Italy this year. Managed to find a villa for the children's holidays.'

'Oh, I know about them. School holidays are when all the men suddenly disappear.' The woman having lunch with Hugh Pargeter opened her eyes to an almost impossible extent. 'I'm going to get desperately hungry in August.' Her name was Mrs Tobias and Hugh had met her when he handled her divorce case, successfully, because Mr Tobias had made a determined rush for freedom, scattering alimony lavishly as he went. Now their lunches were a regular event to which Hugh looked forward with a certain amount of trepidation. Mrs Tobias was kept thin by regular visits to Forest Mere and she dressed expensively. To Hugh she seemed beautiful and he delighted, somewhat guiltily, in having her eat opposite him. When not at Forest Mere, her appetite was more than usually healthy.

'Do you have to go?'

'Oh yes.' He gave her one of his martyred looks. 'I can't disappoint the children, you know. Anyway, I have organized this holiday.' In fact he had worried about it so much that he felt now that he had done it all.

'Is it a nice house?'

'Oh, I think so. Actually I sent my wife to check up on it. You can't be too careful.'

'You didn't take a look?'

'I've been rather too busy here.' He frowned, wondering whether they could recoup the entire cost of the holiday by letting the house in London to an American. But Americans had been rather thin on the ground lately, fearing such Libyan terrorists as might haunt the dark streets round Notting Hill Gate.

'If you're so busy can't you tell her that you've got to stay here? Then we could still have lunch.'

'Of course, I'd love to. But I'm afraid I'm fully committed.' He looked noble, as though he were saying goodbye before catching a troop ship to almost certain death on some foreign front. Indeed he treated his children's holidays and an uninterrupted period of married life as a stern duty for which he was prepared to make the supreme sacrifice. In this solemn moment they both gazed abstractedly at the sweet trolley. 'I'm sorry!'

'Oh, that's all right.' She also was looking brave at the prospect of three weeks in the summer without their regular Thursday table at the 'Dolce Vita' near his office in the City. 'A girl learns to get used to school holidays.'

'I really am sorry,' he repeated and wondered why it was that these lunches, designed as an escape from responsibility, had begun to weigh on him with the weariness of marriage itself.

'Not your fault.' She was giving her doe-eyed look to a pile of profiteroles. 'At least I can indulge myself when you've gone.'

'Actually, I hope you don't.'

'Indulge in dessert?'

'Oh, pudding,' he said. 'I shan't worry about pudding.'

'Just as well.' Marcia Tobias was now disposing of a plateful of chocolate-coated balls with discreet efficiency. To his mind, she represented the sort of rare treat to which he was entitled, sixteen years after he married Molly. Or rather, he often thought, Molly had married him. He had been carried along by his wife's extraordinary power of making decisions, from the time when she had walked into the offices of Glebe and Pargeter, when his old father was alive, and told him that her great-aunt had left her some money and she had decided to invest it in a London house.

At the end of the protracted negotiations with her great-aunt's executors, and the vendor's solicitors, Hugh and Molly had been out to several dinners in bistros, for which she insisted she paid her share. He arranged bridging-loans and a mortgage to make up the price of the tall house with the basement into which she had decided he should move as a lodger, abandoning his awful little bed-sit in Chepstow Road.

Since then, looking back on it, there had been too many children's holidays and not nearly as many lunches with girls in the 'Dolce Vita' as a man deserved.

'Good grief!' Mrs Tobias turned her wrist which was fettered with a thin and glittering watch. 'Such a load of things to do. It's impossible.' In fact she had a heavy date with a lady who undertook to slim thighs with ultra-sound.

'But we'll meet again before you go?' She smiled at him over the table napkin, which was removing a minute trace of prof-iterole.

'Of course we will. Thursday week?'

She nodded. 'And you'll send me hundreds of postcards from Italy?'

'I promise.' He felt safe, now lunch was over, to put his hand consolingly on hers.

So they left the restaurant and Hugh got a taxi for Mrs Tobias before he walked back to his office. As they parted, she pursed her lips and lifted her well-attended face, which didn't look quite so young as it had in the restaurant. Hugh gave her its regular after-lunch kiss, and as he did so he saw, out of the corner of his wary eye, the extremely unwelcome figure of his father-in-law coming down Chancery Lane, carrying a walking-stick and an armful of newspapers. Hugh urged Mrs Tobias into her taxi and walked off smartly in the opposite direction.

'*Three* weeks! You mean three whole weeks?' Henrietta's voice mounted tragically. She looked at Molly as though she had just sentenced her to a lengthy and quite undeserved term of imprisonment.

'Three weeks in Italy. In the sun.' The kitchen table was covered with homework, dictionaries, ring notebooks and 'All you Need to Know about the Russian Revolution' pulled out of the huge pieces of luggage Henrietta took every day to school, books used to erect tottering towers wherever the family was next about to eat.

'Honestly! I don't believe this. I simply can't believe you'd do it to me!' Her daughter's outrage had turned to half-amused incredulity. Where had the long silences gone, Molly wondered, into which she used to retreat in the company of her parents?

'Do what to you?'

'In *August*!'

'Yes.'

'Don't you remember *anything*?' Henrietta started to explain patiently, as though to a child. 'That's when *both* parties are – and the Ball at Hurlingham – and when we were all going to the

Muckrakers Club for a really good evening. And then we were
going to have a day shopping in Ken. High Street and sleep at
Rachel Koo's flat. And I told you Mrs Koo knows all about it.'

'Sorry. We're going to Italy.'

'You really enjoy that, don't you?' Henrietta gave her well-
known hollow laugh. 'You revel in disappointing somebody.'

'Don't be ridiculous, Henrietta. We'll have fun.'

'Can't you all have fun while I stay here?'

'On your own?'

'Rachel Koo would come over.'

'You're not staying here without us.'

'Why not?'

'You know why not.'

'Because I'd shoot up drugs or have parties and get drunk and
sleep with boys? Thank you very much. It's nice to know you
think your daughter's a raving drug addict and a tart. That really
cheers me up!'

'Of course I don't think that.'

'Oh yes, you do. To you I'm just someone who can't be left in
your house alone.'

It was the point at which her mother usually said, 'You *are*
only fourteen,' – an undeniable truth which Molly decided to
save for the endless discussions on the subject which would be
bound to occur in the weeks to come. Of course she couldn't
leave Henrietta alone in the house, the tall building she had
bought with great-aunt Dorothy's money. And it was here, after
the house-warming party which began with hours of few arrivals
and long silences, that she and Hugh had finished what was left
of the Carafino and found themselves in the narrow bed in the
basement where this dramatically argumentative child had been
conceived. She couldn't leave her there alone; she would be safer
with them in Italy.

Her husband came home then and found them quarrelling,
engaged in a power struggle in which he felt he had no place.
Three-year-old Jacqueline ran at him and grasped his knees; he

put down his briefcase and lifted her in his arms, flattered by her attention. Later he said, 'Your father called me in the office.'

'I wish he wouldn't do things like that.'

'It seems his paper's asked him to write a series of articles from Italy. On social problems. Serious stuff, that's what it sounded like.'

'Hugh, you didn't . . .' Molly had the same feeling of doom she remembered when her father wrote to say he'd be coming down to see her at school and would take her out to tea, so she could meet a 'new friend'.

'Well, he said he'd lose his job if he couldn't go. Poor old Haverford, it's really all he's got left.'

'Is that what he said?'

'Not all he said.' In fact his father-in-law had congratulated him on the perfectly splendid bit of crackling Hugh had in his arms in Chancery Lane, and naturally mum was the word, and his lips were sealed as far as Molly Coddle was concerned. And, by the way, he did have this job in Italy, but if it was in the slightest degree inconvenient to join them in the villa, he'd book into a cheap little *pensione* by the railway station in Siena. Hugh was not an absolutely brilliant solicitor but he knew when he'd been out-manoeuvred by a ruthless opponent. 'He said he knew the part of Tuscany we were going to extremely well and all the priests were Communists. Do you think that's true?'

'It will be,' Molly said with considerable feeling, 'when he's finished writing about them.'

At the end of the month Molly received another communication from S. Kettering setting out the arrangements for paying the rent. *Half the sum due should be converted into dollars and placed in the overseas account of Barone Bernardo Dulcibene in the Banco dell' Annunziazione in Siena. The other half can most conveniently be received in lire (cash please) by William Fosdyke, an Englishman who has long made his home in Mondano and who has certain bills to discharge in relation to the property. I intend to travel extensively during the summer and I may not have the pleasure of meeting you. It has, however, been pleasant to do business with you and I am sure you and your little family will be extremely happy at 'La Felicità'.*

So she felt, with an unexpected disappointment, that she would never get to know her landlord. All she had learned was that he was a man whose wife thought him the apple of her eye and who had tastes in Italian painting that were remarkably similar to her own.

Arrival

CHAPTER THREE

'Why can't you sit up and look about you?'

'Because we're feeling sick.'

'We paid out all this money to bring you here.' Hugh, driving a large, family-sized Fiat, blamed his two elder daughters whom he knew to be slumped in varying attitudes of distress on the seat behind him. 'At least you ought to show a bit of gratitude and look about you.' Not only had he paid out money, some of it his own, but he had forgone almost a month of lunches with Mrs Tobias in the 'Dolce Vita'.

'My advice to you, if you want my advice, is never look about you.' Haverford, exercising an old man's privilege, was sitting next to the driver. In the back, squashed in beside two hot and complaining children, Molly tried her best to restrain the youngest on her lap from wrenching open the door and free-falling out towards the autostrada.

'Never look about you as you go,' was old Haverford's advice, 'and then arriving will come to you as a total surprise. Besides which, there's nothing much to see except the motorway and a lot of Krautish industrialists hurrying south in their Mercedes towards the bum-boys of Naples.'

Molly's heart sank. Having her father with them on holiday was going to turn out as disastrously as she had expected. Why hadn't Hugh hardened his heart and refused to accept his ridiculous story of having been commissioned to do his 'Jottings' from Tuscany? Haverford had jotted away from the furthest reaches

43

of the King's Road for the past forty years. His journey was, she now felt, quite unnecessary. 'Why don't you read Jacky a story?' she asked Samantha. And to the desperately wriggling child, 'You'd like a story, wouldn't you, about Postman Pat?'

'I can't possibly read when I'm feeling sick,' Samantha told her. 'And, anyway, what's a bum-boy, Gamps?'

'Look about you, anyway,' said Hugh quickly. 'It's Italy. That's what we've paid to see.'

'A gay tart,' Henrietta explained with what sounded like her last breath. 'Anyway, how many more kilometres is it now?'

'Ask your mother.' Hugh moved out to pass a lorry, disclaiming all responsibility for this endless and ruinous journey. 'She knows all about it.'

'How many miles to Babylon?' Haverford intoned. 'Three score miles and ten.'

'When shall we be there?' Samantha asked with her eyes closed. 'Whenever shall we be there?'

'The only decent journeys are the package tours of the imagination, trips to a wood near Athens or Ruritania. You don't have to queue up at passport control. You don't have to fight your way into a plastic-wrapped leg of hairy chicken, while you're hurtled through space at the mercy of some suburban pilot with piles who thinks only of his duty frees and having it off with the stewardess. You don't have to spend half a day in a moving microwave oven racing lorries down the autostrada. You can travel the world from your own armchair.' Haverford was warming to a theme which he had expanded in some of his best-loved 'Jottings'. Why on earth, Molly wondered, couldn't he have followed his own advice and imagined their progress towards the *raccordo* to Siena.

'We should be there in an hour,' Molly said, 'and Jacqueline says she wants to stop.'

'Don't you think she's lying?'

'It's not worth risking. Anyway, we don't want to get there too soon.'

'Getting there's absolutely all I want,' Samantha moaned.

Molly didn't remind her that they mustn't arrive too early because S. Kettering had told them not to.

Suggested arrival time [his latest communiqué read] *should be about 16.00 hours, after Giovanna has recovered from her siesta. In the normal course of events, she will be at your disposal for three hours in the morning between 9.30 and 12.30. Her cleaning is admirable, but she will not undertake washing (the machine will be available to you provided you take proper precautions) or cooking. Don't be put off by Giovanna's somewhat harsh and peremptory manner. She is an orphan, both her parents having been shot by the Germans. She's matched with a somewhat feckless husband and has the sole responsibility for a large family. She will present you with your personal bunch of keys and explain their uses. You will find each key clearly labelled. Signed,* S. KETTERING.

They stopped at a Motta bar. '*Dov'è la toiletta?*' Haverford asked on the children's behalf, but they had already found it, scampering away through the display of giant dolls, plastic picnic tables, local cheese and wine, and returned resentful at having been glowered at by the resident guardian because they hadn't understood the purpose of her saucer of lire. Haverford ordered a coffee and a *cognac italiano per favore*. Hugh drank a beer; with his sleeves rolled up he looked masculine and masterful, in charge of his family on the journey his wife had planned for so long. He was all the more determined to appear in control because his father-in-law was giving him the half-amused, half-pitying look, which Hugh interpreted as 'I know you're sorry you've got to put up with me. It's just because you're the poor fish my daughter married; but then the unfortunate girl couldn't get a better catch in her particular sea.'

When they got outside, the early afternoon heat hit them like a blast of air from the Underground. The hot car seats stung the children's bare legs and made them cry out in protest.

Hugh remained calm at the wheel, driving with the window open. He accepted his wife's instructions and negotiated Conterchi and San Pietro in Crespi without hesitation or mishap.

Mondano was as deserted as a ghost town, wrapped in the silence of its siesta. As they passed the alimentari (shut, as it might be forever) and then plunged off the road into the shadows of the bramble-lined single track, Haverford quoted, as he had been waiting to do ever since they left Heathrow:

> *'Nel mezzo del cammin di nostra vita*
> *Mi ritrovai per una selva oscura*
> *Ché la diritta via era smarrita.*

"In the middle of the journey of our life, I found myself lost in a dark wood,"' he began to translate for the benefit of the children, but they were all, including the baby, asleep now and Molly thought that for her father to pretend to be in the middle of his life was a bit of a cheek anyway.

So she sat, with the sleeping Jacqueline on her lap and waited, it seemed forever, for the moment she both longed for and dreaded. The pot-holed drive seemed endless and dustier than before, with the fine show of spring flowers over. And then the car bumped and scrambled to the top of the little hill and there, once more and changeless, was 'La Felicità'. No one spoke, no one congratulated her. Her family showed no sign of amazement. Hugh drove neatly into the straw-covered shelter as though he were coming to rest in a multi-storey car park; then he switched off the engine and opened his door. But the family sat on with the inertia of those who have travelled a long way and are reluctant to face the effort of arrival.

Hugh said, 'There doesn't seem to be anyone here.'

'But what do you think?'

'It's a fort,' Hugh said suspiciously.

'Oh, God!' Henrietta now grumbled as she awoke. 'We're not here, are we?'

'"This castle hath a pleasant seat; the air nimbly and sweetly recommends itself unto our gentle senses,"' Haverford orated. The silence that followed was broken only by the buzzing and blundering of insects, the uninterrupted beating of cricket legs.

'Where's the pool?' Samantha opened her eyes. 'I can't see any pool.'

'It's there,' Molly told her. 'Everything's there.' But she sat, afraid to get out and face some possible disappointment. The house looked cooler, clearer, its angles sharper and shadows blacker in the high summer sunshine. There was bougainvillaea in flower, clambering up the stone walls, small white roses on thin stalks among the weeds, and wild flowers in what could hardly be called a garden. And then, when she looked at the high terrace with its pots of trailing geraniums, she could see nothing for the shadow was so intense – not the pale blob of a face or the movement of a hand – but she was suddenly as sure as she could be of anything that someone was standing there, looking down, waiting for them to get out of the car and watching them.

'I suppose the children could go and find the swimming-pool,' Hugh suggested.

'I think Giovanna's got here early. We're in luck.' Molly swung open the car door. Jacqueline was awake and starting to complain. Molly carried her a little way towards the house and then set her down on the pavement by the front door. She no longer felt the presence of anyone on the terrace above her. She pulled the bell; there was no answer. Then she called 'Giovanna!' fruitlessly into the silence. She looked back at the shelter where theirs was the only car. If the maid had arrived and was waiting for them she would have to be driven back to Mondano. And now, as she watched, the car doors were swinging open and the two older girls were struggling out, clutching books, hats and plastic bags full of personal possessions. Her old father was extricating himself from the front seat slowly, painfully, gasping, as though he had to push open a heavy coffin lid in order to rise from the dead.

It was only then she saw what she should have noticed immediately: a bunch of keys with one stuck in the lock, many of them hung with labels. It was a collection she had last seen in the hands of William Fosdyke, Signor Fixit, as he locked up the house after her first visit. She turned the key in the lock; the heavy door swung open and she and her family were admitted to the house.

Ten minutes later she was in possession of the huge kitchen. The children had stood for a moment, awestruck in the hall, as she had hoped they might, amazed at the broad stone staircase, the hanging lantern and the dark portraits of who? Certainly not the Kettering's ancestors as they appeared to be mostly of sly Italian clerics. Then Henrietta and Samantha charged up to the tower, with Jacqueline stumbling after them, to quarrel about their bedrooms.

So Molly stood in the kitchen, the centre of the house, with its door opening on to the terrace, where now, for certain, no one stood watching her. The big wooden table had been scrubbed as white as a bone on the seashore. The knives stood sharp and shining in their racks. Out of the window she could see her father sitting in the plastic chair by the pool. He had stayed awake long enough to remember Dante and Duncan and now he was asleep, the sun on his face and his hat on the grass beside him. She opened the tall refrigerator and found, to her surprise, that it was stocked with white wine, beer, mineral water and coke for the children. There was also butter, cheese, peaches and packets of milk. She opened a wooden chest and found pasta, jam, and, put there even more thoughtfully, packets of Rice Krispies and tins of baked beans. On a marble slab near to the cooker there was a joint of ham and a fat salami ready for slicing. Next to them was a huge watermelon and a bowl of green figs. On the shelves of a tall dresser, she saw tins of coffee and chocolate biscuits and a collection of Twinings teas ranging from Darjeeling, through English Breakfast to Lapsang and Rose Pouchong. Her tiredness seemed to soak away from her, as though she were lying in warm water; she felt not only welcome, but positively needed. She decided to treat herself to a fig from the bowl and found its skin still damp, as though it had been recently washed. Then she heard the sound of a car starting and tyres sliding on a dirt road. But when she pushed open the door and walked out on to the terrace the only car to be seen was their family-sized four-door saloon hired from Pisa airport. The boot was open and Hugh was manfully pulling the remaining suitcases out of it.

'Was that a car?' she called out to him.

'Was what a car?'

'I thought I heard something . . .'

'I didn't. Do these all have to go up to the tower?'

'Not ours. We're in the big bedroom.'

And then the silence of the hillside was rent by a further sound, a high buzzing at first like a gigantic and enraged wasp, and then a roar and a rending of the air, so that Molly felt as though she were standing on the bridge of a warship and some huge Exocet missile was being hurled in her direction. And indeed it was, for over the brow of the little hill a bright-red motor-scooter erupted and upon it swayed the figure of a monumentally built woman, her classic features frozen into a mask of anger and her grey hair flying in the wind so that she had the appearance of a vengeful Medusa. This was no doubt Giovanna aroused from her siesta. She skidded to a halt, threw her leg over the saddle as though dismounting from a charger, and began to harangue Hugh in words he didn't understand. Molly watched the scene feeling calm, even amused, and bit into her fig. Then she walked back into the kitchen and soon heard the hard clatter of shoes on the stone stairs and Giovanna was upon her.

'*Dov'è le chiave?*' The furious figure, stone-faced, and with magnificently controlled rage demanded of her new employer.

'*Ecco su la tavola. Ecco qui.*' Molly pointed to the bright bunch on the scrubbed table and Giovanna gathered them up and strode to a hook on the dresser where they dangled with all their labels. It wasn't fair, just or right for the Signora to come before the hour appointed; she should have been admitted by Giovanna herself and the keys should have remained hanging on their appointed hook; the other set being in the pocket of Giovanna's overall from which she now drew them and held them up making it clear that they would be relinquished only upon her death and then only into the hands of Signor Kettering. What had occurred was quite contrary to the wishes of the *padrone* who would be outraged if he ever got to hear of it. Despite this disastrous beginning, however, Giovanna would be there in the morning, her own family circumstances permitting, and she would be much obliged if the Signora would make sure that her children were up and dressed, and the breakfast eaten, so that she could see that the house was returned to something like the order which Signor Kettering expected of it.

'The key was in the lock of the front door, so we simply walked in. In view of the fact that we have paid half the rent into the Banco dell'Annunziazione.' Molly spoke quietly and in English, only for the purpose of relieving her feelings and not in the expectation that this woman would understand. She had only caught the meaning of the outraged Italian aria in snatches. Then, remembering the tragic death of Giovanna's parents, she spoke with exaggerated courtesy to the elderly orphan. '*Molte, molte grazie, Giovanna. Capito. Domani a la nove e mezzo. Grazie tanto.*'

In spite of Molly's smiles and her anglicized Italian, the woman still stood, wrathful and unappeased. Then the door opened, and old Haverford, rosy from his sleep and the unaccustomed sun, stared at the avenging Gorgon.

'*Signora Giovanna? Bienvenuto. Que bellissima figura.*'

And he went on in English and in the manner of his 'Jottings': 'How many generations ago, when she was a young girl, might she have sat for Pietro and become his Madonna della Misericordia? It's a face which only grows more beautiful with the years.'

Molly's discomfiture at her father's unstoppable awfulness was increased by the spectacle of the hard-faced Giovanna, who appeared to her to be simpering, her eyes modestly downcast. Then, instead of leaving them, the maid began to take plates and glasses off the dresser and carry them out on to the terrace.

'And a few generations later,' Haverford went jotting on, 'she must have turned up as Susanna in *Figaro*. What, exactly, do you think she's doing?'

'Goodness knows.' Molly felt she had lost all control of the situation and was only anxious to withdraw from it. 'I'm going upstairs to see about the children.'

She could hear them as she climbed to the top of the tower. They had returned noisily to life after the journey, consoled by spreading the contents of their suitcases, which always looked to her like carefully collected rubbish, old dresses bought from barrows, ratty bits of fur, crumpled and disorderly history notes, about their new quarters. Jacqueline, naked as a fish, ran screaming with delight from room to room, slithering out of her sisters' hands as they tried to catch her. The tasteful domain of the unknown Kettering children, with its bright bedspreads, art reproductions and posters from exhibitions in Florence, had been taken over by the Pargeters, who would soon reduce it to a tip. Her children felt, it seemed, as immediately at home as she had. Molly moved to a high window someone had left open, fearing that the baby, to escape its pursuing sisters, might leap out. She thought again what a point of defence the tower was, commanding the countryside, and then she saw that there was a back road leading away from the tower, narrower, bumpier even than the drive to the front door, which snaked quickly down the hill and out of sight. That way, whoever had brought the ham and cheese, and she could guess who it must have been, had vanished as they arrived, leaving a set of keys behind.

'Why don't you come down and have a swim? Then you can unpack and get ready for dinner.'

'Dinner.' Samantha laughed at this pretentious way of describing their last meal. 'You mean supper, don't you?'

'No. I mean dinner. I know we're not really settled in yet. But we're all going to have a proper dinner by candlelight. On the terrace.'

'Can I have it in my dressing-gown? I'm going to be terribly tired.' Samantha sank on to her bed to show the helpless state she expected to be in by the evening.

'No. You can put on dresses. We're going to have dinner on the terrace with candles.'

'Why on earth?'

'Because that's the way we do things, out here.' Molly spoke with quiet confidence as though she had become in the few hours since their arrival the owner of 'La Felicità' and the organizer of life in the house.

'When I was staying with your sainted mother in Siena, small hotel in Via dei Cappuccini, and we were just leaving, I handed a postcard to the hall porter to stamp and send to England. Well, your mother came rushing in from the car with a rare display of energy and snatched it from the fellow's hands. Of course, it was written to some girlfriend or other in England. The message was how much I missed her, time dawdling on leaden feet until we could slide between the sheets together; picture on front of a Piero angel, undoubtedly *her* face. Hughie will be acquainted with the sort of thing.'

'I don't know why you should think that.' Hugh in a white shirt, neatly consuming prosciutto and figs, was thinking of Mrs Tobias far away from 'La Felicità'.

'Anyway, the Queen of the Night, always called your mother that, you know, because of her amazing devotion to sleep, which she seemed to prefer to almost any other activity, in particular to that which I believe today's lovers refer to so elegantly as 'boffing' or 'shafting' . . . Do you 'shaft' nowadays, Hughie?'

'Would you like another fig?' Molly found herself strangely unaffected by her father's appalling conversation. There had been half a dozen bottles of red wine left standing in a corner of the huge kitchen hearth. She drank a mouthful of unchemicated Chianti someone had brought from the Castello Crocetto. 'Samantha, darling, do try not to fiddle with the candle. We don't want to set the place alight.'

'You mean *pas avant les jeunes filles en fleur*. Oh, I understand.' Haverford laid a finger upon his bluish lips. He was wearing an elderly white linen jacket and a blue spotted bow-tie, so that, given a boater hat set at a jaunty angle, he might indeed have looked like the late Max Beerbohm.

'Well, then your outraged mother leapt into the car which was loaded with our luggage because we intended to be off to Urbino that morning, and apparently she decided on some kind of *hara-kiri* or *felo de se*, a consummation of our marriage devoutly to be wished but never performed. Anyway, she drove off at high speed, ignoring all *senso unicos*, and finally crashed into a bollard by the *ospedale*. And you, Molly Coddle' – he smiled at his daughter as though it were all, in some comic way, entirely her fault – 'you were in an awful pink plastic carry-cot in the back seat and you never even woke up!'

'That's not true, is it Mummy? It can't be true!' Samantha's common sense was outraged.

'How should I know? Babies don't remember that sort of thing.' Molly smiled, thinking of Jacqueline, no longer a baby it was true, but so trusting, so unperturbed by being transported to the top of a Tuscan tower, that she had not stirred when her mother knelt beside the bed to kiss her. Molly felt similarly safe, brought to this strange place about which she would have clearly so much to learn. It was knowledge which could be postponed until they were days older and more experienced in the ways of 'La Felicità'.

If she looked at her father with tolerance on that first night it was because his flattering of Giovanna had resulted in the table being elaborately laid on the terrace, fresh candles put in the brass candlesticks, and flowers in a big green and white pottery jug set in the centre of the table. She had even found the records to which S. Kettering had directed her. They were piled haphazardly, some put back in the wrong sleeves, and were mainly recordings of Italian opera. Now, a somewhat scratchy and hissing *Turandot*, playing from the small, lit sitting-room which opened on to the terrace, added a mixture of Italian and oriental excitement to the occasion.

'Of course your marriage isn't subject to these accidents, is it

Molly Coddle? You never caught old Hugh trying to smuggle out an illicit view of the backside of the Cathedral to some little angel in Pimlico. Modern wedlock is so terribly much more like the home life of our dear Queen.'

'I'm not much of an expert,' Hugh said, 'but isn't the wine rather good?'

'The Classico of Chiantishire. Grown to suit the palates of N.W. as they turn up at their summer villas. I recall when Nancy Leadbetter and I stayed in a terrible fleapit of a room in Siena. What we drank then tasted like sulphur and ox blood; it set fire to your tonsils.'

'There's one thing we have got to remember –' Molly wondered how she had forgotten to tell them.

'But we were drunk the whole time on the aphrodisiac of youth.'

'– Shoes. No one can walk about in this garden without shoes on.'

'Why ever not?'

'It seems there are all sorts of stinging things. You just have to be careful.'

'Not snakes?' Molly was surprised to see her father looking at her, blue-eyed, smiling, as though they were alone in an entertaining conspiracy.

'No. Not snakes in particular,' Molly told all the children. 'Just everyone be careful.'

'You have your instructions, girls,' Haverford winked at them. 'Keep your shoes on or you will get kicked out of the garden of Eden. I must leave you for a while. When you get to my age life seems little more than one long march to and from the lavatory.'

'What do you mean, not snakes in particular?' Hugh asked after his father-in-law had wandered off into the shadows at the end of the terrace and they heard his stick tapping along the stone floors. But before Molly could answer they all looked out as a car breasted the top of the small hill and lit them as brightly as actors on a stage. Molly and her husband covered their eyes and peered out towards the lights. So whoever it was driving the silent car must have seen them before twisting the wheel, reversing against the dry grass and brambles, and driving away as quietly towards the castle and the village.

'Whatever was that?'

'Who knows? Somebody lost, I suppose. It must be quite easy to mix up all these tracks,' Molly told them. They were no longer shading their eyes, and the terrace was now lit only by the candles and the open door into the small sitting-room.

'But how did they know?' Henrietta was puzzled.

'How did they know what?' Samantha looked at her sister with contempt.

'How did they know they were lost? They didn't even stop to ask.'

In the bedroom cupboard the man's shirt and woman's skirt were still swinging. Molly moved them carefully to one end of the bar before she hung up Hugh's clothes and her summer dresses. She wanted the room to be tidy before they went to sleep as, after only some nine hours' occupation, she felt a proprietorial interest in 'La Felicità' and wanted it to look its best always.

'He's worse.' Hugh came out of the bathroom which was dimly lit and marbled as a side chapel. 'Absolutely worse than he's ever been.'

'I know.' He had a white trace of toothpaste at the corner of his mouth. Molly took a handkerchief and tidied him up as though he were the room.

'Nothing but talk of "bum-boys" and "shafting" in front of the girls.'

'They don't really mind. I mean, they're extremely knowledgeable.'

'Well, I mind. And suggesting I'd creep out and send a postcard to some, well, some girlfriend or another!' Hugh was deeply offended by the suggestion. 'What's he trying to do, split us up or something?'

'Probably.'

'Whatever for?'

'It entertains him.' She was surprised by her tolerance. 'I suppose he hasn't got much else to do, at his time of life.'

'Can't he grow old with dignity?'

'Apparently not.'

'Does he think about sex the whole time?' Hugh was already in bed, his wife still tidying.

'So it seems.'

'I can't imagine being like that, when I'm old.' He gazed towards his mid-seventies with an anxious expression. He hadn't been, in his wife's experience, very much like that when he was young.

'It's his generation,' Molly reassured him, lifting an empty suitcase on to the top of a cupboard. 'Apparently they hardly ever thought about anything else. You like it here, don't you?'

'Yes,' he had to admit. 'Of course, it's very grand.'

'Not really. It seems quite homely.' It wasn't what she meant. She would have liked to say that, in her opinion, it wasn't in the least like home, but in every respect better.

'Grand, and, my god, it's expensive.'

'Much cheaper than a hotel, for all of us.'

He shook his head, hardly able to bear the thought of what they were paying out to have his antique father-in-law insult him at mealtimes.

'Anyway, I'm going to pay for it.'

'I'm not sure I altogether approve of that.'

'It's all fixed. I've fixed it all with S. Kettering. So don't worry.' She resisted the temptation to add, 'Your pretty head.'

But Hugh's brown eyes were closed and his martyred Saint Sebastian head was flat on the pillow. He had had a long drive and, in the face of great provocation, behaved, on the whole, exceedingly well. Molly, now in her nightdress, got into bed beside him. As she stretched out an arm to switch off the light she saw, on the marble-topped bedside table, the book which had been open on the bedcover when she had first visited the house. It was closed now but a dry leaf marked a place. She was too tired to read and fell asleep.

First Week

CHAPTER FOUR

Molly's sleep had been deep and dreamless but she woke up early, saw Hugh unconscious beside her and replaced the sheet he had kicked away as she might cover one of the children. Then she moved quietly into the kitchen and made herself a mug of tea. Framed in the narrow window she saw the landscape, lit and brilliant as the background of a painting. The terrace tiles were already warm under her bare feet; the sunlight, when she looked towards it, stung her eyes and made them water. When she moved, a bright green lizard sprinted up the wall and vanished. She sat and drank the tea and thought about S. Kettering. Then she got the photographs out of her handbag and looked at the view of the swimming-pool. The figure sitting on its far side was a man wearing sand-coloured trousers and a red shirt; he had reddish-brown hair brushed straight back and looked square-shouldered and sturdy. The focus in the distance was not sharp enough for her to be able to tell much more about him. She stood at the foot of the staircase which led up to the tower but even Jacqueline, so well known for her early rising that her grandfather called her the Dawn Patrol, was silent. She wandered back into the small sitting-room with her mug of tea, put it down on the polished surface of a table but removed it hastily in case it left a tell-tale ring which S. Kettering might complain about in the future. And yet, now she had taken possession of 'La Felicità', she no longer felt so much in awe of the absentee landlord as a half-amused curiosity about him. Finding out about Kettering was, she thought, a private

59

game which she might set herself to play on this holiday. The room gave her no help. It was too appropriate, too suitable, to betray any particular personality. There were a couple of oriental rugs on the tiled floor, old maps, comfortable armchairs and sofas, flower vases which tactfully avoided the awfulness of Italian ceramics. Only a picture over the fireplace seemed out of place: an archly primitive painting of a large tabby cat and a Victorian child in a formal garden. It was so painted, Molly thought, that the cat looked considerably more human than the child, who had the embarrassing appearance of a performing animal dressed in frilly pantaloons and a bright blue sash. She avoided its eye and knelt in front of the bookcase.

The books were hardly more revealing, seeming to be less of a private collection than the sort of works which might help visiting tourists dedicated to culture. There was a shelf of art books, another of guides, Italian history and works on wine and Tuscan cooking. There were none of the battered paperbacks usually left abandoned after rainy afternoons in holiday houses, no near pornography and, she thought, no detective stories, until she remembered the Sherlock Holmes collection beside the bed. S. Kettering was either a particularly serious-minded chap or anxious to show off to his tenants. Having reached that judgement Molly felt, for the first time, one up.

So she smiled to herself and pulled out a tall book from the bottom shelf, *Piero della Francesca* by the fellow whom her father always called K. Clark. The plates flickered past, solemn and beautiful faces, sleeping soldiers, angels carrying flutes, and then a page fell open more easily because, slipped into it, she found a sheet of the villa's notepaper on which was typed what she at first thought to be a shopping-list, but, as she began to read, discovered it was no such thing.

'On the floor looking at artworks, crouched in front of for-gotten masterpieces! That's how I always remember you, Molly Coddle.' Her father came into the room, looking like an un-reformed convict in his striped pyjamas, his grey hair upright at the back of his head, a smouldering cigarette held in one cupped hand and his mug of tea in the other. 'Forget art,' he said. 'Life's the thing, isn't it? My "Jottings" will describe Italy as a place where the drama in the streets is never ending. Not as a museum.'

'Don't put your mug on that table,' she said. 'It's going to leave a ring.'

'Life is for living and, for God's sake, tables are for putting mugs down on.' All the same he stood his on the rug as he sat down, inhaled smoke and coughed with pleasure. 'When do you propose to begin life, Molly Coddle?'

'I don't know what you mean.'

'A husband, three jolly girls and a holiday in Italy. Is that enough to satisfy your taste for living? At least there was a bit of drama in your mother's life. She used to crash cars.'

'Only because of the way you behaved,' Molly was angry enough to answer.

'The way I behaved, yes.' He smiled complacently and gulped his tea. 'The way I behaved certainly gave rise to a bit of drama, from time to time. Don't you long for it, Molly Coddle? You must do, as your father's daughter. Tell me honestly, are we as different as all that?'

What he had said was meant to be consoling. He thought, once again, how large she looked and yet how vulnerable, wearing nothing but her nightdress, kneeling on the floor in front of him so that he could see, although he tried not to, the tops of her ample breasts. He had never been much of a fellow for breasts. In a way she was imposing, and as statuesque as the pictures in front of her; it was just that she was not, and never could be, her father's type. He held out his hand to her, feeling, unusually for him, guilty.

'We should try and get on a little better, Molly Coddle. You've never understood me.'

She thought, I understand you all too well.

'I was fifty-three when I used to meet all those wonderful girls striding down the King's Road, blonde hair flying, boots like little musketeers. Only fifty-three. I could feel quite young then. Now I'm seventy-seven and I'm hardly a day older.'

What a pity you can't feel your age, she thought. It would make life so much more pleasant.

'Let's all go into Mondano in search of adventure. Anyway I want to root out the priest. Chase up a few stories. You'll have shopping to do, most likely?'

'Yes,' she said. 'I'll have shopping.' And then she looked down again at the neatly typed list in the book, open on the floor in front of her.

> ASSETS
> *1) La Felicità*
> *2) Being together*
> *3) The children*
>
> CURRENT LIABILITY
> *The existence of B.*
>
> MEANS
> *1) Lawyers (useless)*
> *2) Other means to be considered*
>
> OBJECTIVE
> *B. lost and gone forever*
>
> *Nancy L. Which side is she on?*

'What are you looking at, Molly Coddle?'

'Really nothing.'

'Isn't that "The Flagellation"?' Her father squinted down at the page but she banged the book shut and slid it back on the shelf.

'Yes, I suppose it is.' And then, to her relief, Jacqueline appeared at the doorway and asked, accusingly, if anyone was going to get her breakfast.

'*Lardo*. Bacon. Have you any *lardo*? And *marmellata di arancia*. And matches. *Fiammiferi*. The wooden ones. *Fiammiferi di legno*. Not the little wax jobs.' Molly smiled and laughed nervously.

'*Niente fiammiferi di cera.*' She remembered trying to light the gas at the villa with a flaming wax Vesta, which twisted and burnt her thumb. '*Lardo*,' she repeated, reading from her list with diminishing confidence. The woman behind the counter had been gazing at her through strong spectacles and now scratched doubtfully at her moustache with a thumb-nail. The three old men seated on chairs in the dark shop were looking at her as though she were an amusing variation on their usual routine of watching the shopping.

'Well, *uova* then.' Eggs had not been one of the things left by her unknown benefactor and there had been complaints about the absence of toast soldiers. Now Jacqueline, trotting about the shop telling herself some endless and only vaguely comprehensible story, knocked down a pile of brightly coloured buckets. Being with young children, Molly thought desperately, is like having to take out a geriatric, or a drunk. Samantha wandered out through the plastic strips of a door-curtain to where death-dealing lorries thundered down Mondano's main street. Only Henrietta stood in a silent spasm, her entire body controlled by the Walkman which gripped her head and blared into her ears the sound of her own personal disco, reminding her, to her quiet fury, of the parties she was missing by coming on holiday with her parents. The shopkeeper nodded with eventual understanding, cut off a huge bunch of bright green grapes and threw them on to the scales.

'No, no. No *uva*, grapes. *Uova*, eggs.' Molly tried to speak slowly and rationally but the calm which had sustained her in the villa seemed to have drained away. She could feel the sweat soaking her cotton dress and the red flush rising up her neck like an infection. As she struggled with Italian pronunciation, Jacqueline doubled away behind her and slid out of the shop.

'Where's she gone?' She turned on Henrietta. 'I told you, I told you to keep an eye!' But her eldest daughter only smiled vaguely, deafened by her private music. It was at this moment that Signor Fixit appeared in the doorway with the plastic strips draped over his shoulders like variously coloured spaghetti. He was holding Jacqueline, who seemed to trust him, by the hand and Samantha was on his other side.

'Just caught your nipper apparently setting out for Siena,' Fosdyke said. 'You want to watch out for the lorries. Accidents have been known.'

'It's too bad of you!' Molly heard her voice rise miserably in a forced panic caused by guilt and love. 'I told you not to wander off.'

'But they will, won't they? You can't stop people wandering. Let me tell you, no one shops in here. Absolutely nobody. I'll take you across to Lucca's. He's an old scoundrel but he's got all the Oxford Marmalade you want. Why don't you give me *la lista* and relax.'

Lucca's, across the lorry-ridden road and down a small sour-smelling alley, was as small as the shop from which Fosdyke had led them. But lame Lucca skipped and dived into dark recesses at Signor Fixit's commands barked out in Italian that was not much better than Molly's.

'Thank you,' she said, 'for all you've done.'

'Absolutely *niente*, Mrs Pargeter. Sorry I couldn't get some basic staples up at the house for your arrival. Had to pop down to Rome on a spot of business.'

'But there were all sorts of things there: salami, figs, even baked beans. I thought how thoughtful you'd been.'

'Not me, I'm afraid. I can't take the credit.'

'Then who do you think?'

'Someone, I suppose, used to the ways of offspring. By the way, Mrs Pargeter –' He moved closer to her and lowered his voice; she got a whiff of Imperial Leather and small cigars. 'The bank here stays open until twelve. Would you like to get it over? Then you can enjoy your holiday without thinking of money!'

'Of course. I was going to let you have the rent as soon as we met again.' She hastened to reassure him that she would never be less than totally reliable in her dealings with S. Kettering. To show her continual readiness, she carried her traveller's cheques and her passport in her handbag.

They loaded the car and then Fosdyke offered to take the children for a coke in the café opposite the petrol pumps. They could all meet there and he wouldn't embarrass her by coming into the bank while she did her little bit of business. The children seemed willing, indeed anxious, to go with their newfound friend. Even Henrietta took off her ear-phones as Fosdyke asked her how she liked the villa: and, to her suprise, her mother heard her answer, as she walked away, 'It's absolutely brilliant.'

In the branch of the Banco dell'Annunziazione a girl, whose face was a mask of disappointment nobly borne and from whose carmined lips dangled a cigarette miraculously balancing a tube of ash, clattered calculations as she stood before an upright typewriter and, in less time than she had expected, Molly was in possession of a mound of hundred thousand lire notes. In the café she found Fosdyke nursing a malt whisky ('Kept for me specially by Carlo because I was once able to do him a favour') and the children occupied with a Space Invader machine for which he had advanced them hundred lire pieces. When she gave him the second half of S. Kettering's rent, he put it in his pocket without counting it. 'I trust you implicitly, Mrs Pargeter,' he told her. You won't want a formal receipt?'

'I suppose,' she felt bound to say, 'I ought to have one.'

'Then I'll knock something out for you. Kettering . . . Well, Kettering's travelling.'

Kettering travelling and Fosdyke in Rome? Then who, she began to wonder, had supplied last night's dinner? 'I've been meaning to ask you about the Ketterings.'

'Relax, Mrs Pargeter. You'll have a drink, I'm sure you will.'

'Mrs Kettering, for instance . . .' she asked after Fosdyke had called the pale and sullen-looking girl wearing glasses and a blue overall from behind the zinc-covered bar to bring *vino bianco* to the Signora plus, *ancora malt whisky con acqua*. 'Is she travelling with her husband?'

'Travelling, I think. Not necessarily with her husband.' Fosdyke smiled, as though enjoying a joke.

'But you told me that Mr Kettering was the apple of his wife's eye.' She remembered the curious expression he had used.

'Well, yes, of course.' He seemed to find her questions more and more comical. 'But you can't always travel with the apple of your eye.' And then, no longer smiling, 'What's this, Mrs Pargeter? Some sort of an interrogation?'

She looked round the café, a bleak, concrete erection with plastic chairs and tables. At one of them sat the men who, she was sure, had jeered at her from the wall beside the petrol pumps and were now slapping down playing cards and shouting *Ventidue!* with much of their remaining strength. Behind the bar the wall was decorated with postcards of the Pope and the Madonna. On a shelf stood wilting plants and very small stuffed animals, squirrels and starlings which had fallen victim to the chase. Their table was close to the door of the *toilette* from which came the smell of urine mixed more faintly with disinfectant. 'Naturally, I feel curious about the people who own such a splendid house.'

'You're happy there?'

'I'm sure we're going to be.'

'Then what else do you need to know?'

She thought for a moment and then said, 'Well, do they live at "La Felicità" all the winter? I mean, do they have somewhere in England?'

'Oh, nowhere in England. People like me and the Ketterings have severed all connections. We're the ex-pats.' He said it as though they had settled in some remote outpost of the old British Empire and not in handy, holidaymaker's Chiantishire. The Star Wars machine, eagerly watched by all her children, hummed and twittered.

'And the Kettering children?'

'What about them?'

'They seem very neat and tidy.'

'Kettering, I believe, runs a fairly tight ship.'

'And are they travelling too?'

'I'll tell you quite frankly, I wouldn't know where to put my hands on them at the moment. Any other questions?'

'Yes –' Drinking white wine, she felt bold enough to ask – 'What's the S. for?'

'The what?'

'The S, in 'S. Kettering'.'

'I think we'll leave you to find that out.' He was smiling at her again now. 'It seems to me that you enjoy a bit of detection.'

She didn't deny the accusation, for they were interrupted by the children with hands outstretched for more lire to finance the Star Wars programme. Driving out of Mondano she thought that Fosdyke had, perhaps, understood her. She wanted to be more than an outsider in 'La Felicità', more than a vague summertime nuisance for whose sake the family had to go travelling, someone only to be communicated with by notes or as a new source of rent. She was also, in a way which she found surprising, beginning to feel the remote attraction of a powerful force called 'S. Kettering'. Whatever you thought of Hugh, no one could accuse him of running a 'tight ship'. Then she remembered that she had forgotten to get a receipt from Signor Fixit. She had also failed to pick up her father. Having been driven with the children into Mondano he had wandered off on his own unexplained concerns.

Now she saw him, standing on the pavement outside the church, holding his thumb out to her and grinning beseechingly as though he were some hopeful teenager off on the hippy trail. And beside him, an elderly priest in a black soutane was also holding up a thumb and laughing as though he were taking part in a particularly outrageous joke.

'*Arriverderci, Don Marco. Arriverderci. Grazie mille. Grazie tanto,*' Haverford said to the priest, as he climbed into the car. 'Terrific fellow,' he told Molly as they drove away. 'Red as a baboon's bum. I mean, not just a Euro-Communist or of the pinkish persuasion. Hard-core Stalinism, with strong support from the Holy Ghost.'

'Are you sure?' Molly wondered how far the language tapes borrowed from the Fulham Public Library had allowed her father to penetrate the political opinions of a Tuscan cleric.

'Of course, the old God-botherer speaks pretty good English. Learnt it off an R.A.F. prisoner on the run during the war. And another thing. He's suggested a way we might persuade Giovanna to do the washing. You won't have to spend the entire holiday peering into that steamy little porthole, watching the children's vests revolving in the suds. All we have to do is tell her that we know all about her parents.'

'They were shot by the Germans.'

'Not according to the highest authority. They were a couple of collaborators. The red resisters of Mondano shot them, by popular request. Oh, and the priest gave me a pot of wild boar pâté. It'll be a treat for the children.'

In the back of the car, Henrietta and Samantha made exaggerated vomiting sounds at the very thought of it, and Jacqueline joined enthusiastically in the pantomime. Molly drove skilfully back down the road, taking the short cut to what she had already grown to think of as home.

CHAPTER FIVE

The children lay round the pool and slowly lost the prison pallor of Notting Hill Gate. Sometimes they sent the pigeons fluttering up to the sky and played ping-pong on the white encrusted table. Haverford got up early, sat in the garden jotting away until, as often as not, Don Marco arrived in a small rattling car and took him off on an unknown errand. Hugh would get up purposefully and drive into Mondano, returning with a large number of bread rolls and a few croissants over which the children quarrelled. Later, exhausted by the morning's expedition, he would retire to the poolside where he read yesterday's *Daily Telegraph*, of which Signor Fixit had found him a source. After lunch he formed the Italian habit of taking a siesta and he went to bed early. When Molly joined him he would ask hopefully if she were feeling tired or, even perhaps more hopefully, as though it relieved him of all responsibility, if she had the curse. Almost always she answered, 'yes' because she had come to prefer lying still, with his soft sleeping body behind her, breathing the night air scented with pine wood and wild thyme as it came to her through the open shutters, and listening to the faraway ululation of the Borzoi dog chained beneath the walls of the Castello Crocetto.

She often wondered about the note left in the art book in the small sitting-room and typed she was sure (and her interest in detection took her so far), on the same instrument that had typed the instruction sent to her. '*La Felicità*' came first among S. Kettering's assets, above *The children* and *Being together*. But who or what was *B.*, the only liability? And why was her landlord's object to have *B. lost and gone forever?* Something to do with his business, she thought, but she still had to discover what his business might be. It had been enough for her that he was a man who thought his house a good point of departure for the Piero della Francesca trail.

One night she dreamed that she got up and went to the lavatory, where she found a new, neatly typed notice fixed over the bowl. *The master bedroom at 'La Felicità' is intended for regular sexual intercourse. Visitors are asked to respect the traditions of the house.* S. KETTERING. The note embarrassed her considerably, although she suspected, even while she read it, that it was a dream. When she awoke she was surprised at herself for dreaming so foolishly and resolved to think less about the mysterious Mr Kettering in the future.

A remarkable change had taken place in Giovanna. She spoke and understood more English than had at first appeared but it seemed to be English she had got from the Kettering children, so she was easily understood by Jacqueline who would run to her, climb on to her lap, whenever the maid sat down for a moment and stay there silent and apparently overawed. Giovanna said she often sat in with the Kettering children if their parents were out and would be glad to do the same for the Signora Pargeter.

Now she left with plastic bags full of washing and returned after lunch the next day with Hugh's shirts, Molly's dresses and the children's T-shirts and jeans beautifully ironed. She arranged them on the big table on the terrace where they looked impeccable, like clothes set out for a wedding.

Molly had a bad moment wondering if her father had somehow used the fate of Giovanna's parents to blackmail the cleaning lady. She wouldn't put it past him but in the brilliant afternoon heat she wasn't inclined to pursue the matter. The next day she put her shirt and cotton trousers, even her knickers, out for Giovanna. She could spend more time by the pool, thanks, perhaps, to a long-forgotten act of collaboration with the Nazis.

'I wish I had red hair,' Samantha said to her mother, inspecting herself as she so often did in the tarnished mirror surrounded with gilded laurel leaves and intertwined cherubs. 'Gorgeous thick chestnut hair, considered artistic, like the girl in the Sherlock Holmes story.'

'Which Sherlock Holmes story?'

'The one Gamps was reading to us. He found the book here. "The Copper Beeches".'

'Which one is that?' Molly, of course, knew perfectly well. She was thinking of the book that had been left open on the bedcover when she first visited 'La Felicità'.

'You know. The one where this governess is told to put on a special dress and sit with her back to the window. Just so she can be mistaken for someone else.'

'Yes, of course.' Molly caught sight of herself in the mirror, standing beside her daughter. Strangely enough, the idea which occurred to her, in that first moment of its discovery, didn't make her feel at all afraid.

She went over to the pool and found the book on a table, damp from having been left out all night among towels and goggles, sunglasses, an old *Daily Telegraph* and the girls' bikini bottoms. The story was still marked with a dry leaf. She read it through and then sat for a long time on the white strips of the reclining chair in which she had first seen Signor Fixit. She was afraid then, rather as a skier might feel when he looks down the steep whiteness of a dangerous slope, or a high diver who seems far above the water, but the sensation was so unusual to her that she couldn't be sure that it was entirely unpleasant still strongly mixed, as it was, with curiosity.

'And how many children did you say Mr Kettering had?

'Well, three. At the last count.'

'And girls, of course?'

'Well, yes. Now that you come to mention it.'

'How old?'

'Fifteen, the eldest, I think they told me. Jail-bait, actually. She looks well over the age of consent.'

'And the next?'

'Oh, I think a few years younger.'

'And, finally . . .'

'Little Violetta seems to have come as a bit of an afterthought. She was a surprise to most of us.'

'Only a toddler, Violetta?'

'She's certainly not four, but bright as a button. Knows a few rude words in Italian, I'm reliably informed.'

'And girls don't, on the whole, need very different accommodation from boys,' Molly said, thoughtfully. 'If I'd had three boys I could have fitted them into the same bedrooms.'

'You tell me, Mrs Pargeter. I'm afraid offspring are something of a closed book to me.' She had expected to see Fosdyke the day before when she went shopping. He was so often in Lucca's, tasting a slice of salami, cutting off a sliver of cheese to try or speculatively pinching the melons. He hadn't been there that morning and now she had run him to earth in the café. She had sat down opposite him and immediately started on her inquisition.

'So why did the advertisement say *girls preferred*?'

'*Females preferred*, wasn't it?'

'Exactly. *Females*. I suppose that made it sound more business-like. Why *females* . . . and *three*?'

'I suppose because little girls are less likely to possess catapults, air-guns, or lob cricket balls through windows.'

It was no good, she thought, for Signor Fixit to pretend that he still lived in the age of *Just William*. She had another explanation of the matter entirely.

'Or did he want a couple with the same number of children as he had? The same ages, the same sex?'

'Giovanna may get on better with them. Boys tend to annoy the servants.' He said it as though it were some deep truth, a secret he had been let into.

'I have read "The Copper Beeches".'

'Have you, by Jove?' He looked at her, smiling. 'Super chap, Conan Doyle. One of my own favourites.'

'*The Complete Sherlock Holmes* is one of the books in the house.'

'I know Kettering reads, of course,' Signor Fixit said, 'but pictures are his great love.'

'Oh, I know that.' And then Molly plucked up her courage to say, as casually as she could, 'I wonder why the advertisement didn't tell me what dress to wear.'

'Come again?' Fosdyke cupped his ear in his hand, suddenly afflicted with deafness.

'Mr Kettering might have told me how to dress. When I was sitting at dinner on the terrace. With the candles lit, according to his instructions.'

'Well, I suppose he might. But why on earth, my dear lady, should he want to?' He smiled at her tolerantly, as though there were no accounting for the ideas girls got in their heads. And when that smile, that patronizing masculine smile which she had endured so often, was beamed at her, she felt her confidence drain away and retreat with a scrabbling of small stones like a departing wave. The explanation which had been so clear to her when she shut the book by the pool now seemed only a thought, whimsical and without any solid foundation. And even if it were, as it just might be, true, why should she assume that this old ex-pat, mainly interested in the hunt for gentleman's relish, know anything about it? 'I managed to get hold of this mag from a shop off the Piazza di Spagna in Rome.' Delving into a plastic bag on the seat beside him Signor Fixit unearthed the *Informer* and managed to change the subject. 'It keeps me sane.'

'What keeps you sane?'

'This wonderful fellow.' He opened the familiar magazine. 'Must be thirty years ago I started reading his "Jottings". What's his name? Haverford West?'

'Downs,' Molly corrected him. The bar was hot and the small, stuffed animals with beady eyes staring down at her seemed especially repulsive.

'What wisdom. What true knowledge of life!'

'You think so?' Molly looked at him. Did he really know nothing or was he trying to stop her questions by this extravagant praise of her least favourite weekly column?

'An artist in words.' Fixit was rambling on. 'And with a good deal more education than I've had hot dinners. Wouldn't I be right in saying that?'

'I don't know.' Molly looked at him, anxious to discover what he was trying to conceal. 'I mean, I don't know anything about your education.'

'Kicked out of Oundle before I had a chance to get to grips with the first line of the *Aeneid*, if you want to know the truth. Anyway, you can tell this fellow's educated. And women! From the way he writes, and there's nothing offensive about it mind you, nothing that I shouldn't be ashamed to show my aunt . . . Well, she's quite a racy old girl herself, just between the two of us . . . But from the little things this Haverford Downs slips in about the ladies, would I be right in thinking he's had a fair amount of experience with the sex?'

'I don't think' – Molly was finishing her glass of wine, which seemed even warmer and oilier than usual, as quickly as she could – 'that you should believe all you read in the papers.'

'And the weird and wonderful thing is this week's "Jottings" . . . Here, look.' He flicked through the pages. 'Of course, I'm really saving it up for when the hotpot comes out of the oven, but I just happened to cast my eye and yes, look . . .' He found the page triumphantly. 'It comes from here.'

'From *here*? It can't do.'

'Can't?'

'We only got here three days ago.' Only three days and they seemed to have travelled a great distance.

Fosdyke laughed, showing her an unexpected quantity of gold fillings. 'Don't tell me, Mrs Pargeter, that 'Haverford Downs' is your *nom de plume*. I mean, why would when you got here have anything to do with it?'

'He's my father.'

'That distinguished old gent I've noticed in your company is the author of "Jottings"?'

She admitted it. She had come to question him and, as had happened so often, her father had taken over the conversation.

'You wait till I tell Kettering! He'll be tremendously impressed.'

'You mean he doesn't know? I thought Mrs Kettering must have an old father who wrote somewhere about the place.'

'If she has, dear Mrs Pargeter' – Fosdyke was being almost intolerably gallant – 'he can't be anything like the great Haverford Downs.' He looked at his watch. 'Must go now. I'm sure we'll meet again. It's a small world in Chiantishire, a very small world indeed.'

He left her then, smiling and bowing, carrying the plastic bags full of the good things he knew how to put his hands on. The idea that the Pargeters had been specially chosen because of their similarity to the Ketterings had in no way been confirmed by Fosdyke but it grew in her mind steadily. If the Ketterings had wanted another family to stand in for them, it could only be for recognition by someone they wished to avoid or who might be a danger to them. No doubt she should have been alarmed at this thought but she remained excited by it. And this excitement, and the feeling of being involved in a half-guessed-at mystery, became her private obsession as she went about the house, visited the shops and looked after the children.

'I've met a fan.'

'I thought you might.'

'He's asked me to dine at the villa he's looking after for a few months, just to oblige a couple of ex-pats. It seems he's able to lay on steak and kidney pudding. Remarkable fellow and a devoted reader of the "Jottings". Might be a source of useful information.'

'I doubt it.'

'Well, then, you'll be out tomorrow evening?' Hugh asked his father-in-law from behind the *Daily Telegraph*.

'You'll just have to make your own entertainment.' Haverford finished his cup of breakfast coffee and lit a cigarette. His fit of coughing echoed across the landscape, an early morning salute, as he often put it in his 'Jottings', to an old man still courageous enough to face death at the hands of a packet of filter-tips. Hugh, who had been reading about the dangers of having a smoker as a cohabitee, waved his handkerchief through the air and moved to the edge of the terrace.

'Oh and we're all going to a party. Good thing you brought me along with the baggage, you know. I've got you into Mondano society.'

'A party?'

'Nancy Leadbetter. There'll be young people there.'

'God, how awful,' Henrietta sighed. 'I don't think I can stand young people.' Since their arrival at 'La Felicità' she seemed to have forgotten all the social life she was missing in England and devoted her energies to the narcissistic process of going brown, measuring each day the contrast between her exposed wrist and the satisfying white band left beneath her watch-strap. 'How's your watch mark?' her sister would ask her, to which she was able to answer 'Brilliant'. 'Anyway, what young people?' Probably the most awful little squeakies.'

'They may be quite grown up. Nancy's unbelievably long in the tooth,' Haverford told them. 'Her mind's going too. I met her walking up by the castle, great big straw hat, floating veils, general appearance of a female Friar Tuck out for a constitutional.' Molly waited for an embarrassing reminiscence and got it. 'I greeted her. "Nancy Leadbetter, my old girlfriend." "Who are you?" she said. "Who am I? Well, only the chap who rogered you regularly in the sixties." I told her. "I'm too old," she said. "Far too old to remember that sort of nonsense. So don't ask me anything about it." Then I said I was here with the family and she announced she was having a party for the local English, "a rather disgusting barbecue" which she knew young people liked, and she supposed we'd better come along. Arnold Leadbetter made a fortune in property after the war. Luckily he was away from home a good deal, which was when we got rogering.'

Molly remembered the note still stuck, so far as she knew, opposite 'The Flagellation' in the Piero della Francesca book. *Nancy L. Which side is she on?* She said, 'How do we find a babysitter?'

'I'll ask Giovanna,' Haverford volunteered.

'No. *I'll* ask her.' At least Molly could see there would be no more blackmail.

'Do we really want to go to this bash?' Hugh wondered.

'What's the matter, Hughie?' Haverford ground his cigarette out into the remainder of the butter left on his croissant plate and gave what he described as one of his 'nice loose coughs' as he grinned at his son-in-law. 'Haven't you got a thing to wear, darling?'

The next evening they were deprived of Haverford's company when he went to dine with Signor Fixit. Hugh became more cheerful than usual. He sat at the head of the table in his white shirt, beautifully washed by Giovanna, with a silk scarf knotted at the neck, looking handsome and quizzical as he drank Chianti and told the girls about his less lurid divorce cases and more eccentric clients. He wondered if they'd ever find husbands or boyfriends who would take them on such a holiday as this and rather doubted it. He was glad, at any rate, that he had been able to arrange these weeks at 'La Felicità', a summer which they would always remember. But such occasions, to be really memorable, had to be worked at. Tomorrow they would go into Siena. Molly, at least, wanted to see some pictures.

'Oh, not Siena, *please*,' Henrietta said. 'I want to go *brown*.'

Molly wasn't listening to them. She had seen, like a distant lighthouse, headlamps moving round the castle on the skyline.

Then the light had crept forward, down the rutted track that led
to nowhere but their house. It vanished for a while, but then
shone brightly at them as the car reached the top of the small hill
and again they shielded their eyes to look at it like actors on a
stage. Only this time the car didn't stop or turn but drove on,
slithering a little on the loose gravel, until it stopped by their
front door.

'Whoever?' Hugh began, but Molly was already up and almost
running down the stone steps as if she were hurrying towards
some long-planned assignation.

The car was long, low and extremely dusty. The man who got
out of it left the headlights full on and the engine running. He
was in his early forties with a receding hairline, a plump face and
a small mouth. He wore a short-sleeved shirt and dark blue
trousers; one hand patted his moist forehead with a white
handkerchief and the other held out an envelope.

'*Signora Kettering?*'

She stood facing him, a large fair woman in an embroidered
jacket and white trousers for their formal dinner on the terrace.
She said nothing but put out her hand and took the envelope.

'*Buona notte, Signora Kettering.*'

He got back into the car and she heard the door slam, the
engine accelerate and the tyres slide again on the gravel. She
walked up the stone stairs to the sound of the scratchy long-
playing record, highlights from *Turandot*, which she had put on
as they had sat down for dinner. When she got to the terrace
there were four faces looking at her.

'Well?' said Hugh. 'What was it?'

'Oh, nothing. Just something for the Ketterings.' She took the
envelope into the small sitting-room and put it on the mantelpiece
under the painting of the Victorian child with its crafty cat-like
eyes. It was for Signora Kettering and her English upbringing
told her that it was unthinkable to open letters addressed to
someone else; and yet as she came down the stairs and met the
driver she had been taken, as she felt sure she was meant to be

taken, for Signora Kettering. She had been Kettering's wife, the letter was hers and sometime, perhaps, she would have to open it.

CHAPTER SIX

Nancy Leadbetter's grandchildren and a generous selection of their best friends, teenage lovers and hangers-on arrived by taxi, bus and hitch-hike from the station in Siena to the grandeur of Villa Baderini, her house on the other side of Mondano. Some were dressed in old riding-breeches, boots and grubby lace shirts; many in jeans and flak-jackets; some inappropriately, when the afternoon sun made the paving stones almost too hot for naked feet, in long Oxfam overcoats and black Homburg hats. They looked like a collection of the pallid child revolutionaries who emerged on the streets of Moscow after the Revolution. Their military appearance was emphasized by the fact that some of the girls wore scout knives, compasses, even tin mugs, hanging from their belts, and they carried haversacks and sleeping-bags bought from Army Surplus shops. The boys, especially those with hats and overcoats, carried battered suitcases and rolled umbrellas. All these preparations for living off the land were unnecessary, for between them they knew of a network of wealthy houses, stretching from St Tropez to Mykonos, where bedrooms with a bath *en suite*, swimming-pools and occasional servants in white gloves would be put at their disposal by parents only too grateful to discover that their daughters had not, as yet, been violated by a lorry-driver or their sons arrested for the importation of stuff. Their stay at each of these billets was short and they left behind them minor breakages, burnt saucepans, cigarette holes in the sheets and, as often as not, their forgotten passports.

Nancy moved among them for a while, making them welcome, peering into their pale faces with the object of discovering which were her grandchildren. She had invited four, if she remembered rightly; the product of two families and none much over sixteen. Out by the pool she found a girl who greeted her warmly and, delving into the recesses of her knapsack, brought out a box of nougat and gave it to her. 'Why are you giving me a present?' Nancy Leadbetter asked. 'You're certainly no grandchild of mine.' 'No, but I take these for the people we stay with,' the girl told her. 'It seems more polite.'

Having decided that she was too old for nougat, Nancy stood for a moment admiring her pool flanked by statues painstakingly collected by her husband, two Henry Moores, a Giacometti and an Elizabeth Frink, all concreted to the ground and wired with electrical devices to a central burglar alarm in the Mondano police station. What gave her the greatest satisfaction was the water, now bloodstained by the final, flamboyant exhibition of the setting sun. It had been a dry summer but the pool was full and the young people, many of them travel-stained after a long trek from Portofino, were lying in steaming baths, their toes poised to activate the gilded taps. She went upstairs to change, thinking how proud Arnold would have been of the way she had coped with the water shortage.

Arnold Leadbetter had left the Pay Corps at the end of the war with nothing but his demob suit and fifty pounds. Ten years later he had acquired, thanks to some daring mortgaging and a firm way with sitting tenants, a hold on Notting Hill Gate and a sizeable amount of the East End of London. He moved into Mayfair and bought his first Matisse. He was a shy, lonely man who married the nearest thing to hand, which happened to be Nancy, the entertaining redhead who looked after his fingernails in the barber's shop at the Dorchester.

Once married, Arnold began to give parties, admirably hosted by the young and vivacious Nancy, for the artists before whom he became speechless with respect. His wife, who was never speechless in those days, entertained the painters, art critics and sculptors more successfully than her husband and found herself slipping into various love affairs which her Arnold, smiling quietly and getting on with his business and his collection, seemed to expect. Perhaps she felt it was up to her to enter the 'artistic' world to which Arnold remained a devoted but remote outsider. When she was in her fifties and had grown to a generous obesity, her husband would whisper proudly to his dinner guests as they stood in front of some glowing nude or abstract construction, 'Wonderful artist, wasn't he? And of course, you know, an old boyfriend of Nancy's.' The guests would smile politely at the work and the information, often not quite sure how to take either of them.

After Arnold died, Nancy, feeling more strongly than ever what she had always known, that he was the only man she had loved, came to live permanently in the house where he had always seemed happiest, a piece of property he had picked up for a song in the sixties from Barone Dulcibene's father-in-law, old Count Umberto Baderini. The villa had been built in the days of Lorenzo the Magnificent by a Baderini banker. The Baderini Cardinal gave it its baroque façade and had its gardens laid out with descending terraces, fountains, a grassy-staged theatre, grottoes and a lemon house guarded by statues of antique giants. Into this grandiose villa with its chapel and immense central staircase Arnold Leadbetter had moved his business interests and his collection of modern art. His widow continued to give parties, for that had always been her talent, inviting the owners of neighbouring villas, the local Chianti growers and the aristocratic keepers of boutiques in Siena. She also asked her two sons. They were always too busy to come but they sent their children. Nancy enjoyed seeing them and an occasional painter or writer who asked to renew acquaintance with Arnold's collection. They found Nancy, now in her sixties, had become larger and much quieter. She missed the sight of Arnold padding around in the background filling up glasses and, because he was no longer there to enjoy the effect of her jokes, she had given up making them.

Now she stood looking out of her bedroom window, feeling lonely in spite of the car headlights crawling up the avenue of tall cypresses towards the villa's ornate façade and the first arrivals climbing the twin stone staircases to the central entrance. She saw the old man who had accosted her on her walk that afternoon proceeding at the head of a little posse consisting of a neatly dressed man, a woman with untidy hair and a couple of children. He was waving his stick in a proprietorial fashion, as though he were showing them round his estate.

'A couple of good Picassos. Four or five Braques, a Leger.' Haverford waved his stick in the vague direction of the front door. 'In Chiantishire! Where they'd steal your children if you didn't bolt them to the ground!'

'Oh, do shut up!' said Molly, thinking of Jacqueline left in the sole care of Giovanna. What on earth was she doing, she wondered, climbing the steps of a palazzo, as behind her what seemed like the entire English colony of ex-pats in the province of Siena came straggling. Of course she knew why she had been so anxious to come; there must be some, perhaps many, people here who could tell her about S. Kettering.

'Come along in. I'm Nancy Leadbetter.' The huge woman came billowing down to the entrance hall, dressed in bright orange, which went uncomfortably with her recently revivified red hair.

'I do know you, Nancy.' Haverford reached up to kiss her unoffered cheek. 'In every sense, of course, including the biblical,' he added in a penetrating whisper clearly audible to his embarrassed family. 'And I've brought along the fruit of my loins, my small claim on posterity. This is my Molly.'

'I haven't met you, have I?' Nancy looked at Molly, puzzled.

'Of course not.' Haverford told her. 'When we were together we were far too happy to worry about issue. Molly's old man, Hugh Pargeter, and the young people. Henry and Sam.'

'Young people,' Nancy said firmly, 'are all in the kitchen getting to know each other.' She opened a door into a cavernous room where the young army were grouped round a huge table on which their boots and packs rested, smoking, rolling cigarettes or making each other up. 'Need we?' Samantha whispered in desperation. 'Go along,' said Hugh. 'You know you've been wanting to meet someone of your own age.'

'I've never understood that.' Haverford stood in the middle of the entrance hall, wondering. 'I don't go to parties to meet septuagenarians. We rather hope to be asked to dance by a couple of twenty-year-olds, don't we, old thing?' He started to put his arm round Nancy's waist and reached some of the way towards her mouth before she moved away from him.

'All the men seem to be in the garden helping with the barbecue. That's what men like doing, isn't it?'

'Well, it's not the *only* thing that men like doing is it, Hughie?'

'Of course' – Hugh seemed deeply impressed with his surroundings – 'we'll help with the barbecue. Be pleased to.'

'Why don't you come into the drawing-room? You might meet someone.' Nancy, ever vague, led Molly towards a pair of high double doors and then left her to talk to an English couple coming up behind them. 'It's the Corduroys,' said the man helpfully. 'Ken and Louise.' 'Go into the garden, Corduroys.' Nancy raised a large arm with the authority of a policeman directing traffic. 'Help with the barbecue. That's where you're needed.' Then she sent Molly into a shadowy room which seemed at first to be empty. She paused at a picture on the wall, a grey and beige cubist arrangement of lines and broken planes around a torn fragment of newspaper.

'A bad moment, wasn't it,' a voice behind her said, 'when art surrendered to geometry? By the way, I am Vittoria Dulcibene. We live, you might say, in the next castle.'

The woman who came towards Molly from the shadows by the bookcase was very tall and swaying like a poplar in a high wind. A long arm, seeming likely to snap at the wrist from the excessive weight of a diamond bracelet, was raised in what she thought might be a greeting, but ended in a gesture to brush a wisp of free-flowing grey hair from in front of the Baronessa's eyes.

'I'm Molly Pargeter,' was all she could think of to say. 'I've seen you with your dog. He's very beautiful.' Being English, she thought that a sure way of bestowing pleasure on strangers was to compliment them on their dogs.

'You find him so? To me it is a most hideous brute. Our walks together are painfully boring. Anyway, he is not mine, this Manrico.' She pronounced the dog's name with special contempt. 'He was dumped on me by your friend when he vanished, promising, of course, to be back in a day or two.'

'My friend?'

'Your landlord. I assume you know Signor Kettering?'

'We haven't met.'

'Really?'

'We have corresponded, of course.'

'But correspondence, that doesn't give you, does it, the full flavour of a person? Kettering, I assure you, is nothing like his letters. So cold, so impersonal, so businesslike. Come, shall we sit down? Nancy has not arranged for us to be brought a drink. Her mind is on the young people.' And as they sat together in the darkening room, as flares were lit in the garden and there was a blast of distant pop music through a crackling loudspeaker system, Molly confessed, 'I must say I'm curious about Mr Kettering.'

'It's natural,' the Baronessa smiled at her. 'I would wish to know about anyone whose house I inhabit.'

'The house seems a bit anonymous.'

'There's safety in that, no doubt.' She was still smiling. 'Our Kettering doesn't give things away. But you want to know what he's like, in the flesh? Is that the expression?'

'I'm beginning to find a few clues.'

'How clever of you! But whatever impression you have, it will be wrong, unless you allow for his charm. Believe me, he is a bloody bewitcher. Who else would persuade me to care for his revolting Manrico, a creature who consumes at least two sheep

hearts a day. Believe me, that monster is costing me a fortune!'
Vittoria Dulcibene suddenly clutched her forehead, like a woman
facing ruin. 'Would not your children like a nice pet to take back
to England?'

'I'm afraid not. The quarantine laws.'

'Of course, in England, you have laws against everything. And
I believe you take them seriously!' She was cheered up again and
amused. 'So are you happy in "La Felicità"?'

'The children love it. The house is very beautiful.'

'That is Kettering's doing. He has an eye for beauty I would
say. And of course, you have the wonderful Giovanna.'

'She's babysitting tonight.'

'Then your baby is indeed fortunate. This is a totally loyal
servant.'

'I'm sure.' Molly, anxious again to show that she was not a
stranger to the life of Mondano said, 'Is it true, do you think,
about her parents?'

'Is what true?'

The word sounded melodramatic but she said it. 'Collaborators.'

'You are English, Mrs Pargeter.' The Baronessa was looking
straight at her, speaking seriously. 'I suggest you shouldn't use
words you don't understand.'

'I'm sorry.'

'I don't suppose you have ever killed a person in your life.'

'Well. No . . .'

'Don't apologize.' The Baronessa raised a long white finger,
weighted at the base by a sapphire ring, and wagged it as
though to a child. 'Living in England you would have no call to
do so.'

'Well, have you?' Molly smiled back, by no means certain if
this was a conversation meant to be taken seriously.

'Oh, yes. I had to when I was a child, you know. It was for me
like the young people out there doing their Licenza Classica.
What do you call it? "A-levels".'

'A-levels. Yes.'

'I was sixteen, I think, at the time. My friends and I were of the resistance. With the Communists, of course.'

'The Communists?' Molly looked away to the crackling logs in the huge fireplace, the only light in the dark room. The idea of this elderly, bejewelled woman as a young revolutionary seemed particularly absurd.

'Oh yes. And to join the group you had to have killed a German soldier. You see if you had killed one you were not so likely to betray the others. It was a sensible precaution.'

'I suppose so.' Molly did her best to look at the matter in a practical manner.

'Well, I bicycled round Siena with a gun in the basket on my handlebars, underneath my exercise books and Petrarch's sonnets. It was November, cold and wet and the streets were empty. I rode up the Via Pendo and I saw one. He was a private; he was waiting by a big car, probably for his officer to come out of his mistress's apartment. Well, I cycled up quite slowly behind him and then I stopped with my feet on the ground and felt for the gun. But he took his cap off and he had grey hair. He was an old man with a wife and children, I thought. Grandchildren possibly. Well, I couldn't shoot a grandfather. So I pedalled up the Via San Pietro. And then I saw another Tedesco. An officer, this time. He came out of a restaurant and stood waiting. I said to myself, "All right, this will be it, now I will be a member of the group." And you know what he did, the bastard?'

'Ran away?' Molly suggested.

'He took out a beautiful silk handkerchief. It was a big square, with a green and golden pattern. And he blew his nose on just one corner of it, very carefully. He brought it out rather shyly, as though he didn't want anyone else to see it. And I thought, if a man has a handkerchief like that his heart can't be in the war. So I pedalled on up the Via Capitano. And on the corner by the Duomo a lieutenant in the uniform of the S.S. whistled at me. He had neither grey hair nor a silk handkerchief. I shot him between the eyes and then I was off, down the smallest streets, and I didn't stop pedalling until I was back in this Villa Baderini, which, as a matter of fact, used to be my father's. I slept almost all the next day. My family thought I had been studying too hard. It was the sleep of innocence, or experience, perhaps. All I wanted to say was when you speak of "collaborators", you English don't know what you are talking about.'

'I suppose not.' Never having shot anyone, Molly was doing her best to look apologetic.

'And I don't think you can ever understand Italians. The English are always so complacent. You always appear to be perfectly contented.'

Molly removed the smile from her face, now afraid that she was looking contented.

'We are usually in a mood of black despair. That's why you get all this singing and shouting. All this meaningless laughter in the streets. "*Funiculì, funiculà*", all that sort of balderdash. That is to hide our deep pessimism. Kettering understood that. In many ways Kettering was typically Italian.'

Was? They sat together in the darkness, in front of the log fire which was welcome on a summer night suddenly grown cool, and Molly wondered why S. Kettering should be referred to in the past tense. She wanted to ask, 'Have you any idea where he is?' But the room was suddenly bathed in light and Nancy Leadbetter, who had pressed all the switches by the door, was among them and telling them to go out to the barbecue because that was where the fun was about to begin.

'Not for me, *cara*.' The Baronessa looked more solemn than she had when she described shooting her German officer. 'Squatting on the ground trying to balance a singed beefburger and a paper-cup load of Chianti, that is an occupation entirely for the English. If you don't mind, I will go and make myself an omelette. I do remember where our old kitchen used to be.'

As Nancy led Molly into the garden she said, 'There are a

whole lot of English people here, the local inhabitants. I expect you'll know some of them already.'

'Only a man called Fosdyke,' Molly confessed the extent of her ignorance. 'He seems a very helpful sort of person.'

'If you're being helped by Fosdyke,' Nancy smiled, dimpling several of her chins, 'then you really are in trouble.'

'Oh, not as bad as that surely?'

'Arnold wouldn't put up with the man, not at any price. He tried to sell him a picture. Can you imagine? A religious subject. Anyway, Arnold couldn't ever stick religion. It made him think of death.'

'I was wondering' – single-minded, Molly pursued her investigations – 'you must know my landlord quite well . . .?' *Nancy L. Which side is she on?* She had the words by heart of the note pressed in the page opposite Piero's 'Flagellation'.

'Kettering? Oh yes, of course. We all love Kettering. Now I must try to get the young people dancing.'

She moved purposefully away to the group who lay in the darkness under the cypress trees, or sat on the walls and steps of the garden, and began to activate them so that a light dress, or white pair of jeans could be seen jigging about in the night that had suddenly fallen. There was no wind so that the flares stuck in the earth burnt straight upwards. The dancers avoided the illuminated area, which was left to the middle-aged, balancing plates and only occasionally laughing. Peering into the shadows Molly saw her two daughters, otherwise unpartnered, dancing together. Then she was pleased to see a girl, slightly older than Henrietta and Samantha, talking to them and offering them sweets.

'Quite a party, isn't it? Nancy's an exceedingly generous person.' The couple she had met as the Corduroys, Ken and Louise, were holding plates and looking round for somewhere to sit.

'Absolutely no side about Nancy,' Louise told her. 'Arnold left her all the money in the world and she gives us the sort of barbecue we threw for our friends in Haywards Heath.'

'Of course she does have staff to hand around the nosh,' Ken told her.

'Nancy has staff to a large extent' – Louise seemed proud of their hostess's wealth – 'but there's absolutely no side about her.' She was looking at the maids carrying plates of singed meat to the young people and a servant who was bringing a tray full of raw steaks and sausages out from the house.

'I was in landscape gardening, pools and patios,' said Ken Corduroy, who had heavy hornrimmed glasses and the soft, urgent voice of a salesman. 'But my tummy was playing up and I said to myself, "Ken. This isn't a bit of good to you. Get out of the rat race." We bought our property here in seventy-three.'

'Ken misses the rat race. If you want to know the truth. Settled in, have you now, up at "La Felicità"?'

'Of course I don't miss the rat race. I'd be a fool to miss it.' Ken looked at his wife with sudden hatred.

'In the winter months,' Mrs Corduroy said with smiling determination, 'he misses the rat race. You know you do, Kenneth!'

'Well, I do keep up an entrepreneurial connection with the local pool interests,' Ken admitted. 'Not enough to play up my ulcer, of course, but I do just tick over. I act in a consultative capacity to the Brits, when it comes to pools and patio windows. Yours all right at "La Felicità", is it?'

'Of course, it's all right.' Louise Corduroy answered on Molly's behalf. 'Sandra Kettering wouldn't allow it to be anything but all right. That woman has a genius for organization.'

'And paperwork.' Ken smiled at Molly, retracting his top lip so that his teeth seemed to be aimed directly at her. 'Sandra apparently bombards her tenants with paperwork.'

'Written instructions. That's what we heard.' Louise was laughing. 'Quite frankly, Ken and I couldn't be bothered to let our place and give out all those orders.'

'Be careful not to use the toilet and the hair-drier at the same time,' Ken joined in the laughter. 'Sandra Kettering is an Iron Lady when it comes to issuing commands.'

'Sandra?' Molly looked from one Corduroy to another. The words, spoken casually, had given another shake to the kaleidoscope, entirely altering the pattern her mind had grown used to. Whoever was manoeuvring her, it had now occurred to her that it might be a wife. She felt angry and disappointed at being robbed of her remote contact with her landlord through the letters. She heard herself say, 'So *she's* S. Kettering?'

'Is that how she signs her letters? How very formal.' Louise looked as though it was typical and Ken said, 'That'd be Sandra. Here's your old man.'

Hugh approached and they sat down together, the Corduroys and the Pargeters, and Molly felt that her husband's almost invisible disposal of his food was a criticism of her lack of delicacy and the extent to which she had to open her mouth to accommodate her bun. The tomato ketchup stained her fingers and fell as uncompromisingly on her dress as blood, but her brain was racing. Mrs Kettering had composed the notes. Mrs Kettering wanted three girls and a fortyish couple so that they could sit by candlelight on their terrace, so that she could be taken for Sandra and Hugh for . . . but what was Mr Kettering's Christian name? If he were to be an 'S.' also, a Stephen or a Sam, then how was she to know which of them had given her orders?

'Then what's his name?' Molly asked Louise when the men were talking, so far as she could hear, about the rat race.

'What's whose name?'

'My landlord's.'

'Buck Kettering.'

'Is that his Christian name?'

'I suppose so. Everyone *here* calls him Buck.' To Molly the name seemed ridiculous, a cowboy actor's or the name of an American millionaire.

'A nickname?' Something invented perhaps, to hide the 'S.'?

'No, it's real.' Ken turned to her and knew all about it. 'He gave me a cheque once, after we'd done some work on the pool at "La Felicità". I remember how he signed it because it sounded so impressive: "T. Buckland Kettering".'

Molly looked round at the party. Leaning against a recumbent Henry Moore, a group of English Sloanes, lanky people, all wearing old men's panama hats regardless of sex, shared out the single bottle of champagne they had bought at the Duty Free and laughed loudly. The Baronessa was out in the garden now, a white cardigan slung over her shoulders, talking to a line of young Italians who were sitting on a wall in varying postures of exhaustion. A man with a bald head, brown as a walnut, with a sweater knotted round his neck, was dancing with a fair-haired woman whose face Molly couldn't see, but whose sunburnt arms moved mechanically, like a doll's arms, in time with the music. And then, as she sat watching the dancers, Molly thought of something which made her shiver, so that Ken Corduroy, noticing it, thought she felt cold in the dark garden and offered her the sweater which, like so many of the older guests, he wore knotted about his neck. *B.* is for Buck, she thought. So who had written the note in opposite 'The Flagellation'? Was that another of Sandra's productions, and did she want her husband *B. lost and gone forever*, and was his existence her *Current Liability*? Did Mrs Kettering want Buck to leave her or was she considering a more extreme solution? Because of the story the Baronessa had just told her, Molly thought immediately of death.

'Molly!' Her husband was calling to her, as it seemed, from a long way off. 'Mr Corduroy was asking you something.'

She turned to Ken, feeling it very unlikely that she'd know the answer.

'We were wondering about that charming old gentleman we've seen you with in Mondano.'

'My father,' Molly had to admit.

'We've seen him around with the Padre too. Is he a very religious type of person?'

'I think he'd like to be Pope,' she told them with a sort of weary insight. 'Only he doesn't at all believe in God.'

Molly spent more time with the Corduroys and was introduced to the Tapscotts, a white-haired couple: Nicholas, who had been the British Consul in Florence, and his wife Connie. They had settled in 'Toscana', they told her, finishing each other's sentences, 'to take a pot-shot at painting and . . . jeepers isn't painting difficult! Honest injun, it's a dashed sight harder than the consular service. Nicholas bashes away at the landscape and I did . . . Yes, the missus did the child you may have noticed in the sitting-room at 'La Felicità'. . . . Pretty terrible really . . . Nonsense, old girl. You knock my landscapes for six.' Molly remembered the child in pantaloons and decided that it must have been bought by Sandra and not Buck Kettering. They also met two elderly men, introduced as Tim and Gavin from San Pietro, who ignored Molly and proposed a 'boys' night out in our local "trat" if Hughie wanted a rest from the little ones'. It was to avoid this last couple that Hugh unexpectedly asked her to dance, which they did unsuccessfully, their bodies unused to performing together, and Molly keeping to the shadows in case the children should spot them and never be able to forgive the embarrassment they had been caused.

Towards midnight she went to tell Henrietta and Samantha that it was far past their bedtime. For some time she looked round the garden for them and then went into the house. The lights were off in the big drawing-room but someone had lit the logs which had been piled in the fireplace. The young people were draped about the furniture or lay in couples on the floor in utter silence whilst the firelight flickered. Sitting on a carved stool on the hearthrug, holding forth like the Ancient Mariner, Haverford was bringing some long anecdote to a conclusion. From the expressions on the faces of his audience, which included the two Pargeter girls, it was impossible to tell whether they were listening to him or not.

'There was this Andrea, lived somewhere down Oakley Street,

danced for a time with the Ballet Rambert. Anyway, I used to call
on her, quite unexpectedly, once in every month or two perhaps,
and she used to entertain me most hospitably. Well, I dropped in
one evening, a summer evening it was, as I recall it, after I'd been
to dinner at the Chelsea Arts Club and I felt in urgent need of a
little female company. Well, it was only a bedsitter and Andrea
and I sat on the one divan having a smoke and a glass of the fizzy
stuff I always brought her, and I said, "What about slipping
between the sheets"?'

'Henrietta! Samantha!' Molly called from the doorway, and
then, 'We're going now.' Her voice had no effect on the audience
or on her father's story.

'But she put me off! Unusually, she prevaricated. Not tonight,
she said. Tonight wouldn't be very convenient. And do you know
what? I felt a sort of stirring beneath me, the faintest possible
movement. And then, damn me, it was clear that I was sitting on
someone! Do you know who it was? It was a little husband who'd
been sleeping under the covers.'

Haverford was laughing and some of his audience nodded
solemnly, as though they understood. 'Come on,' said Molly to
the children. 'You really must come on. We're going now.'

'Going? And we've never had a chance to get together all the
evening.'

Mollie turned. It was the woman with sun-browned arms and
the white dress who had been dancing. Now she was smiling,
accompanied by a very young Italian who might have been one of
the waiters her old school-friend saved for the last.

'Don't say you don't remember me! Rosie Fortinbras.' Of
course she remembered when they first saw Siena together.
Before she could think of an appropriate greeting, Rosie said,
'Welcome back to Italy. Better luck this time.'

'I'm not quite sure what you mean.'

'Well, you didn't do all that well on our grizzly school trip, did
you? Not if you were on the look-out for adventure.'

CHAPTER SEVEN

On the sixth day of their holiday, the water ran out.

Nancy Leadbetter's party had ended late on Wednesday night. Rosie Fortinbras had proved to be of minimal use as a source of information. She had known Nancy for years, of course. She and Carlo were staying a night, possibly two nights, because Carlo hadn't felt up to snuff all the summer (here young Carlo groaned wearily and leant against a wall in confirmation of his feeling considerably below snuff). Had she met Mr Kettering? Well, of course, absolutely everyone knew Buck. Charming? What a question to ask! I suppose it depended on whether you went for the older man, which, speaking for herself, Rosie didn't and never had done and was, anyway, leaving to stay with the Spratlings at Porto Ercole and then, perhaps, driving down to Rome to see poor old Jack Gerontius, who hadn't long to go, and after that, who knew? Positano, perhaps, or Capri? She, Rosie, was game for anything, but poor Carlo hadn't been feeling exactly chipper.

In the car Henrietta said sleepily, 'That girl was frightfully snooty and superior.'

'Which girl?'

'The girl talking to us.'

'She gave us nougat,' Samantha said. 'It was disgusting.'

'Why was she so snooty and superior?'

'Because she said we were in her house.'

In the dark front of the car Molly felt another tingle of

excitement, as though, in her childhood fantasies of detection she had found, at the scene of a crime, a clue which was going to unlock the whole mystery. '*Her* house? Whatever did she mean by that?'

'Her parents' house.'

'Parents? Who is she?'

'Chrissie Kettering.'

Molly had gone round the party trying to pick up information, listening for hints dropped during casual conversations and there, talking to her own children and eating nougat, was the girl who might have told her almost everything.

'Do you know' – she did her best to sound unconcerned – 'this Chrissie Kettering at all?'

'Oh, yes. She's always in the Muckrakers Club.' Henrietta's tone was accusing. The Muckrakers, a teenage disco which occupied, on Friday nights only, premises in the Charing Cross Road, was the Mecca of that young teenage set which those who had reached seventeen called 'the squeakies' and who were prepared, according to their older critics, to take over the world. On the two or three occasions when Henrietta had been allowed to go there, Molly had insisted on collecting her. She had waited long after midnight in the empty street until the Muckrakers doors were thrown open and 'the squeakies' filled the street with shouts of resentment at being fetched from their pleasures so early and the sound of long, passionate, gossiping farewells until school on Monday morning. And among that crowd, while she waited, might well have been Chrissie.

'So she lives in London?'

'Oh, yes. Well, she must do if she's always in the Muckraker.'

'Nowhere in England. We've severed all connections. People like me and the Ketterings, we're the ex-pats.' Molly remembered what Fosdyke had told her. Once again she would have to review her ideas.

'She lives in England, with her mother and father?'

'Honestly, Mum. Well, I mean it's not the sort of thing you ask people.'

'She did say her father hated letting his house to strangers during the summer.'

'He said that, did he?' Molly was wounded.

'Oh, apparently he doesn't mind letting it to you.' Samantha, a tired but considerate voice, comforted her mother from the back of the car.

'Why me in particular?'

'He said you sounded as if you were really fond of pictures.'

'He thought you'd appreciate it, that's why.'

'We would?' Hugh was driving fast along the bumpy, stone-skittering road, longing for sleep.

'No. Mummy in particular,' Henrietta told him. At which moment their car headlights lit the stone walls of 'La Felicità' so that they appeared golden against the black velvet of the sky. Forgetting all her questions, Molly could only feel a secret satisfaction.

Inside the domestic fortress all was well. Giovanna, smiling as she left, said that the *bambina* had never stirred and she had taken the opportunity to do a pile of ironing.

'Plays funny tricks on you, does the mind,' Haverford said as he poured out a final nightcap of Chianti. 'I never thought old Nancy Leadbetter would forget that I rogered her. Over a longish period, too.'

That was all the talk of 'rogering' Molly heard that night. Hugh lay on his separate pillow; it was strange, she often thought, how he managed to sleep without getting his hair untidy and his inert body showed no interest in her. She lay awake for a long time, looking at a pattern of moonlight on the stone floor of the bedroom and listening to the distant complaints of the chained dog she now knew to belong to Buck Kettering. Buck, the man who was possibly in danger, the man whose wife wanted him *lost and gone forever*, the man who might perhaps already . . . 'But you don't know that,' she told herself, 'you don't really know anything.' At last she fell asleep, but it seemed to her that she woke up some time in the night. She was lying on her side and Hugh was on his side also, clinging to her back, as though for protection. And then, somewhere in the house, she heard a sound which gave her a dry, tingling sensation in the mouth like a small, electric shock. It was the feeling she had had as a child when she frightened herself with a detective story. It now hardly entered her life except for the time when, in the dark patch of garden below the bedroom window, she had seen the snake. Somewhere in the house she was sure a handle was turned quietly, a door was opened and then closed again with care. She would not, of course, have been surprised to hear her father making one of his many nocturnal pilgrimages, but he would have taken his stick, banged doors, bumped against furniture, turned on lights, even sung an old pop song from the sixties if he could have been sure of waking the children. This door was closed too carefully, perhaps too stealthily, for it to have been any of Haverford's doing. The bedroom was on the same level as the terrace, the small sitting-room and the kitchen, and so she waited for the sound of another door or footsteps on the stone staircase down to the entrance hall. But, hearing nothing more, she decided that she must have been mistaken and went back to sleep.

The next morning, alone in the small sitting-room, Molly took out the Piero della Francesca book, as a scholar might take a work from the shelves to check a reference. Molly's special subject was the Ketterings; but when she turned to the reproduction of 'The Flagellation' the book was empty, the list gone. Puzzled at first, she turned every page, then she held up the book by its spine and let the pages flutter; no sheet of paper fell out. And yet she knew it had been there when she closed the book and put it back on the shelf. Someone had taken it, someone, presumably, who knew where to find it.

'You should have come with us. The pool's wonderful.' Hugh with his hair wet, carrying Jacqueline and leading his two other daughters, all of them making wet footmarks on the stone floor, came in from the terrace. He looked very young and, she was surprised how irritated it made her feel, innocent. She thought of telling him that a note from their landlady, contemplating the disappearance of her husband *forever*, had gone, vanished, and just who, did he think, was likely to have taken it? But she could imagine his tolerant lawyer's smile as he demolished her fears and speculations. He would cast doubt on the words of the note for which there was now only 'secondary evidence, as we lawyers would say'. What fears she had, and even cherished, she decided to keep to herself.

'Only one thing about that pool,' Hugh said, depositing Jacqueline wrapped in a damp towel like a warm parcel in his wife's arms, 'the tide's gone down a bit. Perhaps it's leaking.'

'I'll see about it.'

'All right. Call on me if you have any trouble.. I thought we might have a treat and drive into Siena.' Hugh went away to get dressed. Molly rang the house which Signor Fixit was guarding but there was no reply. The house-sitter was sitting somewhere else and the phone echoed in an empty hallway.

Then she rang Nancy Leadbetter who was fetched by a servant and, after a long interval, answered sleepily.

'Whoever is it?'

'It's Molly Pargeter.'

'Molly *who*?'

'Pargeter. We came to your party. It was so kind of you . . .'

'I can't remember.'

'I thought I should drive over and thank you personally.'

'No need for that.'

'And my children would love to meet all those young people again. Apparently Chrissie Kettering was there . . .'

'Chrissie who?'

'Kettering. You know' – she almost had to force herself to use the strange name – 'Buck Kettering's daughter.'

'No. He's away. Travelling.'

'Who?'

'Buck. He's not here. He's let his house to some English people.'

'Yes, I know. That's us.'

'Who are you?'

'Molly. Molly Pargeter.'

'And you say your children were here last night?'

'Yes. That's right.' She tried to sound as bright as possible. 'Two young girls.'

'Well, they're not here now. They've all cleared off. Vamoosed. Moved on at dawn to Athens or Antibes or somewhere or other. I'm sorry I can't help. They left no phone numbers. Your two girls will probably be sending you a postcard.'

'My two girls are here.'

'Where's here?'

'The Ketterings' house.'

'You know the people he's let it to? Do tell me, what're they like? More boring English?'

'Is Chrissie Kettering still with you?' Molly raised her voice slightly as though speaking to a foreigner and tried to get to the heart of the matter.

'No. I told you. They've all gone. All the young people. And they've left the most terrible mess in their bedrooms. Do let's chat again some time and you can tell me all the gossip about Buck's new tenants.' And Nancy Leadbetter rang off.

'The thing about the Sienese,' Haverford said, voicing a thought he intended to use in one of his 'Jottings', 'is that they always want somebody else to do their dirty work for them. I mean, take the time when Cardinal Alfonso of Siena wanted to murder Pope Leo the Tenth. *Niente fotografie per favore.*'

However, the waiter in the Piazza del Campo had taken Hugh's camera off their table and was waving to them to sit closer. 'Oh God,' said Henrietta and pulled her hat over her eyes. Hugh moved his profile a little towards his family, conscious of the fact that he always looked his best in a snap whereas the sight of a lens made his wife flustered.

'I mean, he didn't go and strangle Leo himself. He corrupted the surgeon Battista da Vercelli, who was to treat a fistula just below the Pontiff's left buttock . . .'

They had arrived in Siena when the recently washed streets smelled fresh and metallic. They had parked by the stadium and walked down towards the Campo. On the way the children straggled behind them or dived down lanes where archways blocked out the steadily mounting sun. They inquired the price of medieval patterned paper diaries and portfolios for the girls, and bought them small address books as a concession to their shrill demands. They gave Jacqueline a bright parish flag to flap and trail along the ground. In the Palazzo Pubblico they saw Martini's cavalier, dressed in the same golden, diamond-patterned cloak as his horse. The landscape he rode through was as white as a desert.

'Bloody dry, the hills around here,' Hugh had said. 'No wonder the pool looked empty.'

And then they had sat in the line of cafés and restaurants on the northern side of the cockle-shaped square, behind the fountain carved with women and wolves and dragons, opposite the tall, pink bell-tower. Samantha led Jacqueline out to buy a paper bag of corn to feed the portly, over-privileged pigeons and Haverford Downs gave them a taste of his 'Jottings'.

'The Sienese Cardinal persuaded this surgeon to poison his patient, you see. Well, of course, the whole plot was found out and the unhappy doctor drawn and quartered or whatever. Can't remember what happened to the Cardinal. Did he get beatified or secretly strangled? Can't you tell me that, Henry? I suppose not. Schools never hand out any *useful* information.'

'Who's coming,' said Molly, collecting her bits of shopping and standing up, 'to the picture gallery?'

'I'm *dying* for a swim,' Henrietta panted. 'When are we going back to "La Felicità"?'

'We've seen pictures.' Samantha returned with the youngest Pargeter, leaving a flurry of disappointed pigeons.

'Oh, honestly, need we?'

'Isn't it rather a long walk?'

'Anyway we haven't had an ice-cream. You promised.'

'I must confess I'd rather sit on and view the passing scene.' Haverford, his head cocked on one side, was casting an eye over blonde girls from Sweden, Guildford or Saskatoon, quite undiscouraged when they didn't return his smile but merely quickened their pace towards the souvenir stalls. 'At my time of life there's more pleasure to be had from the rear view of a pair of Levis than in all the Martinis the old rascal ever painted. Wouldn't you agree with that, Hughie?'

Hugh looked into his glass of white wine. It was hard to tell if he was more discomforted at being accused of being as lecherous or as old as his father-in-law.

So Molly walked alone and ended up in front of another Martini painting in the Pinacoteca. The tall and helpful Saint Agostino stood surrounded by disasters, someone was attacked by a wolf, a child fell from a window, a horse fell into a ravine. As soon as a flying angel whispered news of these events into his ear, the Saint put down his book and flew, like Batman, to the rescue. So he swooped to catch the falling child, drive away the wolf or restore the horse – all these miracles being depicted in small panels round the central figure of the Saint.

'Signor Fixit,' a voice behind her spoke her thoughts. She turned to see Nicholas Tapscott the ex-consul and painter. Dressed in a white shirt and trousers, and with his white hair and a face apparently never submitted to the sunshine, he looked as though he had been rolled in flour preparatory to cooking. 'Doesn't that remind you of old Fosdyke?'

'I was thinking that,' Molly agreed. 'He seems to be fixing everything.'

'Wonderful painting.'

'Yes.'

'Full of life, of course.'

'It seems to be.'

'Neither Connie nor I could touch it. That's what we can't seem to get into our pictures. Life . . .'

'I suppose it's hard.'

'Not that we expect to be Martini. Nothing like it. But all the years we've been trying. Might have been able to capture "life". Can't think why not, in fact.'

'I'm sorry.' Molly hardly knew what to say.

'Dedicated painters, both of us. A.1 light out here. Old masters to study. Long winter days with nothing else to do. One problem. We're so jolly rotten at it. Know what you're going to say. Why not give it up?'

'No. Of course not.' Molly had, at least, thought it.

'Dedicated, you see. All the great ones dedicated. Van Gogh, Raphael, even old Martini. Easy to be dedicated if you're a blooming genius. But to go on being dedicated when you're a rotten painter! I tell you. That calls for heroic devotion.' He smiled at her, revealing strong, yellowish teeth. It didn't seem to her as though he were joking.

'Gift of ubiquity,' he went on, looking at the picture. 'All the saints had it. They could turn up wherever they liked. Several places at the same time. Only not everyone wants all that helping, do they? It's a bit disconcerting to be minding your own business. Just getting on with things. Then having a blooming great saint swooping down. Interfering with everything. People resent that. Why didn't Nancy ask old Fosdyke to that excellent party?'

'I don't know.'

'Not universally popular, Signor Fixit.'

When they got back from Siena, the pool was three quarters empty. Deprived of a swim, Henrietta decided to wash her hair but the bathroom tap could only be persuaded to emit a trickle of dark brown water, after which it coughed, spluttered and ran dry. By six o'clock there was no water in the loos. Molly rang the blessed Saint Fixit for the fourth time but there was still no reply. Then she rang Nancy Leadbetter again.

'I'm sorry to disturb you. This is Molly Pargeter. I rang this morning . . .'

'About your child. Of course, I remember quite clearly. You won't have got a postcard yet.'

'No. It's about the water at "La Felicità". We seem to have been cut off.'

'You can't keep them at home forever, you know. You've got to let go.'

'I mean all the water's gone. In the taps and everything. It's terribly inconvenient. Do you know who I ought to ring? The plumbers?'

'Never heard of them.'

'What?'

'They must be new here.'

'Who?'

'The Plummers. Where do they live?'

'I just wondered if you knew . . .'

'Anyway, if there's no water in the Ketterings' house I don't think you should take it. Not if you've got children who'll need a regular wash.'

Molly gave it up and drove into Mondano. She now knew where Giovanna lived, in a surprisingly large house opposite the café. The windows were dark and she got no answer to her repeated knocking on the front door. She went into Lucca's shop but he had no idea where Giovanna and her family had got to. And when she tried to interest him in *niente acqua*, he laughed as he limped round his shelves serving several customers at once and, shrugging his high shoulders, said, '*Non c'è pioggia, non c'è acqua.*' It was all very well for him to talk, Molly thought, as she saw Signora Lucca washing a lettuce under a running tap in the kitchen. In the café the sullen girl in glasses merely muttered, '*Fuori,*' when she asked where Giovanna and her family were. She wrote a note on a postcard she had bought in Siena about the *acqua* and slid it through Giovanna's letter-box. She still felt, in some calm and detached part of her mind, that Buck Kettering was alive and wouldn't want their holiday ruined.

When she got home she had to boil spaghetti in *acqua minerale*. She was determined to appear unworried in front of her dispirited family.

'There's something wrong with this house,' Hugh said when they sat at their muted dinner. 'I always felt it.'

'There's nothing wrong. It's just been a dry summer. Lucca in the shop was saying that. *Non c'è pioggia, non c'è acqua.*' She drank a quick second glass of wine and did her best to smile round the table.

'If we bath in mineral water,' Samantha said, 'I'd like to try the fizzy sort.'

Only Haverford encouraged his daughter. 'A man can live without water,' he said. 'Hughie, you'll join me in a bottle of duty-free gin, purely for shaving purposes?'

'Giovanna'll be here in the morning,' Molly said with determined brightness. 'I'm sure she'll do something about it.'

'"And Noah said to his wife as they sat down to dine, 'I don't care where the water goes as long as it doesn't get into the wine'"', Haverford quoted gleefully. 'Splendid writer, old Chesterton, even if he wasn't all that expert in the sex department.'

Before they went to bed they had filled buckets with what was left of the pool to use in the lavatories. The children became excited, as though they were preparing to withstand a siege.

CHAPTER EIGHT

The next day the sun woke them early, beating down from a clear sky, baking those tiles it could reach on the terrace so that the children hopped over them, nimble as cats on hot bricks. The distant hills were burnt to the ashen colour of the landscape Martini's horseman rode through, each crowned by its sweltering farmhouse, now turned into a holiday home. Jacqueline ran naked, pulled at skirts and trousers, whining at the heat, but no one was prepared to take a hot and heavy child in their arms. Hugh wore a pair of neat white shorts which made him look ready for tennis. Haverford fanned himself with his panama hat and wheezed like a rusty concertina. Molly stood on the battlements of the terrace and kept a look-out. At last she was rewarded. A cloud of dust appeared on the horizon, the air was again torn by the sound of a high-pitched buzz and Giovanna rode, as Molly hoped, to the rescue.

The powerful maid didn't seem to take the situation seriously. She turned on taps that emitted nothing but a despairing sigh and she laughed. Then, as though it were the most natural thing in the world, she heated up a kettle of pool water to do the washing up. At last a pick-up truck came bumping up the track, containing Giovanna's fat and apparently unsatisfactory husband and a detachment of villagers, including the old men, Molly was sure, who had sat on the wall by the petrol pumps mocking her. Other villagers came straggling over by bicycle and motor bike as though the disappearance of 'La Felicità's water were a kind of annual festival at which prizes would be given and refreshments served. Finally Don Marco came rattling down the track in his battered Fiat and shook Haverford enthusiastically by the hand, ignoring the rest of the family.

The pool was now empty; only a few rapidly drying puddles stained the bottom. The villagers looked down at it with the satisfaction of those who couldn't swim and certainly wouldn't want to try. In time they were joined by a certain Valentino, an elderly man with spectacles and a purple birthmark, who unlocked a shed beside the pool, turned taps and wheels, and announced, in his role as the Ketterings' regular pool attendant, '*Va bene adesso.*' He then went off to cut the nettles under the straggling roses, satisfied that water, should it ever reappear, would no longer escape from the pool.

Meanwhile Giovanna's immense husband had waddled off to a patch of rough grass in which he hunted until he found a small metal square. He began to pull at it, stooping, sweating and shouting, '*Il pozzo!*'

'*Pozzo*,' Haverford translated for the benefit of the English present. 'The stout party's found the well!'

It was at this juncture that Molly was distracted by Jacqueline, who had to be taken back to the house into one of the lavatories sluiced only by a bucket of old chlorinated pool water. Meanwhile the villagers crowded to peer down the open manhole as though it were an interesting accident. What they saw by the further light of a bicycle lamp was a chamber about six feet square and the opening of two pipes, half in and half out of the water-level on opposite walls. If the liquid was meant to flow into the chamber from some high point on the hillside and then out to the tank supplying the house, it had given up in the hot weather and was no longer doing so. Giovanna's husband acquired a long garden cane, which had been supporting a tottering mallow, and with it established the depth. He poked the stick hopelessly towards the mouth of the pipe and grunted, '*Bloccato.*'

'Blocked,' Haverford explained. 'He says it's blocked.'

'*Qualcuno deve scendere.*' The huge man whose belly flowed over his belt and seemed to cascade down the front of his trousers pointed with the cane. They all looked at the dark square and saw that it was hardly a manhole, more of a child-hole. Even Hugh, although able to look like a *jeune premier* from time to time, had filled out as a result of an underdemanding marriage and a sedentary occupation, and would have been a round peg for such a small square hole. The other villagers, eyeing each other speculatively, saw that they were all too full of pasta for the adventure. Henrietta, tall for her age and spectacularly thin, stood by them in the bikini she had put on for the sunshine and the wand, hovering round the crowd, finally pointed at her.

'*La ragazza.*'

'No,' said Hugh. 'Quite definitely no.'

'I don't see why,' Henrietta said. 'It'd be something to do.'

'It'd be a bit of fun!' Haverford, too old and far too tubby to be lowered down any manholes, was enjoying a vicarious adventure.

'*Sì?*' Giovanna's husband raised his eyebrows at Henrietta.

'Why ever not *sì*?'

So the voluminous man held her wrists and lowered the girl's body, small-breasted with protruding hip bones and long legs which, when stretched out together, still showed light between them, into the dark square where she stood with water up to her thighs. He handed down the cane and the bicycle lamp and she waded away into the shadows as the curious faces of the villagers, the anxious face of her father, peered down at her.

Molly had buttoned up the braces on Jacqueline's trousers and found her youngest child a biscuit when she heard the screams. They were high-pitched, terrified and rent the silence of the house. Going to the kitchen window, the biscuit tin still in her hands, she saw an extraordinary sight. The crowd of villagers seemed to be standing round a patch of earth from which the thin, naked arms of a young girl were desperately waving as the screams continued. She picked up Jacqueline and ran out into the garden.

Hugh was coming towards her carrying their tall eldest, whose arms and legs fell haphazardly like a doll's while a long strip of green weed circled her ankle. The sobs still racked her.

'She's all right. Nothing's broken.'

'Hetty! What is it, Hetty? Darling . . .'

'She just panicked, that's all. She must have panicked in the dark.'

'Darling. What did you see? Did you see anything?'

The sobs were less frequent now. But there was still a terrified child's face on a body almost a woman's.

'I thought she'd enjoy it.' Haverford was trotting beside them.

'It was perfectly safe.' Hugh knew that his wife would blame him although he shouldn't be blamed. 'It was quite shallow. They only wanted her to clean out the drain with a stick.'

'And she was the only one thin enough to get down the hole. You'd've stuck there, Molly Coddle. Wouldn't she, Henry? Your mother would have been stuck just like Pooh Bear.' In saying which old Haverford, as usual, brought no help or comfort to anyone.

'What did you see?' Molly asked the question again when she was alone with her daughter in her tower bedroom. Henrietta lay wrapped in a blanket, her teeth chattering, pale in spite of the tan she had been cultivating so carefully.

'I told you. I didn't see anything.'

'Why were you frightened then?'

'I . . . I don't know.'

Molly thought she must have seen *something*. 'There was nothing there? Nothing peculiar at all?'

'I suppose I was stupid, really.'

'But you're not stupid, darling. You know that.'

'I suddenly thought they'd shut me in there. I thought I'd never get out. It was stupid.'

'You know Daddy wouldn't let them do that.'

'I know.'

'So wasn't there anything else?'

'Not really.'

What did that mean, that 'not really'? 'They shouldn't have put you down! They should never.' Molly put her arms round the girl in an unusual demonstration. She had brought them to a place with snakes, although none had appeared to alarm the children, snakes or secrets. She felt guilty as she held her daughter until the shivering and the teeth chattering stopped. And yet she didn't mean to leave 'La Felicità'. She meant to find out more, as much as possible.

In the hallway she found Giovanna telephoning. It sounded as though she were talking to someone she knew well, or at least had dealt with previously, because she called her interlocutor 'Tonio' and smiled continuously as though engaged in invisible wooing and sometimes she laughed.

'*Acqua.*' Molly used the word, unable to make a joke, or a tragedy or even, for the moment, a sentence of it. And Giovanna stood with her hand on the telephone which she had put down and spoke slowly, loudly, as though to an imbecile. Molly understood that water would come by lorry during the afternoon or at least by the evening. Tonio at the Water Board had given her his promise. That should have been arranged before. The *ragazza* should never have been put down the well, that was the fault of her husband who didn't fully understand the house and was ignorant of its ways.

. . . *The purchase of water by the lorry load may strain the budget of even the best-heeled family.* She remembered the warning in the letter written, it now seemed, by Mrs Kettering. Well, Mrs Kettering would have to pay, the woman who wished Buck Kettering *lost and gone forever* would eventually, Molly decided, be responsible for the intake of water.

Giovanna left. Henrietta came down to lunch, still shivering slightly, in a sweater and jeans, and refused to discuss her experience, telling Jacqueline not to be bloody silly when she asked if she'd seen crocodiles.

All that afternoon they waited for the water to come. Molly and Hugh sat on the terrace unable to concentrate on anything else. At the distant sound of a lorry on the Mondano road he would start up, shade his eyes, and then sink back in his chair, disappointed. 'Bloody disaster,' Hugh said, 'this holiday's turning out to be.'

'I don't see why.'

'If it's your idea of fun to sit here . . . waiting for water. We might as well have gone on holiday to the Sahara Desert.'

'It's interesting when things go wrong. That's the way you find out about a place.'

'Find out how much they charge for water. Probably a fortune.'

'We've never bought water by the lorry load before. It's rather an adventure.'

'Well, I don't see why I should pay for it.'

'You won't have to.' But Molly knew he would say when they got home, 'For what I shelled out for the water we might as well have filled the loos up with Chianti.'

He stood up again at what he thought was the sound of a lorry, which also might have been an aeroplane or a dry gust of wind in the trees behind the house. When he sat down he said, because he felt guilty, 'I thought it'd be an adventure for Henrietta.'

'Is that why you let her do it?'

'Of course that's why. Being let down an Italian well, by a crowd of villagers. I thought, that's something she'll remember all her life.'

'Perhaps it will be.'

'But of course she didn't enjoy it. That's the trouble with adventures. People start out on them and then they go wrong. A bit like taking this house for instance.'

'What upset her?'

'Was that a lorry?'

'No. What do you suppose upset her?'

'It was cold and dark down there, I imagine. Perhaps she wondered if she'd ever get out.'

'That's all?'

'What else do you think?'

'I don't know. Anyway, nothing she wants to talk about.'

By six o'clock the water hadn't arrived and Haverford, looking at their despondent faces, said, 'It's like a death in the family.' Being, as he said, temporarily flush, he took them all for a plate of spaghetti in a 'trat' in Mondano. In fact he had telegraphed the *Informer* for some expenses 'to entertaining priest', and, bewildered by this unusual demand, the editor had wired back money. 'This is the little spot where the locals eat,' he told the family as they took their places under the umbrellas in the small Piazza Emanuele. The locals consisted of the party of Sloanes Molly had seen at Nancy Leadbetter's and another English family with two teenage sons whom Haverford, loudly and explicitly, urged his eldest granddaughter to 'get off with' or 'drag away to the disco', although he didn't suggest where a disco might be found in Mondano. These invitations made Henrietta feel that she would do anything, even return to the well, to avoid the company of the two youths one of whom bore across his chest the legend MY MOTHER WENT TO ISRAEL AND ONLY BROUGHT ME BACK THIS LOUSY T-SHIRT.

After some confusion over the ordering, Haverford gave them a lengthy account of his love affair with one of a pair of identical twins whom he'd met at a *Red Mole* party in 1965. 'And it was only when we were tucked up in her *freezing* room in Charlotte Street that I got this strange feeling and I said, "But you're not Janet, are you?" And she gave me the immortal reply, "No, I'm Heather, but won't I do?" I made a short story of the business and sent it up to *Encounter*, but the puritanical buggers in charge sent me a rejection slip! Do you find that believable? Even

Haverford Downs receives the occasional rejection slip! It was ever thus with genius. Thomas Hardy always included a stamped, addressed envelope with his contributions. Magnificant title that, don't you think Hughie – *I'm Heather, but Won't I Do?* The whole problem of identity raised in a single sentence. And *still* the buggers rejected me.'

Of all the family Jacqueline had received the warmest welcome by the waiter, was always asked what she wanted first, and called *Bellissima*. Now she was asleep, her fists clenched and her hair half-way into a quarter-eaten plate of spaghetti, so Haverford called for *il doloroso* and to his daughter's surprise pulled money out of a back pocket, new ten thousand lire notes. 'I told you, I'm flush at the moment. Flush and eager to show a little hospitality to the best daughter an old man ever had to comfort his declining years,' he added with patent insincerity.

And then, on the way home, something happened which raised their spirits almost to the point of singing. On the dirt road from the castle, headlights blinded them, great tyres crunched to a standstill and Hugh backed on to the bramble bushes. What he made way for was the long cylindrical body of a lorry. A dark giant of a man, possibly Tonio, leaned out of the lorry's cabin to thank them for pulling out of the way. '*Acqua?*' '*Sì, acqua.*' '*Grazie, grazie tanto.*' 'Thank God.' '*Grazie mille.*' The cries of gratitude sounded from the car and heartfelt from Haverford, 'You're a better man than I am, Gunga Din.' Even the child in Molly's arms smiled sleepily when her sisters told her that the water had come at last.

As soon as she got into the house, Molly ran up the stone stairs to the kitchen tap before she switched on the light. There was a cough, a splutter in the darkness, but no water. Hugh called from the loo to tell her that pulling the chain produced a cascade of silence. Depressed and disappointed, she went to the square of kitchen window and looked out on to the pool, which glittered in the moonlight, now flowing with the precious and expensive liquid which should have filled their most urgent needs. 'Oh,

Italy!' she said to herself, on the verge of tears, 'whatever are you up to now?'

'I don't suppose you paid the almighty lire, did you?' Hugh had gone into San Pietro in an effort to find the *Daily Telegraph* which had disappeared from their lives with Signor Fixit. Giovanna was in the house, banging the washing up unhappily into a bowl of chlorinated water. The rest of the family sat huddled round the pool, rather as rose bushes, shallots and date palms will crowd thirstily round an oasis in the desert. Haverford was writing his 'Jottings', young Jacqueline was splashing in her arm-bands while her two older sisters tried to further define the watch marks on their wrists. Molly stood looking at the lapping water with Ken Corduroy, expert on garden pools and pergolas, who had arrived quite unexpectedly in his Volvo estate.

'We couldn't have paid them. We went out to eat in Mondano and they just dumped all the water in here.'

'Well, there you are, you see. They do like to be paid.'

'But they came at *night*. Under cover of darkness. They came when we couldn't possibly have expected them.'

'That's what they tend to do.'

'But *why*?'

'Please don't ask me to explain what goes on in the mind of an Italian Water Board. It's been a complete mystery to me ever since I arrived here. It's like their attitude to religion and their bloody Communist Party. Totally confusing, to say the least. It comes as a shock, I have to tell you, to anyone who's spent a lifetime dealing with the perfectly decent chaps you run into at Thames Water.'

'I suppose I don't know exactly what Giovanna told them.'

'Of course you don't. And you don't know what their game is exactly.'

'Their game?'

'Might it be, I'm only hazarding a guess, you realize that, but might it be that they want you to get them out here again?'

'Will they come?'

'Who knows? Unless you pay them.'

'What would they do?'

'You mean where would they put the water next time? Maybe on the sitting-room carpet. Your guess is as good as mine, Mrs Pargeter.'

Molly imagined a dehydrated house turned into a swamp and said hastily, 'Of course I'd pay them. But they never left a bill.'

'Like their taxi drivers. Haven't you had that at the end of a journey. 'What's the fare?' 'What you like!' With an ever so charming shrug of the shoulders. They trust you to get into a panic and err wildly on the side of generosity.'

'The Water Board would behave like that?'

'Especially the Water Board.'

Molly fell silent. The sun lulled her brain. Henrietta dived into the pool and her head emerged, neat and glossy as a seal's. It was too hot to argue. 'How much,' she said, 'do you think would be reasonable?' He had, after all, some experience of pools.

'Five hundred and thirty grand. In lire.'

'Two hundred and fifty pounds?' Molly's mathematics were instantaneous. The Ketterings would have to pay in the end, but it was a sizeable chunk of their holiday money. 'All right, if that's what it costs.'

'I should think it costs at least that.'

'I'll send it.'

'In the post? How long do you imagine that's going to take? You'd next clean your teeth back in England. Look, I happen to be calling at the office this afternoon. Pool business.' He had little difficulty in persuading Mrs Pargeter to run into Mondano with him and cash some traveller's cheques. When she left the pool side, she said to her father, 'I'm just popping into the bank with Mr Corduroy.' 'Oh, yes,' said Haverford, 'of course you are,' and didn't look up from his 'Jottings'.

So, shortly before noon, Molly trusted Mr Corduroy with her money and at six o'clock when she was in the kitchen opening a packet of cornflakes for Jacqueline's supper the tap, left on, coughed discreetly and loosed off a generous gush of what looked to her like particularly clean and upmarket water. She gave Jacqueline a hot bath and later, with a feeling of gratitude for some sort of deliverance, she laid dinner out on the terrace. They ate by candlelight, with highlights from *Turandot* playing, but received no visitors of any sort.

After dinner Molly, who had taken to reading there in the afternoons, went into the big downstairs sitting-room to find her book. She saw it, a paperback Margery Allingham, on the shadowy sofa and moved towards it. Outside the tall windows the darkness came suddenly, unexpectedly, without any long twilight. Then she felt a breath of air and the creak of the door she hadn't altogether shut and which led out to the courtyard. The visitor, whoever it was, came in silently, and looking round, not knowing who or what to expect, Molly saw the tall sad-looking dog, its eyes wet and its pink tongue lolling, which Buck had apparently abandoned to the Castello Crocetto. It moved uncertainly towards her, its uncut claws rattling on the tiles, and gave her hand a soft, wet greeting. At that moment the telephone rang.

She waited for three rings, but she knew that Hugh wouldn't pick up a machine that might buzz and shout '*Pronto*!' at him. Then she lifted the receiver while still holding out her other hand for the dog to lick.

'Vittoria Dulcibene,' the telephone announced. 'I am missing that horrible dog. Has it gone off to look for Buck?'

'Yes, it's here.'

'It should be kept chained. My gardener is too soft-hearted. Shall I come and pick it up or will it do in the morning?'

Molly thought it would do in the morning, and then she said, 'Was it *Mr* Kettering who left the dog with you?'

'Well, no. It was Sandra, actually. She dumped Manrico here, with compliments of Buck.'

'I expect you know how to get in touch with her, in case of trouble, I mean. Is she in London?'

'London? I don't know about London. There or in Rome, perhaps. It's hard to know where they get to. Why do you ask who left the dog with me?'

'I don't know. Mr Kettering going off without the dog and his wife bringing it round to you – it all seems a bit odd if it's so devoted to him.'

'People may be devoted to us and we're not so devoted to them. Haven't you found that?'

'Not really.'

'Then you are lucky, Mrs Pargeter. Shut that appalling Manrico up in a shed somewhere. I'll send the gardener in the morning.'

The line went dead and, unfolding itself from the mat, the dog gave a single, peremptory bark that might have been the result of an interrupted dream. The sudden sound brought down the children and Hugh, who looked nervously at the Borzoi.

'What's that? The Hound of the Baskervilles?'

'I think it's the Ketterings' dog. It seems to have come home.'

'Well, we can't be expected to look after it. Not on top of everything else.'

However the girls took the dog upstairs where it wolfed all that was left of the lasagne and went to sleep in front of the hearth, quieter than it ever had been at the Castello Crocetto.

CHAPTER NINE

JOTTINGS FROM TUSCANY
by *Haverford Downs*

As I told my faithful readers last week, this particular old gent was transported by an extremely uncomfortable magic carpet (B.A. steerage, Apex ticket, with all the delights of plastic food and stewardesses trained by the Obergrüppenführer at Heathrow) to Chiantishire, that old-established suburb of Wimbledon, which can't have changed much since Britannia ruled the waves and wogs stopped at Calais. It's true that there are a few natives here (known as 'Eyeties' to the British colonials), who are useful to serve as maids, waiters or 'chaps to look after the swimming-pool'. Speaking of which, when one such status symbol ran dry here the other day, a child was lowered into a pit to clean out the drains, so the nineteenth-century tradition of infant chimney-sweeps is alive and well and living in Tuscany.

Is there, Informer readers may well ask, no underground movement, no Maquis, no risorgimento fighting British Imperialism? Well, the wartime resistance movement was run by the Communists, who stood almost single-handed against the Nazi menace, and suffered heroically for it. The 'maid' in the villa in which I am lodged for the purposes of research (she is a statuesquely beautiful and highly intelligent woman who is called 'maid', rather in the way the South Africans call elderly black servants 'boy') suffered the horror of seeing both her parents shot by the Germans whilst the aristocrats from the local castle entertained the S.S. officers to black market dinners of wild boar and chocolate sauce.

At this point in his writing a white pigeon which had been fluttering round the swimming-pool alighted on the table, took two steps forward and excreted on the 'Jottings', no doubt in the interests of historical accuracy. Haverford took a new sheet of paper and continued to compose, undeterred.

By and large, of course, your average Euro-Communist is about as far to the left as an English liberal, but here, among these dry Tuscan hills, they have a tougher breed, who hark back to the guerrilla fighters of 1943. Typical of them is our local priest, Don Marco. In many ways, the good arciprete *is nostalgic for the days of Stalin and he regards Russian* glasnost *rather as he would the Vatican bank investing heavily in Durex. 'If you English tourists get too powerful around here,' he told me over a glass of grappa, and with a particularly charming smile, 'I think I can remember where the old machine-guns are buried.'*

Footnote. I happened to meet a former girlfriend while out for a constitutional among these perfumed hills and blow me if, much to her chagrin, I couldn't remember ever having slid between the sheets with her. Half-way through the conversation, of course, the penny dropped but how was I then to say, in the words of that potent piece of cheap music, 'Ah, yes, I remember it well.'? A bottle of Chianti Classico for the reader who suggests the most tactful way out of this conversational senso unico *before next Saturday.*

Haverford wrote in a small, meticulously neat hand. He would telephone in his copy but didn't want to be overheard by the family who might be critical, so he decided to call on Fosdyke the next day and use the telephone in the house his fan was guarding. He watched the slim body of Samantha dive into the pool and thought that by the time she came of an age for love he would no doubt be drifting round eternity in the unwelcome company of his wife with all rogering out of the question. In the hot sunshine his body stirred uselessly to life and he fell asleep.

*

But Haverford's daughter found sleep that night hard to come by. It was very hot and she lay under the single sheet staring up at the high moonlit ceiling and thinking about T. Buckland Kettering. Her mind vacillated between laughing at her fears and suspecting a terrible mystery. Surely, she told herself, there was nothing unusual about a family who let their house and left no address. Had she not wildly exaggerated the significance of the advertisement? Might not the Ketterings specify girl children only as reasonably as 'no pets' or 'using the premises for business purposes forbidden'? Perhaps the dinner on the terrace by candle-light was no more than a helpful suggestion intended to add to their pleasure in 'La Felicità', as was the idea of a trip across the Mountains of the Moon to Urbino. All that seemed to her to be like a man writing, a foreigner to Italy, advising other foreigners, a teacher displaying his wisdom to likely pupils. And yet . . . (Far away now she heard the dog Manrico, chained up once more, lamenting its departed master.) And yet, the letters were signed 'S.' for Sandra Kettering, and Sandra must have left the typed note of her most private intentions in the Piero book opposite 'The Flagellation'. Had she been wrong in all her first impressions?

And 'B.', she thought, what did that mean *B. lost and gone forever*? Surely no more than that the Ketterings were splitting up, like so many of their acquaintances, as even the Pargeters might have done, had it not been for the late, unexpected, un-planned arrival of Jacqueline. The Ketterings also had a young child, Signor Fixit had told her, little Violetta, who came 'as a bit of an afterthought'; but that wouldn't prevent a separation, even a divorce, which, it seemed, Sandra Kettering welcomed. So Buck had gone off somewhere. No doubt, he had found another woman, and to Sandra and to Molly, he was gone for ever.

Then she remembered the car that had interrupted their dinner on the terrace. She had walked down the stairs and for a moment been taken for, and almost become, Kettering's wife. She couldn't guess why Sandra Kettering in her detailed instructions had arranged for her to be there and for that mistake to be made. And then she thought of how she might find an answer to some of her questions.

When the envelope had arrived she had put it on the mantelpiece in the small sitting-room, but almost at once she had decided to take it more closely into her possession. She told herself that it must be kept carefully, to be left out for Mrs Kettering when their stay was over, so she had put it in a compartment of her handbag. It had remained there, she was sure, even after the note in the Piero book had vanished. So now she got up carefully, her nightdress clinging damply to her body, and laid the sheet back over her sleeping husband with as much respect as if he had been dead. Then she lifted her bag from the chair, turned the door handle with exaggerated care and made for the kitchen. Safely there, she lit the gas, with one of the solid and reliable wooden matches Signor Fixit had been able to find for her, and put on the kettle. She made herself a cup of English breakfast tea and then, with the kettle still boiling, steamed open the envelope. When the gum was melted she opened it and slid out a single sheet of unheaded paper on which a short message was written in Italian. She took it into the sitting-room where the dictionaries were kept and did her best to translate: *It is excellent news that the whole business has been done successfully. Now we can enjoy the future without anxiety. We will meet very soon, I hope. For the moment I send this messenger. Distinti saluti. Claudio.* Molly turned the paper over and found a list of figures prefixed with lire signs and equipped with what seemed to her to be generous allowances of noughts. This list was headed with the letters, A.I.C., which meant nothing to her.

She remembered a tube of gum Samantha had bought to stick postcards and photographs into her project ('My Italian Holiday'), and refixed the envelope, returning it to her handbag. Then she went back to the kitchen, poured herself another cup of tea, and crossed to the window. She looked out at the moonlight in the well-filled pool and her brain was racing. The business that had been done successfully was undoubtedly the business of seeing Buck *lost and gone forever*. Might he have been despatched by those means, other than useless lawyers, which were considered by Sandra when she wrote the list? So now Mrs Kettering could enjoy the future with her Claudio, whom she would meet again after a decent interval. That was the message Molly had received when she had come down the stairs and left her husband at the dinner table. And as she stood at the window she seemed to hear again, as clearly as she had heard it two days before, the sound of Henrietta screaming. The remembered sound had an extraordinary effect on Molly. She ran down the stairs, unbolted the heavy wooden door and was off, running in her nightdress, barefoot across the garden, holding the torch which she had snatched from the chest in the entrance hall.

Through all this Hugh slept. Had he woken up and looked out of one of the bedroom windows he would have seen his wife in the moonlight pulling desperately at the handle on a manhole cover. When she had lifted it, she prostrated herself on the ground and peered into the blackness below with the help of the well-provided villa's torch. She saw the water at a higher level than it had been when Henrietta had been lowered into it and the mouths of the two pipes were almost submerged. And then she saw that there was a narrow, open doorway in the wall opposite her, which opened on to another chamber. There was nothing the big, anxious woman could do to investigate the matter further and although she played the beam of the torch on every inch visible to her, she couldn't see whatever it was that might have made her daughter scream other than the damp and secret darkness of the place.

After a while she felt exhausted and walked slowly back to the house, shutting the front door carefully behind her. Hugh didn't wake as she lay down on top of the sheet beside him and before dawn she fell into the heaviest sleep she had enjoyed that holiday. In the morning she wondered if her inspection of the villa's water-works might not have been part of a dream and looked carefully to confirm that the letter to Signora Kettering was still in her handbag. Later she locked it away in her own empty suitcase, a place where she was sure even Giovanna would never find it.

The house from which Haverford Downs intended to telephone his 'Jottings' belonged to the Harrisons, an elderly couple who had set off to visit their daughter in Toronto. They had arranged a tenant but been let down, and Signor Fixit had promised to go and sit in their villa, having let his own house. The arrangement suited him well. The Harrisons' home was perfectly kept, equipped with all the latest devices, with its cream carpets and matching walls, with its rôtisserie and dishwashing machine and its large television set on which the Harrisons played videos of their favourite movies which they swapped with a group of friends who lived around Siena. So, in the winter evenings, they would draw the curtains and watch *The Sound of Music* or *Bridge over the River Kwai* and feel as though they had never moved out of Twickenham.

Mrs Harrison had always been a keen gardener and they had built a rockery, down which a small stream flowed with the aid of an electric pump. Their pool was oval-shaped and illuminated at night by carriage-lamps, fixed to the posts of the pergola which surrounded it. Their poolside chairs had plastic covers patterned with bright flowers and their poolside barbecue was electric because Mrs Harrison didn't like the mess made by charcoal. Everything the Harrisons had was well ordered and extremely neat. In the middle of all this tidiness Fosdyke created his own particular mess. His jackets were hung on the backs of chairs, his triumphantly acquired groceries were stacked in the sitting-room, his cigar butts filled the ashtrays and his glasses had made rings on the surface of the poolside table. He spent a great deal of time on the telephone and he was often out of the house on various missions, not returning until late at night.

It was at the Harrisons' villa, named by them 'Sole Mio', that Fosdyke had entertained his hero and admired writer, Haverford

Downs, on the night before Nancy Leadbetter's party. Having managed to come by a decent bit of steak and kidney, he stood over the young maid, who came in once a week, until she had managed to produce a pie, later warmed up for dinner in the microwave. There were potted shrimps to start (a collector's piece anywhere past Calais) and apple crumble, Stilton cheese, charcoal biscuits, Bath Olivers and a bottle of Warre's port.

Bald and pink, with his face peering above the white folds of the napkin stuck into his collar, Haverford looked like a particularly contented baby at feeding-time. 'The continentals have never understood the delights of nursery food.' He tried out a possible 'Jotting' on Fosdyke. 'Come to think of it, they've probably never had nurseries. They've never known the delights of being shut in a cupboard and smacked with a hairbrush by a Nanny whose starched apron crackled across her bosom like approaching thunder. That's why Mrs Thatcher could never become Prime Minister of Italy.'

'I thought it right to feed you, sir,' said Fosdyke, 'in the style of an English gentleman. They're not particularly thick on the ground around Mondano-in-Chianti.'

'Am I a gentleman?' Haverford wondered as he dug into the steak and kidney. 'I suppose I have some of the right characteristics. I have always owed money. I usually stand up when a lady enters the room (if the lady in question is one of those battling Berthas from Bermondsey who staff the *Informer* office, her subsequent confusion delights me), and I have always been anxious to place my education and superior talents at the service of the Radical Left. My grievance against our present masters is that, quite frankly, I find most of them rather common. I dress myself untidily, my family despair of me, and I have absolutely no sympathy with any technological advance since the invention of the shoehorn. I suppose you might call me a gent.'

'Or a genius?'

'Well, that,' Haverford was forced to admit, 'of a sort, yes. We may not be in the First Eleven, but we are a pretty strong team,

Hazlitt, Charles Lamb, Beerbohm, Chesterton and Haverford Downs. We who do battle with the weekly deadline.'

'I believe I've told you how much pleasure your writing gives me.'

'I believe you have. I must say it gives me a certain amount of pleasure too.'

'Beautiful prose style. Not that I'm an expert.'

'Kind of you to say so. I believe I was born with a certain ear. The gift God gave to Mozart.'

'Mozart?' Fosdyke looked confused.

'Of course *he* wrote music,' Haverford explained patiently, 'but it's much the same thing. One has to hear one's paragraph. One word cut and hark, what discord follows! It's something I can't make my Pictish editor understand. The fellow makes marks on my copy like the abominable snowman.'

'Whatever you say, of course, I'm no judge of these things. You always seem pretty wise to me.'

'One has lived a certain amount of life,' Haverford admitted, swigging the Guinness Fosdyke served with the steak and kidney ('no particular point in just opening another bottle of Chianti in Chiantishire'). 'But tell me, dear boy, I don't see you as a regular *Informer* reader?'

'Well, I wasn't until I managed to put my hands on a source for old Lord Pottleton, the Labour peer who had the castle outside San Pietro. Hell of a fellow for crystallized fruits and waiters. Well, when Paddy Pottleton snuffed it, I still got the rag, entirely for your articles. I can't say much for the rest of the paper.'

'Quite honestly' – Haverford was wiping his mouth with the napkin still festooned about his neck – 'neither can I.'

'I always thought, if I were in a hole, you'd be the sort of chap I might turn to. Much sooner than any of the politicians –'

'Poets,' said Haverford, who wasn't one, 'are the acknowledged legislators of mankind. And of course,' he added hastily, 'certain prose writers also.'

'– Or sooner than, well, a priest for instance.'

'Don Marco's a remarkable fellow. Red as a watermelon. One of the old-fashioned sort.'

'Well, there now! That's exactly what I mean.'

'*Are* you?' Haverford looked curiously at Fosdyke, who was changing the plates, stacking the dirty ones for the moment on the Harrison's video recorder. 'In a hole, I mean?'

'Not so much a hole –' Fosdyke poured cream on his visitor's apple crumble. 'Let's say, more at a crossroads.'

'Ah.' Haverford ate his pudding tactfully and with some respect. People had rarely asked for his advice and he found the idea of playing the role of Signor Fixit's confessor novel and strangely flattering. 'A crossroads, did you say?'

'It seems to me, do correct me if I'm wrong, but reading the weekly "Jottings" one would say you've had a certain amount of experience with women.'

'Over the years' – Haverford did his best to sound modest – 'you might speak of me as one who has loved not wisely but too well.'

'Love! Well, that was what I wanted to ask about. I don't just mean the other stuff.'

'What other stuff?' Haverford got going again with the cream jug. 'What are you referring to exactly?'

'Well, you know. The below the belt. All that side of the business.'

'My dear Fosdyke. You can't be quite so English. You can't live by the Queensberry rules, you know. Most of what's most interesting in life goes on below the belt.' He absorbed another spoonful of nursery food, thinking that he had said something rather good which could be used in next week's article.

'I'm not referring to what is available for fifty thousand lire in the back streets of Siena.'

'Really?' Haverford did his best not to look interested. 'Which back streets are those exactly?'

'This is a country,' Fosdyke said, 'where you can get most things if you know where to look for them.'

'Can you really?'

'Oh, yes. If I told you what you can lay your hands on, if you're prepared to pay the price, you'd be astonished.'

'In the words of Diaghilev to the young Jean Cocteau, astonish me, Fosdyke.'

'Well, I mean, you can always find someone who'll do it for money.'

'And I imagine you always have been able to from the dawn of time.'

'Not that anyone should avail themselves of it, of course.'

'Well, I don't know. Provided you take reasonable precautions.' Haverford smiled tolerantly.

'But if you have any particular quarrel with anybody. I mean if there's anyone you find standing in your way.'

'A quarrel?' Haverford gave himself the credit for being reasonably quick-witted, but now the old ex-pat's meaning had eluded him.

'They usually do it, you know. With lorries.'

'Lorries?' Haverford's mind began to boggle. Did you do it in the cabin or was there a bed made up in the back? And what about the driver? Was there a man at the wheel who would be present throughout? Or was Italy full of slender, available girls driving ten-ton trucks.

'A fellow can't live out here, winter and summer both, without getting to know the ropes,' Fosdyke told him. 'I've heard about a chap who's in close touch with a fellow who can always manage it. It could happen crossing the street in Mondano, and you know what a menace those lorries can be. Well, it might be a big one with a misleading number-plate which simply doesn't stop that gets your mortal enemy. Pure accident, that's the name of the game.' Having delivered himself of this, his longest speech, Fosdyke sat apparently shrouded in gloom.

'I thought,' Haverford said, puzzled by the turn the conversation was taking, 'that we were talking about love.'

'Love –' Fosdyke adjusted himself to the change of subject. 'I thought I'd got over it completely. My lady wife behaved exceptionally badly, as I think I may have told you. Scarpered, not to put too fine a point upon it.'

'Love isn't a thing you get over, Fosdyke. It's not influenza.'

'I realize that now.'

'It's not something I shall get over, I'm afraid, this side of the Styx.'

'Even at your age?'

'I don't quite know what you mean by even at my age.' Haverford looked miffed. 'It's always the same person of course, although over the years she has had different names and come in various shapes and sizes. Fundamentally she is a slightly delinquent page-boy with small buttocks and an upturned nose. She is the archetype of the imagination. The obsession that never dies' – Haverford drank Guinness – 'whilst there is a spark of life in this old carcass.'

'Small buttocks . . .' Fosdyke was thoughtful. 'Well, I suppose it takes all sorts to make a world.'

'Unfortunately that's true.'

'But that's not what's brought me to the crossroads.'

'No?'

'Not that at all. I suppose you might say it's the real thing.'

For an unusual moment Haverford was silent, looking, when it came to the real thing, a little out of his depth.

'Quite honestly, it's rather thrown me.'

Fosdyke got up and cleared the pudding plates, stacking them also on top of the video. He put Stilton, biscuits and port at the disposal of his guest. As he did so he moved in the dreamy way of a man in a state of shock.

'Is it the unrequited sort, this love?' Haverford felt he should ask for more particulars. 'Does the person concerned . . .'

'Whom I will not name, if it's all the same to you, Mr Downs.'

'Or does, whoever the person in question is – of course, I'm not expecting a name – reciprocate the passion?'

'Fully reciprocated,' Fosdyke said with some gloom. 'Mutual in every way. I'm telling you this in the strictest confidence of course.'

'Oh, of course. But what, dare one ask, is the problem?'

'I'm worried, quite frankly, about the responsibility I might be taking on.'

'Oh, responsibility.' Haverford was clear on the answer to that one; he had mentioned it in several of his 'Jottings'. 'Responsiblity is like income tax, V A T, string vests, open-toed sandals worn with socks, tights and grubby bra straps – one of the great anti-aphrodisiacs. Breathe the word "responsibility" and the most dauntless cock-stand collapses. Responsibility detumesces.'

'I do feel' – Fosdyke didn't seem to have been listening – 'a strong sense of responsibility.'

'Because you and this lady . . .'

'Who shall be nameless.'

'Of course. Because you and Miss Nameless happen to fancy each other?'

'Coming into someone's life is a bit like taking over their house,' Fosdyke said. 'It may land you in something you didn't bargain for. I'm not boring you, am I?'

'Not at all. No, my dear fellow, of course not.' But whether it was because of the conversation or the nursery food, Haverford's eyelids were beginning to droop.

'So what would your advice be, speaking from experience?'

'Taking over other people's lives? Not on, if you want my opinion. I've always had quite enough to do taking over my own.'

'I'll have to think it over,' Fosdyke said. 'But I'm enormously grateful to you for your time. I say, I do hope I haven't embarrassed you, talking like this?'

'Think nothing of it,' Haverford told him. 'I don't get embarrassed easily.'

Eventually, Haverford was driven back in the Metro the Harrisons had left at Fosdyke's disposal. It was the night a driver had put a letter into Molly's hands and called her Signora Kettering.

Haverford had got home after the children had gone to bed, earning Molly's frowns for slamming the car door, shouting good-night to Fosdyke and singing 'Lydia, the tattooed lady' all the way upstairs.

Second Week

CHAPTER TEN

Ken Corduroy drove round to the Harrisons' with an ingenious pool-cleaning device, a mechanical object that swam round scrubbing at the walls, he had ordered for them from England. He walked up to the front door and pushed a button but the chimes went unanswered. So he went round to the pool and noticed, at first, how the neat tables were littered with old newspapers and the ashtrays loaded with cigar ends. A couple of chairs, plastic with the appearance of cast-iron painted white, had been knocked over, a glass had been broken and an empty whisky bottle lay on what he would call, with his expertise, 'the pooldeck'. He saw that the little waterfall in the Harrisons' rockery had run dry.

Then he noticed that the level of water was low. Stepping nearer he saw that it was, in fact, non-existent and that the pool had only a few rapidly drying puddles. It was not until he was standing on the very edge that he saw Signor Fixit. He was lying face downwards in the shadow of the short diving-board, fully dressed in a blazer and white linen trousers. Blood from his head discoloured the blue tiling pattern of the plastic liner around him. The terrace door was open and when he went into the house Ken Corduroy found further disorder; another chair knocked over, dirty glasses and a smell of spilled whisky. He telephoned the police in Mondano.

'What dramas!' Haverford came home in a state of nervous

excitement. 'Don Marco drove me over so I could telephone my
"Jottings" and the house was crawling with *carabinieri*. There was
a doctor there, the whole works. They'd fished poor old Fosdyke
out and the ambulance was just leaving.'

'Dead. Did you say dead?' Molly had been laying out the lunch
on the terrace. The sun sparkled on the plates and, wet-haired
from the pool, the children were being unusually helpful in the
kitchen. Nothing that day had seemed threatening at 'La Felicità',
until her father came panting up the stairs with his news. The old
priest came steadily up after him; his car, small and dusty, parked
under their thatched shade.

'Not sure. Wouldn't give much for his chances, though.'

'*Morto. Forse morto . . .*'

'I invited Don Marco to lunch. You won't mind. He's had a
terrible shock.'

'Of course not. Father, do please sit down here. We're
honoured.' Hugh, who never went to church, adopted a tone of
peculiar reverence when faced with the old man whose cassock
showed traces of tomato sauce.

'*Grazie. Non ho fame.* No hunger.' But the priest allowed
himself to be seated and to have a glass of wine poured for him.
Haverford also sat, lifting his panama to mop his flushed forehead
with a red and white spotted handkerchief. Molly went on laying
the table, placing knives and forks neatly as though her sanity
depended on it. It was true she hadn't entirely trusted Fixit.
Sometimes she'd found it difficult to believe a word he said, but
he had been there to meet her when she'd arrived as a stranger.
He had shown her round and helped with her shopping. Now he
had vanished with no reasonable explanation whatever. She felt
bewildered and suddenly lost.

'It all seems quite obvious. Fosdyke was all alone, had been for
a few days since I had dinner with him in fact.'

'He drove you home on that night?' Molly started to investigate.

'You saw him?'

'Yes. When you got out of the car.'

'*Ubriaco*,' said Don Marco sadly. He raised his glass with a dirty-nailed little finger cocked and drank disapprovingly. 'Drunk.'

'*Ubriaco* as a newt. I'm afraid so. He must have been staggering a bit out there by the pool. Just his luck it didn't have any water in it.'

'Had it?' Molly asked her father.

'Had it what?'

'Water in it. When you went there to dinner?'

'Oh yes, I'm sure it did. We had a drink out there before we got stuck into that amazing menu. Yes, I'm sure I remember I saw water lapping.'

'Pools can empty pretty unexpectedly round here,' Hugh said. 'As we know to our cost.'

'Old Fosdyke certainly didn't expect it.'

The children had finished laying out prosciutto and cheese and hard-boiled eggs. Molly brought out a big bowl of salad and sat looking at it, eating nothing.

'What's wrong with Mr Fosdyke?' Samantha said.

'He had an accident. He dived into the pool with no water in it.' Henrietta had heard more of the conversation.

'Silly thing to do,' said Jacqueline, her teeth stained yellow with hard-boiled egg.

'He didn't dive. He fell. So you must all be very careful.' Hugh looked round at his family nervously. It had turned out to be a strange sort of holiday. Now they were all sitting round discussing a fatal accident in muted voices, with an old priest who smelled of garlic beside them, cutting a piece of cheese into wafer-thin slices. On top of it all, the remorseless heat was becoming too much for Hugh, his sunburn itched and he felt sick. At that moment his dearest wish was to be back at work and having lunch with Mrs Tobias.

'We had a long talk when we had dinner together,' Haverford said out of a silence in respect of the dead. 'He confided in me. It was a sort of confessional.'

'*Confessionale*,' the priest smiled at Molly and took another genteel sip of wine and surprised her. 'Your father is naturally religious.'

'He seemed to be worried about taking over someone's life. He said it was like taking over their house,' Haverford remembered. 'That's what worried him.'

The next day Giovanna came to work and couldn't stop herself weeping. Her small crushed handkerchief was quite inadequate to contain the huge tears that welled from her eyes after she had heard of the death of Signor Fixit.

CHAPTER ELEVEN

JOTTINGS FROM TUSCANY
by *Haverford Downs*

The sack of Rome, when the brute and lascivious soldiery of the Emperor Charles V raped the women, robbed the churches, and broke open a long-dead Pope's tomb to steal the ring from his finger, was only one of the invasions of this long-suffering land. It was followed by the deprivations of greedy Swiss, repressive Austrians, revolutionary French, barbaric Germans and the huge, unpaid army of tourists and expatriates who live off the land and commit their own atrocities. They're not, it's true, much given to murdering old men and children; they don't force Cardinals to ride facing the tails of donkeys through the streets. They have not, as yet, imprisoned Pope John Paul II. However they do desecrate the holiest places with their flash-bulbs and hand-held video cameras; they invade peaceful monasteries and sleep on the outskirts of towns in their evil-smelling 'campers'. They display their scarlet, sunburnt shoulders and huge backsides flaunting shiny 'jogging shorts' round the Piazza del Campo in Siena. They do their best to make even our delightful local trattoria in Mondano sound like a Berni Inn in Basingstoke as they call raucously for prawn cocktail and steak and chips, having to settle with obvious disgust for the pure poetry of Signora Sparanti's risotto con funghi. Ever since the Marquis of Mantua failed to defeat the French at Fornovo in the 1490s (a period which must have been almost as barbaric and unpleasant as the 1980s), this sunsoaked land has had to endure invasion and rely on the assassin's knife or the patriot's bullet to even the score.

In the context of such a history, how are we to interpret our local sensation, the death of an obscure Englishman, who acted as house agent, courier, travel guide, purveyor of groceries in short supply, house-sitter and, it has been daringly suggested, pimp to the English army of occupation in Chiantishire? He was a man of considerable literary taste (I must report, in all modesty, that he subscribed to the Informer *and never missed these 'Jottings') who died, so the authorities would have us believe, by falling into an empty swimming-pool when drunk on hard-to-come-by malt whisky.*

I attended Fosdyke's funeral. The English masters he served so well, and to whom he was universally known as 'Signor Fixit', were conspicuous by their absence. My own family stayed away. My son-in-law, being a solicitor, said it was too much like work, as he is constantly attending the funerals of clients in England. My daughter, although clearly distressed at the tragedy, preferred to stay at home with the children. In the local cimitero, *opposite the old Mondano church, I was, at first, the only mourner. The graves around us on a stifling hot morning (funerals here are not long postponed for obvious reasons) were decorated with wilting flowers and photographs of deceased mamas and departed children. As my old friend, the Communist priest, performed the last rites, did I see a half smile on those weatherbeaten features? How many fascists did he bury with public grief and deep private satisfaction in the last year of the German Occupation?*

Did Fosdyke die, I wondered as I stood by that hastily dug grave, to avenge the humiliation of Fornovo? Remember this is the country, as Signor Fixit himself told me, where a lorry can be hired not only to move your furniture but to run over an unpopular citizen. And if Fosdyke had been popular, it's strange that his funeral was so poorly attended.

However, I was not alone at the graveside. A little later a car drove up and two women in veils got out and joined me. One I recognized, the local Baronessa, whose family has always been friendly with the occupying forces. The other was a middle-aged woman, also Italian, who seemed to be her friend. I intended to ask the Baronessa Dulcibene why she had come to pay her last respects to this mysterious Englishman but she gave me a glassy look of non-recognition and moved rapidly away with her companion. As my old girlfriend Nancy Leadbetter used to say, 'There's no snob like a foreign snob.'

A reader has suggested that the belated realization that you're talking to an ex-lover is best expressed by the old Tallulah Bankhead crack: 'I didn't recognize you with your clothes on.' Well done, Mr A.B. of Bromley. A bottle of Chianti Classico will be winging its way in your direction with the Informer's compliments.

CHAPTER TWELVE

In the second week of their holiday Molly felt that they had been living in 'La Felicità' for ever. Notting Hill Gate, Mrs O'Keefe and the children's schools seemed part of a distant world she could barely remember. Her life centred round the villa, the sunlit early mornings with their promise of great heat, fulfilled during the long afternoons, and dinner on the terrace when the darkness fell suddenly. She still laid the table there, and lit the candles, and put on the scratchy and neglected golden moments from *Turandot*, although no unexpected car came again with any message.

What occupied her mind all day, as she shopped, tidied the children's bedrooms in order not to further distress Giovanna, or swam up and down the pool with her deliberate, tireless breast-stroke in search of weight loss and a youth she had not particularly enjoyed, was 'her mystery'. She had come to think of it as hers because, apart from Fosdyke, now deceased, she had shared her thoughts on this ever-engrossing subject with no one. Molly had not had a religious upbringing. Early in her life, Haverford had told her that if God existed He would be an extremely unpleasant old gentleman with a taste for smiting Philistines and little sympathy for the delights of love as they were understood down the King's Road in the fifties and sixties. Her mother, having been brought up in an icy vicarage on the outskirts of Birmingham, had no faith and said she suffered from a nervous skin condition whenever she was lured, for weddings or funerals, into churches.

Molly's longing for mysteries had found its satisfaction in Italian paintings and English detective stories; but never before had the mysterious circumstances of living people come so near her. As she cut up toast soldiers to dip in Jacqueline's egg, or sat with a towel spread on her lap smiling vaguely whilst her youngest child swam and splashed her way through her bath, she speculated endlessly. Fosdyke? What was the real importance of the man with the squint, the potted shrimp provider, the house-sitter and general factotum of the Brits? Had he been able to answer her questions; was he about to explain the Ketterings' strange requirements about three children and dinner on the terrace to her? Is that why Signor Fixit had ended his long and useful life in an empty swimming-pool? But then she steadied herself, reined in her galloping imagination and felt that she was behaving ludicrously, as she had when she had run out into the garden in her nightdress and dragged the manhole cover off the cistern by the swimming-pool.

But two pools, she thought, as she turned for the twentieth time and did her breaststroke towards the white hills under a dry and remorseless sky – their pool and the pool in the house where Fosdyke was staying – had been emptied without apparent explanation. Surely these two events must be connected? But that was reasoning falsely, and such accidents must happen to many people, mustn't they? And why, she asked herself, as she swam towards the steps, why should an apparently full and cared-for pool (her father had told her that when he visited Fosdyke for dinner, the water was lapping) be suddenly emptied? An act of God or an act of man? Molly knew which explanation she preferred.

Looking up and shaking the water out of her hair she saw the willowy figure of the Baronessa wearing white silk trousers and heavy bracelets, shimmering against the sun and the sky.

'Venus rising from the sea.' The Baronessa was laughing, Molly thought unkindly.

'Hardly!' She felt more than ever awkward and overweight in

her bright red bathing-dress and was conscious of the dimpling of her thighs. Manrico the dog, straining on the short leash Vittoria Dulcibene was holding him by, slapped his tongue round her wet ankles in friendly recognition.

'You will forgive my calling, unannounced.'

Oh, no, Molly felt like saying, you should at least have sent on a couple of heralds with trumpets, followed by your butler, to check up on the state of the lavatories. Instead, she said, 'Of course not. Won't you come in? I mean I could get you a drink or a cup of tea?'

'Tea, of course. I love a cup of Darjeeling at four o'clock in the afternoon. I am also absolutely mad for Harrods' bangers but God knows where we're going to find them since Mr Fosdyke left us. Shall I tie the wretched Manrico up somewhere?'

'He can come in. Anyway, he looks in need of water.'

In the small sitting-room the children were sprawled on the sofa listening to their Beastie Boy tapes and re-reading the copies of *Smash Hits* and *Seventeen* they had brought with them from London. Jacqueline was colouring her Postman Pat book brilliantly but inaccurately. Molly didn't want their father to see them indoors. Although he was busily engaged in a long siesta he thought that his family shouldn't waste the expensive sunshine. She closed the door on her children and led the Baronessa to the kitchen where she put on the kettle and stood watching it with a towel tied round her waist.

'I wanted to bring you my sympathy.' The Baronessa sat at the table and produced a packet of Italian cigarettes and a gold lighter which seemed almost too heavy for her to lift. 'After your unfortunate experience.'

'Which unfortunate experience was that?'

'The wretched trouble you had with your water. Our *Idraulica* workers are so stupid. Of course, they are all Communists.'

'I thought you were a Communist once.' Molly felt she had scored a point.

'That was in the war when being a Communist was a pleasure. It is not so amusing now.'

'Anyway, it seems rather common round here.'

'What seems common?' The Baronessa put a cigarette between her lips and failed to make her lighter work.

'Trouble with the water supply.'

'It's these wretched Tuscan hills. Water is like gold here. One of my family, on the Baderini side that is, not the Dulcibenes – they were merely court jesters if you want my candid opinion. Well, anyway, Paolo Baderini led Mondano in a pitched battle against San Pietro in Crespi for the well on the Arezzo road. Six men were killed but Mondano got its water.'

'When was that?'

'I think 1398,' the Baronessa said as though it were yesterday.

'In spite of your heroic ancestor' – Molly showed some spirit – 'we still seem to be having trouble with the water.'

'Oh, yes. There must have been some mistake. Something perfectly stupid must have gone wrong. Things like that don't happen at "La Felicità", of all places.'

'You mean "La Felicità" is different from everywhere else?'

'Well, things usually run pretty smoothly here. On the whole, "La Felicità" doesn't dry out entirely, any more than we do at the Castello or Nancy does at the Villa.'

'The house where Mr Fosdyke was staying wasn't so lucky.' Molly felt that the Baronessa was at some disadvantage, that she was saying things she didn't want to have too closely questioned. She pressed on however, as ruthless as Holmes or Poirot interviewing a suspect. And the fact that the woman, sipping Darjeeling tea and fiddling with a gold lighter, looked so cool and elegant, whereas Molly knew that her hair was in rats'-tails, her shoulders sunburnt and the damp towel in danger of coming undone at her waist, merely added to her determination.

'That seems another mistake,' her visitor conceded.

'What sort of mistake is it, I wonder,' Molly asked with a

carefully assumed air of innocence, 'which dries up somebody's swimming-pool?'

'I told you –' The Baronessa spoke patiently, as though explaining to a child. 'It's a very dry place, Tuscany. We are not Manchester.'

'Perhaps not.' Molly's answer came sharply as she felt she had been patronized. 'But however dry the weather is, it wouldn't make a whole swimming-pool full of water vanish overnight.'

'No doubt, there are reasons for that.' The Baronessa looked terminally bored. She clicked her lighter again uselessly and then dropped it back into her handbag with a sigh of disgust at all mechanical objects.

'What sort of reasons?'

'*Please* don't ask me that. When I was a schoolgirl in Siena I learnt Dante and a great deal of Virgil. I regret to say that I took no course in hydraulic engineering.'

Yet you know a good deal about resistance movements and possibly sabotage, Molly thought. At last she said, 'I can't understand why a swimming-pool should suddenly empty.'

'No doubt there are devices, certain mechanisms, to control these things.' The Baronessa waved a hand, dismissing the tedious subject. 'If someone turns the wrong wheel or pushes the wrong button, then whoosh! It's probably like pulling the plug out of your bath water.' Anxious not to have it thought that she was ever to be found in a swimming-pool engine shed, dressed in a pair of oil-stained overalls and fiddling with the controls, she crossed the room and looked out over the hills towards her castle. 'Buck was so clever to make this window tall and narrow like an altar panel.' With a loud slurping Manrico finished his second bowl of water.

'I had to pay out a huge sum of money to get the water back,' Molly told her. 'Mr Kettering will have to be responsible for that.'

'Who knows what Mr Kettering will be responsible for?' The Baronessa had been half joking during her tea-time chat and her answers were casual, almost flippant. Now her concentration increased. 'You have told him this?'

'No. But I will when I find him.'

'And you haven't found him yet?'

'I shall have to have some of the rent back.' Molly was determined. 'I would have asked Mr Fosdyke, but . . .'

'That was terrible.' The Baronessa shuddered. 'It was the act of a coward.'

'You mean his suicide?'

The Baronessa didn't answer and after a silence Molly said, 'I paid half the rent into your husband's account at the Banco dell'Annunziazione.'

'Italian drinking habits have changed,' the Baronessa said sadly, now making use of a box of kitchen matches. 'Men in cities no longer go home at lunchtime for a bottle of wine and a plate of pasta. They take a sandwich in a bar near the office and drink beer or' – she whispered the detested word – 'Coca-Cola! There are few men now working in the fields, keeping going on a litre of wine. It is sad. My husband is travelling abroad to find new possibilities for us. When he gets back you can speak to him about it, if money really interests you.'

'Money interests me very much.'

'Oh really?' The Baronessa smiled. 'Now I must get back and give some sort of instructions for dinner. We are expecting people but I'm afraid they can't be of any help to you, Mrs Pargeter. They are not the Ketterings, or anyone who knew them. Come, Manrico, you appalling hound.'

Then she was gone, leaving nothing but a trail of perfume and the cigarette, which she had only just lit after such difficulty, suddenly stubbed out in a small silver dish Giovanna used for the salt. Molly was left wondering about the exact purpose of her visit.

Dearest Marcia, Hugh wrote to Mrs Tobias, on a postcard of Martini's horseman he had bought in Siena. *Wish you were here*.

Am missing you and the 'Dolce Vita' very much indeed. As you see from this p.c. I have been giving the children some basic art instruction. But I'll be delighted to be away from the joys of family life! Roll on September. Fondest. Hugh. It was very early in the morning and he wrote on his knee sitting in the car, waiting to take the children on the breakfast run to Mondano. He had a stamp and meant to drop this message into the box outside the post office, and no one would be any the wiser. As Henrietta, Samantha and Jacqueline straggled out to join him, he slid the postcard into a hiding-place behind the map in the pocket of the driver's door. From there he meant to remove it hastily whilst the children were consuming their doughnuts in front of the café – their reward for getting up early enough to fetch the bread.

He had started the engine and was backing out of the shade when he heard his wife calling him to stop. It was something Hugh hadn't bargained for. She wanted, it seemed, to be taken to the post office.

'We can go there for you. Anyway, all post offices are hell.' Hugh hadn't been into a post office in England for a decade.

'I'd like to come.' Molly opened the car door and sank into her seat, and then turned to smile at the children. 'I'll buy you all doughnuts.'

'I do that, anyway,' Hugh grumbled as he drove too fast in his irritation and bumped up the track. He hoped that he would be able to palm the postcard and whisk it into the letter-box while his wife was engaged elsewhere. As for Molly, she was going to ask if there were any letters in 'La Felicità's cubby-hole at the post office. Nothing had been delivered to the villa. If there were letters for the Ketterings she meant to take possession of them and, though she hadn't yet promised herself to take to the steaming kettle again, she might feel driven to such a step.

They parked in Mondano's central Piazza Cavour and all sat. The church and the deliciously smelling breadshop were visible from the car. Hugh said, 'I thought you were going to the post office?'

'And aren't you going to buy the bread?' Molly felt a wave of lethargy in the hot car and didn't move.

'Of course we are.'

'Then why don't we meet in front of the café?'

'Come along, Dad,' Samantha sighed and opened the back door. Hugh was forced to join the children as they set out across the square. He would have to think what to do with his postcard later. Left alone in the car, still reluctant to make the effort to heave herself out of the passenger seat, Molly saw the edge of Martini's horseman protruding from behind the map in the driver's door. Because of her compulsion to investigate she took the postcard out and read it.

'"*Dearest Marcia*." Who's Marcia?'

'I told you. Just a client.'

'Don't be ridiculous.'

'Mrs Tobias.'

'And who's *Mister* Tobias?'

'Long gone. She divorced him.'

'It sounds to me as though he should have divorced her.'

'I did her case. I won it.'

'I'm sure she was enormously grateful!' Molly astonished herself. She was eloquent and angry, as though the house had given her a new courage. She stood in the middle of the big bedroom, a commanding figure in her white nightdress, and Hugh sat on the edge of the bed, longing to escape in sleep from this attack. When he had got back to the car with the rolls and long loaves that morning he had found Molly gone and his postcard with her. He had looked forward to some sort of scene and a bad quarter of an hour, but he had been kept waiting all day, until the rest of the household was asleep, and then had been amazed at the intensity of his wife's rage.

'Anyway, what's this sweet life you seem to enjoy with Mrs Tobias?'

'What sweet life?'

'This "Dolce Vita".' Molly spat out the words with full-blooded contempt.

'Oh, the "Dolce Vita".' Hugh felt on firm ground and gave her a smile which she found patronizing. 'You've got that entirely wrong. The "Dolce Vita" happens to be a restaurant.'

'Oh, yes. And what goes on there?'

'Mrs Tobias and I have lunch . . .'

'Lunch.' The word seemed to excite Molly to a new level of disgust. 'How often do you have lunch?'

'Occasionally.'

'Oh. And how often is *occasionally*?'

'I don't know.'

'What do you mean, you don't know? Do you go through lunch with Mrs Tobias in some sort of trance? The person you're missing so dreadfully.'

'*Very much indeed.*'

'What?'

'I didn't say dreadfully. I said *very much indeed*.'

'What difference does that make?'

'I don't know.'

'Well, you should know. You're a lawyer. I asked you, what difference does it make?'

Hugh shrugged his shoulders. He didn't want to argue, but he found himself unable to leave the witness-box.

'I'm sure you miss her. How many times have you had lunch with her?'

'Not more than once a month.'

'And when was her divorce case?'

'Almost two years ago.' Hugh had a memory for such things and hoped, now he had told the truth, she would let him sleep.

Molly had no such intention. 'And do you take all your clients out to lunch every month, for the rest of their lives, when you win their cases?'

'Of course not.' He did his best to smile again.

'I don't suppose you win so many cases.'

'I do well enough' – he looked hurt – 'to bring you all on this holiday.'

'*You* brought me on this holiday! You know *I* brought you. I paid for it. With my money. Does Mrs Tobias pay for your lunch?'

'I did the car hire,' Hugh said with justice, 'and the air fares. I even paid for your father's ticket.'

'Of course you did. You're two of a kind, you and my father. Two old womanizers. You should have lots to talk about.'

Seated on the loo, with the door open and his pyjama trousers round his ankles, Haverford was listening to the quarrel with great pleasure. Upstairs Henrietta said to Samantha, 'She's shouting at him. That's a thing that's never happened before.'

Samantha said, 'Do you think they'll get a divorce?'

'So what did you do after lunch?' Molly asked what she felt was the deadliest question.

'Nothing.'

'What do you mean, nothing?'

'I mean, nothing in particular.'

'Oh yes. And where did you do nothing in particular? In a sleazy hotel bedroom? Or did someone at the office lend you his flat? Men do that, don't they? Here's the key, old boy, and don't forget to replace the bottle in the fridge.' Molly heard her voice rising but she had no idea where these thoughts, these words, were coming from. The room with its high ceiling and the long curtains seemed to encourage such arias.

'Or I suppose you can go back to her place now she's divorced. I can just imagine it. Her little maisonette in St John's Wood! Full of frilly pelmets and a cover for the lavatory seat.' Mrs Tobias did, in fact, live in such a place but Hugh had never seen it.

'We didn't,' Hugh said truthfully, 'go to any of those places.'

'Perhaps you crept back to our house, when I was at work, and Mrs O'Keefe had taken Jacky to the nursery. I wouldn't put that past you.'

'Of course we didn't.'

'Why, of course? You're her *fondest*, aren't you? *Roll on September*, so you can have a chance of doing it again.'

'We didn't do anything.'

'What?'

'I tell you, we "did" nothing. We just had lunch.'

'I don't believe you.' She stood in the middle of the room accusing him.

'I swear,' he said, and tried a faint smile. 'The whole truth and nothing but the truth.'

'Nothing? Just had lunch?'

'That's all.'

'Absolutely nothing else?'

'Absolutely nothing.'

'I think' – she was looking at him as though all her worst fears were confirmed – 'that's the most terrible thing I have ever heard.'

'Why?'

'Well, of course, it is.'

'If we'd done something, that might have been terrible. If we'd been guilty as charged. But we haven't. It's entirely innocent.'

'It's the most appalling thing I ever heard.' Again it was as though there were something, some presence in the room itself, voicing her derision. 'You've brought me all this trouble. You've made me read how much you hate this family, how you can't wait to be rid of us. You've slobbered over this Tobias woman all through lunch – twenty-four lunches to be exact – and you haven't had the courage or the passion even to screw her.' 'Screw', where had that come from? It was a word she never used. 'Move over, will you, because I must say you disgust me.'

He lay down gratefully on his side of the bed. She lay on hers, after she had turned out the light.

'I didn't slobber over her at lunch.'

'Be quiet,' Molly told him. 'I don't ever want to talk about it again.'

He was relieved to hear it and found his usual refuge in sleep. But his wife lay awake for a long time, angry still but in some way triumphant. Oh, T. Buckland Kettering, a voice within her said before she fell asleep, I shall find out what's happened to you.

'She's stopped shouting,' Henrietta said to Samantha and sounded disappointed. 'I suppose that means no divorce.'

Haverford stretched his pyjama'd legs out comfortably in bed and chuckled to himself. The dirty old bugger, he thought, he's been sending her postcards.

CHAPTER THIRTEEN

The row over Mrs Tobias's postcard had the effect of elevating Molly, at any rate for the time being, to the undisputed leadership of the family. No longer was she an obscure power whose plans were laid in secret and operated without recognition. The children treated her with a new respect. Hugh was remarkably anxious to please her. Even her dissident father seemed muted. He appeared at breakfast in a clean shirt and his best grey flannel trousers and refrained from uttering dubious anecdotes in the presence of the children.

'I wonder' – Hugh looked anxiously round the table – 'what we'd all like to do today?'

'I want to see the Piero della Francesca's,' Molly told them. 'I must make some plans for that.'

'The place to be avoided,' Haverford said, 'is Siena. Because of the Palio.'

'Whatever's that?' Henrietta suspected that it was some kind of an infectious disease.

'A particularly brutal kind of horse race. It all goes on in the square with a parade of flag-wavers in medieval costume, knights in armour – all the delights of the Middle Ages without the stink and the fear of plague.'

'Let's go. Mum, can we?'

'It'll be packed out,' Haverford said, and, making little of an experience he'd never had, 'I never got to see it myself. Always had something better to do during my salad days in Siena.'

'Perhaps it'll be on the television in the bar in Mondano.'
Hugh suggested a compromise which he knew would be unacceptable. Molly had no desire to watch the race on a wide screen
set among stuffed squirrels.

'Can we go, Mum? Why can't we?' The children were appealing
to the highest authority.

Molly said, 'I don't see why we shouldn't try it. Just to see
what we can see.'

'Molly Coddle has spoken. Let no dog bark,' said Haverford,
and when she had gone he whispered to his unhappy son-in-law.
'Got any postcards to send in Siena, dear boy? Why don't you
trust me with them?'

The parishes they walked through were hung with silk flags of
the Dragon, the Hedgehog, the Panther and the Giraffe. The
horses had been prayed for in the parishes' churches and those
that left a steaming mound in the aisles were considered by their
supporters to be particularly blessed by God. The long procession
with its beating drums and twirling flags and pages in medieval
uniform was winding its slow way to the Piazza del Campo. The
Pargeter family, having discussed the matter all day, and, so far
as the girls were concerned, perfected their wardrobe most of the
afternoon, were surprised by the emptiness of the streets, not
realizing that almost the entire population of the town was packed
into the shell-shaped centre of the Piazza. From there, those that
fainted away would be plucked by the ambulance men like
chestnuts from a fire as they waited for the race to be run around
them on a sanded track between the padded stone bollards and
the bolstered buildings.

As they got to the Via di Città Molly looked down the
steep, dark alleyways between the houses and saw the sea of
faces in the middle of the Piazza. She began to regret her decision
to take her family to the Palio. Just possibly Jacqueline, on
her father's shoulders, might catch a glimpse of the three-
minute race; perhaps the children, clinging to the shutters of a

restaurant in a side street, might have a view of an occasional flag thrown up above the crowd or the heads of the riders as they flashed past. That would have to be the limit of their success. And then she heard her name called and saw Rosie Fortinbras, followed by the clearly exhausted figure of her Carlo, going into the cool entrance at the back of a tall palazzo on the square.

'Not here with the family, Molly? Poor you.'

'Rosie Fortinbras! By all that's wonderful.' Haverford greeted her effusively. 'I had the pleasure and privilege of taking you out when you were at school with Molly Coddle. Toasted tea buns, as you may remember, in the Trusthouse Forte. I must say you don't look a day older. Going to the races?'

'We're going to watch from a window in Doctor Marocetti's apartment. It's the only way to see the Palio.'

'Oh, I do so agree. The good doctor has invited us too.' Her father said this with such confidence that for a moment Molly almost believed him.

'Orlando has invited *all* of you?' Rosie looked startled.

'Well, he can afford it, can't he? Best gynae man in Siena. This way, my group!'

As Haverford set off with her old schoolfriend and her old schoolfriend's lover across a plant-filled courtyard and up a marble staircase, Molly allowed her family to straggle after them. When Hugh said nervously, 'Is this all right?' she whispered back, 'Of course it's all right. Where's your sense of adventure?' The house she was living in, the investigation she was engaged on, had given her a new feeling of recklessness. She wanted, in this instance, to see how her father's elderly daring would be rewarded and had also, when it seemed impossible, become determined to see the Palio.

'As a matter of fact,' Rosie Fortinbras said, when they arrived at the open door of a first-floor apartment, 'Orlando Marocetti's a dentist.'

'Sorry, got hold of the wrong end of the stick.' Haverford

laughed and threw up his arms. 'Ah, Dottore! How extremely good to meet you.'

'Rosie, *cara*!' Doctor Marocetti turned out to be a small man in a lemon-yellow silk suit with large sunglasses. He had to rise on his toes to kiss Miss Fortinbras; he squeezed Carlo's forearm and looked at Haverford and his entourage in some doubt.

'Haverford Downs, *lo scrittore inglese*,' said the old man. 'I'm delighted to discover that I am read in *vostra bellissima città*.'

'You are a writer?' The dentist's English was not perfect but at least better than Haverford's Italian.

'I am charged with the task of writing about your Palio as seen from the windows of your superb apartment for the famous *giornale inglese*, *La Spia*, the *Informer*. Obtainable in Italy, as I have also discovered.'

'You are to write about my apartment?' Rosie's host seemed improbably flattered.

'Mainly. I will also describe the Palio, if you have no objection.'

'You have brought your family' – Dr Marocetti looked more doubtful – 'in order to write about my apartment?'

'A point in my article will be the great hospitality shown by the Italian people to children of all creeds and colours. As you see they are thin children, undernourished, as we are all poverty-stricken in England. They will take up little or no room at your windows.'

'*Si accomodi, prego.*'

Hugh and Molly were thanking the little man effusively as he stood aside and counted their family in. 'Your father,' Rosie Fortinbras whispered in her best Kensington accent, 'hasn't half got a nerve.'

Inside the apartment tall windows looked out on to the finishing and starting point of the race. The room was full of Italians greeting each other, sipping white wine and peach juice, wearing the silk scarves of the parishes of which they were the aristocratic patrons. Vittoria Dulcibene swayed towards Molly and said, 'You get everywhere, my dear, don't you? Even to Orlando Marocetti's. You know I don't wish to sound snobbish but for most of the year we who move in society do not know dentists. On the day of the Palio one such person becomes our oldest friend.' Molly smiled vaguely. She was thinking of something else. On the way through the streets she had seen a small Italian girl stumble and fall. The child's mother tottered insecurely forward on high heels calling, 'Sandra, Sandra!' with mixed anger and concern. Sandra, to Molly, was an unexpected Italian name.

When she thought of the day at the Palio, the Middle Ages seemed to be passing, often unwatched, outside the windows, and the more immediate and important drama was taking place in the apartment, beside the long table set with crostini and slices of pan forte and silver jugs of wine at which, from time to time, she exchanged words with Rosie Fortinbras. Outside, the drums continued to beat, the flags were whirled round and thrown as high as the apartment windows, the musicians played, knights in armour with their visors down to represent defunct parishes rode solemnly by, and the Palio itself, a white banner surmounted by a silver plate (the winner's prize), arrived on a cart drawn by white oxen. Then came the long wait for the race to start.

'Poor Carlo is exhausted,' Rosie said. 'I have been rather putting him through it. We've done the entire Piero della Francesca trail.'

'Really? We're going to do that too.'

'I thought you might be. Well, you always were an art buff, weren't you? The only pictures Carlo likes are in his comics.'

'You haven't seen Buck Kettering lately?' Molly asked the question as casually as she could.

'Not all that lately, I suppose. We are good friends though. Over the years. He sometimes says I'm the only one of the Brits he feels he can trust.' Rosie looked pleased with herself, as though close friendship with Buck Kettering was considered a particular honour in Chiantishire. 'Why do you ask?'

'I want to get in touch with him, that's all. About the trouble we had with the water.'

'Oh Buck's terribly sorry that happened.'

'He knows?' Molly asked quickly.

'Well, I mean I'm sure he would be sorry' – Rosie back-tracked – 'if he knew. I'm sure he wants you to have a super holiday. Could you just pour me another dollop of that peachy stuff? That's the trouble with the Italians, they're not serious drinkers.'

'I was thinking,' Molly said, 'about Sandra.'

'Were you? I thought you did more of your thinking about Buck, for some reason.'

'Well, "Sandra",' – Molly remembered the thought that had occurred to her on the way to the Piazza – 'that doesn't sound at all an Italian name.'

'Of course not. All the same, it is, you know. Buck and I both have this thing about the natives. I think he found her behind the counter in a chocolate shop in Siena. But she turned out pretty well. Good at business and all that sort of thing. Well, you could never accuse my Carlo of being any good at business. Keeps his brains strictly between his legs, don't you, my darling?' Carlo, licking his fingers after eating a crostino, wandered up and stared at Molly in a way she found disconcerting. All the same she felt that she had made a genuine discovery. Sandra was Italian. There was something, surely, about that fact which didn't fit at all easily into the pattern of events as she thought she knew them. She couldn't imagine the girl from the chocolate shop in Siena, who had turned out to have a good head for business and who had become the mother of three, writing the suggestions, which came, it seemed to her, in something like the voice of an English schoolmaster, about the Piero trail to Urbino.

'You seem to be unusually interested in the Kettering family.' Rosie smiled at her.

And then, angry with herself, Molly knew that she was blushing. 'We're living in their house. Isn't it natural to wonder what they're like exactly?'

'Is it? If I took a house I don't think I'd wonder what the

people who lived there were like. I don't think I'd worry about that at all. But then, of course, I don't live with such a gigantic family. Poor old you, Molly. You must have an awful lot of time on your hands to wonder about other people.'

A roar from the crowd called them all back to the windows. The horses had emerged from the Palazzo Pubblico, with jockeys wearing hard hats and what looked like pyjama suits in the parish colours riding bareback. They were got with difficulty to the starting rope where they pranced, bucked and jostled each other, some race horses finding it strange, no doubt, to be under starter's orders in a city square. All the faces of the crowd turned in one direction; the pigeons, deprived of anywhere to settle, flew round in increasing panic. At Molly's side the Baronessa Dulcibene said, 'In the Palio it is less important to win than to see your enemy lose.'

'Winning is a disaster.' The dentist had joined them and looked politely out over the children's heads. 'There are bribes to pay and such a lot of parties to give. The only thing to be said for winning is that it saves you the terrible humiliation of coming second. I' – he showed Molly the scarf tied round the top of his silk trousers – 'am a member of the Ostrich. I can only pray that the Ostrich will not come second.'

The race started. The horses streaked past the line of restaurants, the jockeys slithering on their sweating backs. Two of the riders fell at the first corner and lay still.

'Those men will need a police guard in the hospital tonight,' Vittoria Dulcibene said. 'Their supporters will know they were bribed to fall.' Other horses and other riders crashed to the sand-strewn pavement before, after three laps which went almost too quickly for the crowds to turn their heads, the Hedgehog won. Then the crowd stormed on to the course, seizing the Hedgehog jockey, lifting him into the air and putting him, it seemed to Molly, in far greater danger than he had ever been during the race.

'I am cock-a-hoop!' said the dentist.

'But I thought you belonged to the Ostrich?' Molly was puzzled.

'That is true. And the Ostrich got nowhere. But the Dragon was second and the Ostrich has hated the Dragon since the Middle Ages. All the Ostriches will be celebrating tonight and the Dragons will hide their heads in shame!'

Hugh was letting Jacqueline down from his shoulders and the children, who had behaved surprisingly well, were coming away from the windows in search of cake. Molly could see her father in a corner with Rosie Fortinbras. An unlit Italian cigar wobbled between his lips and he was flirting with her as he had, to his daughter's intense embarrassment, when she and Rosie had been in the sixth form together and he had taken them out to tea.

And then he must have asked Rosie for a light because she felt in her bag and produced a book of matches. Haverford took them, lit his cigar, bowed his thanks and then slipped the book of matches into his pocket. Her father, Molly was confirmed in her view, was not even to be trusted with a book of matches.

'Wasn't that a splendid spectacle, Molly Coddle?' Haverford was coming towards her now, puffing like a steam engine. 'And doesn't it come in useful sometimes having a father who can tell a thumping lie when the occasion demands it?'

The day after the Palio the Pargeters were, as they say in the package-tour programmes, 'at leisure'. The children returned to the pool; Hugh, after offering help which his wife rejected, sat reading in the sun; and Haverford snoozed over a blank piece of paper. Molly washed up and put away the plates after lunch and wondered if the house had any more secrets to offer. She swept the floor, scrubbed the kitchen table to the colour of the dry and chalky landscape, and was still reluctant to go outside. She wandered round the room when her work was finished, hanging up cups, straightening plates on the dresser, and then she took the bunch of keys off its hook. She read the labels, thinking of the rooms, *salone grande*, *salone piccolo*, *cucina*, *porta d'entrata*, and

then the one on a smaller key *granaio*. What did that mean?
Granary? She knew the outbuildings by heart, the swimming-
pool shed with the filter, the stone outhouse where the wheel-
barrow and the gardener's tools were kept, the old pigsty now
used to store firewood and dried lavender. What would the
Ketterings be doing with a granary? With the bunch of keys still
in her hand, she went into the small sitting-room and looked the
word up in the dictionary. Then she toured the bedrooms, looking
at the ceilings.

She couldn't think why she hadn't noticed the trap-door in the
larger of the children's rooms long before. The ceiling was not
high there, and standing on a chair she could fit the key into the
lock. The end of a folding ladder was then revealed to her and
she was able to pull it down and climb into the loft. She saw a
switch on a beam and illuminated what seemed to her to be a sort
of Tutankhamun's tomb, so full was it of relics of the earlier
Kettering period. Drowsy flies buzzed, hot air was heavy with
dust.

All the mess, all the jumble of living had been swept out of the
orderly house and pushed up into the attic. There were children's
toys, a pile of abandoned, grown-out-of clothes, odd shoes, an
old croquet set in a wooden box, a torn badminton net, wounded
cushions, a dressmaker's dummy, a treadle sewing-machine, torn
magazines with their covers eaten by mice, and a heap of what
Molly took to be dressing-up clothes – bright squares of material,
hats with feathers, toy swords, masks and paper crowns, an old
opera hat and the dusty coat of a set of tails. There was a card-
board box full of maps and one packed with what looked like
account books filled with columns of lire. There were also piles
of paperback novels – best-sellers from airport bookstalls and
Italian stories of passion with covers on which men with shiny
black hair could be seen kissing girls in frilly underwear whilst, in
the background, the moon shone on gondolas or knives dripped
blood. Who was it, Molly wondered, so ashamed of these pub-
lications that they hid them in lofts, leaving only the art books,

guides and collections of Tuscan recipes on display to the tenants?

Then she found what she had hoped to discover – some boxes of photographs of the house, of the pool as it was being built, and of the progress of the woman she took to be Sandra Kettering from a delighted girl, already tending to plumpness, holding a baby, to a matronly figure, square-shouldered, frowning at the camera as though it were an intruder, with two spindly girls beside her in the garden and Violetta, the afterthought, stuck solidly on her lap. There were many other photographs of the female members of this family at various stages of their development, but either the husband and father was of a singularly retiring disposition or he was holding the camera.

Molly sat in the dust on an empty trunk and went through them all. Then she noticed a portable typewriter in its case. Under it she found a folder full of papers. She took out one and read words which had long been familiar to her: *Villa to let near small Tuscan town. Suit couple, early forties, with three children (females preferred). Recently installed swimming-pool may compensate for sometimes impassable road. Owner suggests preliminary viewing to prevent disappointment or future misunderstandings.* She picked up another page and read words which were also familiar: *General remarks. The villa 'La Felicità' can only be enjoyed by the observance of strict rules and a certain discipline . . .*

All of these documents – the letters she had received ending with the words 's. KETTERING' (but composed by who, she wondered) – had been photocopied, not once but many times. Some of them were discoloured with age, as though they had been prepared for previous years. So, if there was a mystery about the house it wasn't, as she had at first suspected, that she had been specially chosen to be mistaken for the Ketterings and to cover their retreat. Such a tactic could scarcely have been repeated year after year. She understood, with some disappointment, that she hadn't been singled out to play any role in the Ketterings' lives. And how self-regarding her landlords must be to only want families that were an echo of their own to inhabit their house, and to instruct them to behave as they did, to eat in the same place and play the same music. No doubt they so worshipped 'La Felicità' that they thought it would suffer from any great change in the perfect life within it. She restored the duplicated papers to their folder. Never had the fascinating Mr Kettering seemed so far away.

When she came downstairs, having washed away the dust of the loft, she found her family wrapped in damp towels, drinking tea and eating chocolate biscuits. She told them she had found nothing much up there except a lot of old dressing-up clothes and when Samantha asked if they could borrow them she really didn't see why not.

CHAPTER FOURTEEN

'They're not splitting, are they?' Samantha lay on her bed, still young enough to fear the break up of a marriage, however fragile.

'Oh, I shouldn't be at all surprised.' Henrietta was at her mirror making elaborate preparations for a day on which nothing in particular was going to happen. She sucked in her cheeks, put her hands on her hips, jutted her pelvis and became the cover of *Honey* magazine, wearing a pair of yellowing long johns bought from an Oxfam shop, a lacy blouse also bought to feed the starving, glossy lipstick, Doc Marten's thick-soled shoes, and one of the straw hats she had found in the hall downstairs. 'So many people do split nowadays. Practically all my friends . . .'

'*Why* are they?'

'Well, you heard them. That night. Rows and arguments.'

'They don't usually do it.'

'Things have probably come to a head.' Henrietta decided to add a wide leather belt and a pair of braces to her ensemble. 'Holidays impose a particular strain on a marriage. It's called the twenty-four-hour-a-day contact crisis.' She was quoting now from the woman's page of an outdated *Guardian* her father had bought in Siena and left out by the pool (the *Daily Telegraph* had disappeared with Signor Fixit). 'They're both missing the supportive job situation where attentive secretaries or glamorous bosses act as effective spouse substitutes and proxy partners. In the first week of a holiday watch out for diarrhoea and domestic rows.'

'It'd be awful,' Samantha said, lying on her back staring at the ceiling with itching eyes, 'if they split.'

'It might not be so awful. My friends all say it's much easier to get out to the Muckrakers and all that if there's only one of them to stop you.'

'What friends say that?'

'You know. My friends.'

'Whose fault is it, anyway. Is it Dad's?'

'You mean, has he got a girlfriend?'

'He couldn't.' Samantha shook her head in disbelief. 'He's much too old.'

'I don't think he's that much interested. I don't know about *her*.'

'What don't you know about her?'

'She's different, isn't she? Haven't you noticed that? Well, it's as though she's thinking about someone else all the time.' Henrietta tried another pose: this time one hand flat on the crown of her hat, her body twisted towards the door, her head turned back to the mirror, wide eyes gazing into the imaginary camera. She had reached the age when she needed to challenge Molly and was ready to disapprove of her.

'Someone else? Whoever . . .?'

'Oh, I suppose it might be . . .' Henrietta tried a selection of poses as the camera whirred and the photographer called out 'I like it!' from beyond the glare of the lights. She was conscious of the lack of hard evidence to bring against her mother. 'Someone she met at that party.'

'Who?'

'Well, I couldn't see that, could I? It was much too dark.'

'Not . . .' Samantha worried, 'not that man who came when the water ran out?'

'Him?' Henrietta remembered the grey-haired Ken Corduroy. 'Well, I suppose he might be about the right age for her.'

So the two sisters considered the possibilities whilst downstairs Jacqueline sat, unexpectedly quietly, on her grandfather's lap.

She knew nothing of Haverford's defects of character and as he told her the plot of *King Lear* she gave him her undivided attention.

Later the telephone rang in the hall and Henrietta, who was on her way to the pool, answered it. The call was for her and when she had finished speaking she went back upstairs to change all her clothes. She was singing and felt that her holiday had definitely taken a turn for the better.

The discovery that she had made in the loft, that she was only another photostat copy of a long line of tenants or prospective tenants, had the effect of taking Molly's speculation about the Ketterings off the boil. As she no longer felt that she had been in any way chosen to stand in for them, so her feeling of particular involvement in their lives receded. At the same time she had taken complete possession of 'La Felicità', and as their intangible personalities withdrew so she became, in her mind, the undisputed chatelaine of the villa. She knew its ways, she was prepared to keep quiet about its secrets and she supplied it, decorated it with jugs of wild flowers and roses from the garden, and saw to its tidiness in a way to which she thought the house responded.

Since their original quarrel about the postcard, Hugh had been more than ever content to leave the running of the house and the holiday to his wife. Once or twice when, contrary to her wishes, they were left alone together he tried to apologize.

'You're angry?'

'I'm not. Not angry at all.'

'I do feel terribly guilty.'

'Whatever for?'

'Well, of course I feel guilty.'

'You've no need. It seems you've got nothing to feel guilty about. That's really the worst part of it. All that deception just so you couldn't do anything except have lunch.'

'What did you want me to do?'

They were in the kitchen, clearing up before they went to bed.

It was a quiet quarrel and one the children had no chance of overhearing.

'Oh, I don't know. Feel something for a change. Perhaps that's it. I wanted you to feel something.'

'What's happened to you?' Hugh stood with a tea-towel in his hand, drying one of the Ketterings' cups. 'Something's happened to you.'

She said nothing because, at that moment, she felt nothing had.

'You've changed. You never used to spy on me like this.'

'Me spy on you? Really! I've got better things to do.' Or better things to spy on, she might have told him. 'I don't spy at all. You just leave things out for me to find, that's all.'

'Things. What sort of things?'

'Postcards.'

Molly's expertise in running the house was now extended to shopping and going round Mondano she felt that she had acquired much of Fosdyke's knowledge. She had found the freshest vegetables in the shop behind the church and discovered that the best olive oil was not to be had at Lucca's but bought with the Chianti in the courtyard at the Castello Crocetto, where it was fetched from some cavern by an old man who was still in his pyjamas at midday and who could only be summoned by pulling a bell rope. She had found a cache of Ribena in the *farmacia* for Jacqueline and in a small *supermercato* on the road to Arezzo she had tracked down Shredded Wheat.

Although she had done her best to banish the Ketterings, and whatever their doings might have been, from her mind, she still called at the post office to see if there were letters for 'La Felicità'. On one such visit, her inquiries, as usual, met with no result and she was wondering if her landlords had given other instructions for their mail when she heard a young English voice, half frustrated and half amused, say 'Water Board! What the hell's the Italian for "Water Board"?'

Turning from the nest of little boxes she saw a young couple, tall and thin with fair hair, interchangeable faded blue jeans and sweaters. They were struggling with the local telephone directory, entertained by their inability to make any sense of it.

'*Acqua*. It must be *acqua* something. Go for the "A"s.'

'Not necessarily.'

'Why not necessarily?'

'Well, it probably starts with something like "T" for Toscano . . .'

'Excuse me.' Molly moved in on them. 'I couldn't help overhearing. You're not having trouble with your water?'

'You're English!' The young woman looked at Molly in wide-eyed astonishment, as though she'd just met her next-door neighbour in the depths of some South American jungle or on an Arctic ice-floe.

'Well, yes.' Molly gave the impression that she might, at some unspecified time in her past, have had some vague connection with what Signor Fixit would have called the U.K. Indeed she was sufficiently self-aware to hear in herself something of the late, lamented Fosdyke's tone of knowing helpfulness as she explained, 'Water's always a terrible problem in these hills. That's why they tell you that watermelons are wonderful to eat *and* wash your face with.'

'Yes. But can you bath in watermelons?'

'Tim can't exist without his bath in the morning and the house quite suddenly dried up.' The couple introduced themselves as Tim and Hermia Greensleeve and they'd taken their villa through Paradise Palaces of Fulham. When they first saw it they were overcome by the bougainvillaea, the cool stone floors and the little pool, quite big enough really. 'It seemed to have everything, but what's everything without water?' The maid only came in twice a week and spoke no English and when they rang Fulham the idiot in the Paradise office actually told them to pray for rain.

'*You* don't know what the Italian for "Water Board" is, do you?'

Molly didn't, so she could no longer carry on the Fosdyke

tradition of swooping down to help those in trouble. But then, no doubt on the intervention of Saint Agostino, she saw through the open door of the post office a grey-haired man getting out of a Volvo Estate and setting off towards the butcher's on the corner of the Via Garibaldi.

'Wait there,' she told the Greensleeves, 'I think I can find a way to help.'

'Water Board.' Molly took the message to Ken Corduroy, who had by that time reached the safety of the butcher's. 'Someone else is in trouble.'

'I'm not surprised.' The pool expert smiled at her. 'It's this damned high stuck over Europe. If they want rain they should stop in the U.K. Hailstorms back home, apparently.'

Mr Corduroy stood smiling at her. They were surrounded by the *macelleria*'s excellent supplies of roasts, meatballs and Tuscan shishkebabs prepared with fresh herbs, juniper berries and red peppers. Sausages flavoured with fennel dangled from the ceiling, long-boned pork chops and chickens tied in parcels of herbs decorated the steel trays on the marble counter. Somewhere behind Ken Corduroy a pale pig's head wore a carnation behind its ear like a Spanish dancer and a crucifix hung among the hams. Old women sat on chairs, as silent as though they were in church, whilst the butcher went through his painfully slow rituals. A fan buzzed and fluttered plastic streamers; they breathed in the sweet smell of dead meat.

'They want to get in touch with the Water Board, but they can't find it in the book.'

'Sound idea. Somebody may not have paid a bill.'

'They're renting through something called Paradise Palaces. Surely *they* should have paid it.'

'Never can tell with these villa companies. You're inclined to run into a load of cowboys. Quickest way would be to go up to the *Idraulica*.'

'The what?'

'Bloody great concrete building about fifteen kilometres out on the road to Siena. You can't miss it. By the way, you haven't heard anything of Buck Kettering, have you?'

'No.' At the mention of the name Molly's interest in the Ketterings came flooding back and she could feel that Corduroy, although much occupied in putting his wallet back in the small leather handbag strapped to his wrist, was waiting for her answer in some suspense.

'No, I haven't. Not a word since we got here. Should I have done?'

'Not really, I suppose. Odd sort of fellow, Buck. He seems to have vanished without trace.'

When she returned to the Greensleeves, who were now standing outside the post office waiting for her obediently, Molly was in control of the situation and able to give them the full benefit of her experience.

'The likely thing,' she told them, 'is that your wretched Paradise Palaces never paid the water bill, but it might take weeks to get the money out of them. So why don't I run you over to the *Idraulica*, which is actually what we call the Water Board round here . . .'

'And we were trying to find *acqua*.' Tim smiled at their stupidity.

'It takes a bit of time to get to know the ropes. Anyway, it's only about fifteen kilometres on the Siena road. We'd better call in at the bank and change a traveller's cheque or two. I can show you where *that* is.'

'How much?' Hermia wondered.

'Could be . . . well. Might be up to five hundred and fifty thousand lire if they haven't paid it for half a year. There have been cases like that,' Molly quoted Ken Corduroy. 'That's not quite as bad as it sounds,' she tried to comfort the young couple who looked stricken. 'About two hundred and fifty quid. And Paradise whatever's bound to pay you back in the end. I mean, you can't live without water, can you?'

Molly took them in her car. On the way they recovered their spirits; after all they could wire for more money from their bank in England. It might make a bit of a dent in what Tim had cleared on his TSB shares but after all you couldn't bath in TSB shares or even swim in them. The pool water, didn't they tell her, had also somehow evaporated overnight? They had just got married and this was the first proper holiday they had taken together since their honeymoon, which had been a bit of a disaster. St Lucia. Hermia had been laid low by some highly dubious prawns which was unfortunate to say the least. But they'd been looking forward to Italy and of course they were going to enjoy every minute when the water was fixed. What ought they to see?

'The Piero della Francescas are the best thing. Start with the murals in Arezzo. Then you can do Monterchi and Sansepolcro. If you're feeling very adventurous, I'd advise you to take the trail over the Mountains of the Moon to Urbino. See what's probably the greatest small painting in the world.'

They were in the bank by them, waiting for the girl with tragic eyes and a cigarette adhering to her lower lip to count out an enormous amount of lire.

'What's the greatest painting?'

'Another Piero. "The Flagellation".'

'Sounds a bit kinky.'

'It's a mystery,' Molly told them. 'No one can quite explain it. That's why it's so marvellous.'

The Greensleeves looked suitably impressed and Tim pushed the wad of notes into the back pocket of his jeans, where it would have only temporary accommodation.

So they drove by the Siena road and Molly composed sentences of shopping Italian in her head. '*Per favore, vogliamo pagare il conto dell'acqua per la casa "Perdita", Mondano-in-Chianti*,' which she hoped might be sufficient to meet the situation. Hermia Greensleeve sat in the front seat but twisted round to hold her husband's hand and point out the miracles on the way: the fields of sunflowers past their prime, the terraces of vines and the grandeur of the Villa Baderini high up on a hillside. Molly wondered if her first year with Hugh had been anything like that and decided that, on the whole, it hadn't. In what seemed no time at all they found a grim building, perforated with small square windows like a prison, up a short driveway. Over the gates Molly read the words AZIENDA IDRAULICA COMUNALE. 'There you are,' she said, 'the *Idraulica*,' as though it were a secret known only to her. They parked in a yard beside a row of big tankers of the sort that had dumped water into her swimming-pool and found a door marked UFFICIO.

'*Per favore, vogliamo pagare il conto dell'. . .*' she started off to a man with a haggard, distinguished face who might have been an overworked priest or a university professor suffering from insomnia. 'Yes,' he nodded at her, saving her the trouble of further Italian, 'you want to pay the bill?' There were no papers on the desk in front of him, nothing in fact but a small tin lid piled with a mountain of cigarette ends, and yet he seemed to have expected her coming. When she had explained the Greensleeves' problem, he retired into a back room from which he later emerged with a handful of carbon copies on flimsy paper and confirmed that the villa's owners had ignored their bills for water.

'Do you know Croydon?' he asked as he wrote out the receipt. Molly had heard of it.

'No shortage of water in Croydon. I was there as a student. My subject was philosophy. Now I am working for the *Idraulica*. Teachers of philosophy are poorly paid in Italy.'

'I'm sorry.' Molly felt embarrassed at this confidence, as though the man, who looked extraordinarily thin, had confessed that he was suffering from a fatal disease.

'I don't mind.' He coughed and lit another cigarette. 'One can still read philosophy without having to teach it. I hope very much that I will see Croydon again before I die.'

They emerged from the office with the back pocket of Tim Greensleeve's jeans emptied and a promise that an official would have reconnected the water by the time they got home. In the courtyard a man was getting into a long and dusty motor car. As he did so, he raised his hand to Molly as though in recognition. He had a receding hairline, a plump face and a small mouth, and she had no doubt that he was the man who, it seemed half a lifetime ago, had called her 'Signora Kettering' and handed her a letter. She returned his salute and then, as he drove away, wondered why the words AZIENDA IDRAULICA COMUNALE written over the gate were somehow familiar.

CHAPTER FIFTEEN

'What're you doing, Mum?'

Molly was pulling down one of the empty suitcases from the top of the bedroom cupboard. Her purpose was to take another look at the letter addressed to Sandra Kettering which she had put there for safe keeping. 'I'm just' – Molly offered an unsatisfactory explanation – 'well, seeing that everything's unpacked.'

'I know you're going to say no to this.' Henrietta sat on the edge of the huge matrimonial bed in which her parents were now unfriendly and looked resigned to disappointment.

'How do you know?' Molly looked at her daughter, envying her thinness and the possibilities her life had to offer.

'Because you say no to everything, don't you?'

It was an unjust attack and Molly was stung by it. She had said yes to an adventure, an investigation which she had decided to undertake with no help from her family, in secret and entirely alone.

'Of course I don't, darling. That's ridiculous.'

'Oh, you say yes to some things, like us tidying the bedroom or looking after Jacky for the afternoon. But no when it comes to going out to meet my friends.'

'What friends exactly? Have you got many friends here in Mondano-in-Chianti?' She smiled: she was doing her best to understand her daughter. 'I don't suppose they've got a Muckrakers Club here, have they?'

'Actually you're wrong. I don't mean about the Muckrakers Club. I mean about me not having friends here. It just happens that one of them phoned me up. Don't you want to know who it is?'

'If you want to tell me . . .'

'I thought you wanted to know the names and addresses of everyone I went out with, just so you could phone their parents to make quite sure we're not sniffing glue or anything. As a matter of fact, it's Chrissie Kettering. She's back. And she doesn't have to ask her mother every time she goes anywhere. If she did, she says, her street cred. would suffer.'

'Oh, really.' Molly did her best to sound calm, but she was consumed by a kind of envy. She had been inquiring, probing, consulting the most unreliable sources and making the most dangerous deductions, working, so it seemed to her, in the dark. And her daughter was entering the Ketterings' lives without any effort and no doubt had access to the best information. 'So what's the plan?'

It turned out that Helena Tapscott, the Tapscotts' grand-daughter, had also been at Nancy Leadbetter's party and was a great friend of Chrissie's. So they were all going to meet at the Tapscotts' around six and then they might go and eat at the 'trat' in Mondano with some Italian boys Chrissie knew and who had promised to come out from Siena. And why on earth wouldn't that be all right and need Samantha come too because she'd only feel left out with everyone older than her? 'Now tell me I can't go.'

'Of course you can go. I'll drive you over.'

When Henrietta had left to start the long process of deciding what to wear, Molly opened the empty suitcase and rediscovered, zipped into the pocket in its lining, the letter to Signora Kettering. She considered boiling another kettle but she couldn't be sure of being alone in the kitchen. She decided to renew the cheap brown envelope and might even go so far as to forge the writing of her landlady's name on it. So she tore it open and found the message from Claudio; this she turned over and saw the three letters at the top of the column of figures: A.I.C. She was sure, now, why the words on top of the gates had seemed familiar to her: AZIENDA IDRAULICA COMUNALE.

The Tapscotts lived in a small, ochre-coloured farmhouse outside San Pietro in Crespi. They took Molly into a barn converted into a studio and sent Henrietta out to join the young people in the garden.

'All right,' the tall, sadly smiling Nicholas Tapscott, who looked more than ever as though he'd been rolled in flour, said, 'honest injun, now. I haven't caught it, have I? Whatever it is, I haven't caught it.'

One wall was covered with his landscapes. These were views of Tuscany painted in oils in which the soft colours of the countryside had become hard and metallic; they were the sort of pictures which, had the artist more talent, might have gone on sale in Boots together with Eurasian ladies and tearful clowns. On another wall Connie Tapscott's foxy-faced Victorian children had more originality but caused greater embarrassment.

'Ought to be so blooming easy. Wonderful views round here. Spectacular light. Nice little studio. No expense spared on Reeves colours. Why can't I catch it, Mrs Pargeter?'

Through the open door Molly could see the young people on the sun-baked grass. The boys stood silent and aloof as the English girls chattered to each other and occasionally, like daring children who ring doorbells, tried a challenging word to the Italian visitors and then retreated. She saw a fair-haired girl she took to be Chrissie Kettering put her hand on Henrietta's shoulder, tell her something and then double up with laughter. Molly envied her daughter such confidences and wondered how she too might earn them.

'Do you think I ought to get drunk?' Nicholas was asking, his pale face very close to hers. '"Smoke pot"? Go "on the needle"? Or do I have to "sleep around" a bit?' He raised his eyebrows as he mockingly placed inverted commas round each of these activities. 'I mean, when I was in the Consular Service, we weren't meant to do any of that. Otherwise you'd take early retirement. Or get posted to New Zealand. But to be an artist! Must say, I'd be prepared to take on anything. Not a word to Connie.' Nicholas said this with a heavy wink and his wife standing two feet away from him.

'Nicholas is far too modest about his oils,' Connie Tapscott said diplomatically. 'I really do think he's *seen* something in these Tuscan hills.'

'But not the right thing, my dear. Oh, I do love it. Jeepers, yes. Art's the greatest thing in the world. Even if you do make a bit of a pig's breakfast of it.'

'Will you excuse me for a moment? There's someone I ought to talk to.' Molly escaped out of the barn door with Nicholas's voice following her, 'Have a drink before you go, and look at Connie's stuff,' and Mrs Tapscott's cheerful, 'Don't bother. I'm no good either.'

'You must be Chrissie Kettering.' The girl was shorter than Henrietta, although perhaps a year older, and had darker, golden skin, no doubt inherited from her mother. 'We're so much enjoying your house. It's kind of your parents to let us have it.'

'I'm glad you like it, Mrs Pargeter. Hetty told me about the water. I hope it's all right now.'

'Oh yes. I don't know how that happened,' she lied, as by now she had a very clear idea about the water. 'I think it must have been some sort of a mistake. I mean, it shouldn't have dried up in *your* house, should it?'

'It never has.'

'Then perhaps we were just unlucky. Hetty says you've met in London,' Molly went on with her questioning, although Henrietta was making eyes at her, beseeching her to go away please, to talk to the old grandparents or, better still, drive home and stop embarrassing her in front of her friends. 'Do your parents have a place in London as well?'

'Not now. My sister and I stay with our aunt in the school

terms. Holland Park, actually. I think Mummy and Daddy like to spend all the time they can in Italy.'

'And the baby. Violetta, isn't it?'

'Oh, she's with Mummy, really all the time.'

'I would like to ring your mother. Just to tell her how we're getting on and to put her mind at rest about the water. She's not in London?'

'Oh no. Rome. Staying with friends. I've got the number.' It all seemed far too easy, but then Chrissie, who had been searching in a huge woollen shoulder-bag, said, 'Sorry. I left it at the house we're staying in. Nancy Leadbetter's.'

'It doesn't matter. Just an idea. I suppose I could ring your father, actually.'

'Well, that's a bit harder. He's gone off somewhere. Business, I suppose.'

'He was going to take Chrissie on a trip.' Henrietta spoke for the first time to point out the unreliability of parents in general.

'What fun.' Molly tried to sound not particularly interested. 'Where was he going to take you?'

'Oh, to see a lot of paintings. He said it was time I learnt about them. We were going to stay with him at "La Felicità" before you came too, but he couldn't fit that in somehow.'

'I'm sorry.'

'Oh, it's all right. I've been travelling. We've been to all sorts of places.'

'She's allowed to travel' – Henrietta looked at her mother rebukingly – 'without her parents.'

'I go with my friends,' Chrissie said. 'It's much better.'

Then they discussed how Henrietta would get home and Chrissie said the Tapscotts would drive them, or one of the Italian boys who had a car. Before she went, Molly thanked Chrissie again for the loan of her house and, as she turned back into the unfortunately hung studio, said, 'Those pictures your father was going to take you to see. I suppose they were the Piero della Francescas.'

'Oh yes,' Chrissie told her. 'He's been promising to show me those for years.'

The next morning Molly rang Nancy Leadbetter only to discover, after the usual confused series of questions and answers, that Chrissie and her friends had moved on. It might have been to Orvieto. She might be coming back that way, but then again she might not. No, Nancy had absolutely no idea of Sandra Kettering's phone number in Rome. Molly put down the telephone in the kitchen as Giovanna came sweeping in from the terrace where Haverford, jotting in the shade, called out, '*Ciao bellissima!*' as she left him.

'*Giovanna, lei sa il numero di telefono della, Signora Kettering a Roma?*'

'No.' Giovanna pressed her lips together and brushed even more energetically at the clean kitchen floor. Then she got a dustpan on a long handle and introduced a minute quantity of dust into it.

'*Giovanna. Il vecchio signore fuori . . .*' Molly had worked on her *Teach Yourself Italian* from the time when she had first answered the advertisement; she could make herself ungrammatically understood in most shops and restaurants. But now, as when she quarrelled with Hugh, the house itself seemed to come to her aid, suggesting words and phrases for the complicated speech she was about to utter about the old gentleman on the terrace. '*Il vecchio signore,*' she said, 'is a great English writer. He is a historian. He is studying the history of Mondano-in-Chianti during the war. He will write which families worked with the Tedeschi and which fought for freedom. He would like to write down the story of Giovanna's family.' Meanwhile she wished to speak to Signora Kettering in Rome, so would Giovanna please give her the number. *Tante grazie.* Giovanna gave her a look of intense hatred from basilisk eyes and then yanked out a drawer of the dresser. She took out a tin which contained crumpled shopping-lists, old bills, notes of laundry done and slapped a small square of graph paper, decorated with a row of figures, on to the kitchen table. '*Grazie, Giovanna*.' Molly was unsmiling. '*Grazie mille*.'

She rang the number and it was answered with an immediate, gentle, '*Pronto*. Mrs Kettering? I will pass you to her.' The voice was in no way deceived by Molly's Italian. There was a silence, then footsteps and she imagined high heels crossing the marble tiles of a dark Roman *piano nobile*. Then a voice said, 'Yes?'

'It's Molly Pargeter here, Mrs Kettering.'

There was a moment's pause, it seemed a small intake of breath, and then, 'Oh yes, Mrs Pargeter. It's good to hear from you. I hope all is well at "La Felicità".'

What could she say? All well, Mrs Kettering? Suppose you tell me. I have discovered a note written with the typewriter you used to write to me on. It seems that one of your objectives was to have your husband *gone forever*. He has disappeared, Mrs Kettering. Even his child seems to have no idea where he is. I have sleepless nights on this subject and at one moment I thought that the remains of Buck Kettering might have been seen by my daughter down a well. I have rejected that idea, but how do you explain your list and your objective: *B. lost and gone forever?* In fact she said none of these things, the time not being, she told herself, ripe for such a confrontation. 'We had a bad moment when the water ran out.'

'I heard about it. It was terrible.'

'A terrible mistake?'

'No. I mean a terrible thing to happen.' Sandra Kettering had a rich, contralto voice and only a trace of an Italian accent. She sounded concerned.

'It seems to be happening to a number of people.'

'My concern is that it should happen to you.'

'And it led to a tragedy at the house where Mr Fosdyke was staying.'

There was a longer pause then, and the answer came, 'It has been a *maledetta* summer.'

'We've had to pay five hundred and thirty thousand lire for

water they delivered. Mr Fosdyke was going to get it back from the second half of the rent I gave him.'

'You shall have your money, Mrs Pargeter. After such a tragedy money is not always the first thing one thinks of.'

Molly felt rebuked. But she couldn't help saying, 'Doesn't it seem rather strange that so many people ran out of water? You can't really blame it on the weather, can you?'

'I don't know, Mrs Pargeter. I can't explain it.'

'Can't you? Then perhaps you should ask your friend Claudio.'

There was silence, then a click and an angry buzzing. Molly put down the phone and dialled again but there was no reply, no friend picked up the phone and offered to pass her to Signora Kettering in a voice which she thought she had identified as that of Vittoria Dulcibene.

'My God, what a crafty old manipulator you've become.' Haverford, his straw hat on the side of his head and his papers under his arm, came in from the terrace. 'Pure Italian Renaissance guile, mixed with some not very covert threats. Have you become Molly the Machiavelli?'

She moved away from the phone and put on the kettle to make coffee, pretending to have no idea what her father meant. Two days later, when she called at the post office, she found a letter from the Banco dell'Annunziazione informing her that the sum of five hundred and thirty thousand lire awaited her collection at their branch in Mondano-in-Chianti. She couldn't be entirely sure whether she was receiving hush money or the payment of a debt.

CHAPTER SIXTEEN

JOTTINGS FROM TUSCANY
by Haverford Downs

'Marriage,' wrote Robert Louis Stevenson, who may have some cause to know, 'is a battlefield.' Although this is undoubtedly true, hostilities are carried out in a very different way in Italy and England. At home we believe in the uneasy truce and the balance of terror. A pre-emptive strike may lead to the divorce court, crippling alimony or a lonely old age without the comfort of a domestic quarrel. So the war remains cold with, at best, formal exchanges and, at worst, the severing of diplomatic relations.

In Italy they order things differently. It was here, among these very hills, that in 1610 the highly aristocratic Lucia Baderini married her major-domo. For this offence the unfortunate husband was flung from the top of the campanile in Siena, during the Palio, by members of the family. It is said that in the excitement of the race this act of execution passed unnoticed.

Up the road from the villa now inhabited by your man in Chiantishire, as I have already mentioned, is the Castello Crocetto, home of the Barone Dulcibene and some of the world's best Chianti Classico. In the eighteenth century an old and crusty Dulcibene lived in Rome with his beautiful young wife. At a ball given by the British Ambassador to the Holy See she danced once too often with a cavalry officer. That night the Barone ordered his wife from the ballroom and took her in his carriage to this distant and isolated castle. She was never seen again in public and the Barone, whose life was given over to guarding his prisoner, devoted his leisure hours to blending black and white grapes to produce the pure wine we pour down our throats each night without the slightest fear of a hangover. Things didn't end so happily for the young cavalry officer, who was found floating face downwards in the Tiber a few weeks after the fatal ball.

To what extent does this extreme manner of regulating your domestic affairs persist in Italian culture? I put the problem to my old friend Don Marco over a glass of grappa in his stifling little study in Mondano (the good priest, who risked his life fighting the Nazi war machine, now lives in daily fear of draughts, an unreasonable terror with the temperature hovering in the eighties). I asked him how many of his flock might, at some time or another, have been guilty of a crime of passion, but I couldn't get him to reveal the secrets of the confessional. However, my favourite cleric (who would have made the Red Dean of Canterbury look an uninteresting shade of watery pink) told me that Italian women take it as a huge compliment that murders might be committed on their account, even if they often become the victims. He also said that Englishwomen have become nervous and unhappy because their husbands no longer care enough to resort to assassination. The crime passionnel *is, according to my religious adviser, the greatest compliment an Italian can pay to a marriage: at least it means that the husband has found something to feel* passionnel *about.*

Haverford sat by the swimming-pool and read what he'd written so far. 'Can I do work?' Jacqueline asked and, climbing on to his knees without invitation, began to draw minute shapes, said by her to be fish, on his sheet of paper. Hugh had taken the two older girls into Siena, Henrietta being particularly depressed by a return to family life after a brilliant evening out with Chrissie Kettering, who had now moved on. It was a still day and very hot, a dragonfly dipped and skimmed the water of the pool, the child who unaccountably loved him frowned with concentration and wriggled on his lap. In spite of all he had written about marriage, Haverford wondered if he might not, perhaps, given the most favourable circumstances, try it again. 'I'll go no more a'roving,' the old man thought, giving his past a romantic glow which it had hardly had at the time, 'so late into the night', round the Gargoyle in Soho just after the war, or the Arethusa in the King's Road in the sixties, or even until closing time in the Nell Gwyn pub at the World's End. 'For the sword outwears its sheath', but not yet, not quite yet. And Haverford thought that seventy-seven was no age at all nowadays: being old was still safely five years ahead of wherever he was. The sword still had a little life in it, particularly when he woke up in the mornings. It was only his legs that hurt him. 'Get off now, darling,' he said to Jacqueline as the child's weight induced a stab of pain in one swollen ankle. Well, what did the legs matter? The best things in life, after all, can be better enjoyed lying down. The thing about you, Haverford, he confided in his more private and not as yet published 'Jottings', is that you have had the most prolonged and perhaps the most pleasurable adolescence in the history of mankind. But settling down, that was something he might make a go of now. His own marriage, of course, had clearly been impossible; his wife had lacked the essential talent of being able to turn a blind eye.

'My God, Molly Coddle. Aren't you putting old Hughie through the ordeal of fire and ice?' His daughter came to sit by the pool to read Henry James's *Italian Hours*, one of the books which the Ketterings kept on display.

'Chaps do send the odd furtive p.c. when on a family holiday, you know. It's a fact of human nature. Has been, I suppose, ever since the postcard was invented.'

'You were listening to our quarrel.'

'Of course. What do you expect? You can't keep secrets in a family.'

'Hugh hasn't been unfaithful.'

'No. I do see that's very hard to excuse. Poor old Hughie, all froth and no Guinness. It makes you despair of the fellow.'

'I really don't think you know very much about it. Don't go into the pool without your arm-bands, darling!' Molly called across at Jacqueline who was wriggling in the white plastic reclining chair in which she had first seen the late Signor Fixit.

'I know a good deal about it. As I told you, exactly the same thing happened to me when I was with your sainted mother. You call to mind when I postcarded a girlfriend from a hotel in Siena?'

'I remember what you told us.'

'Two differences in that case. One, your mother did crash the car into the *ospedale*, but two days later she'd forgotten the subject and we were rowing about something else. Two, I had more than an academic interest in the girl concerned. I mean, we'd got a bit further than consummating our relationship through the post.'

'Do you call regular little lunches and not saying anything about them "academic"?'

'Of course I do. And so is kissing a bit of crackling goodbye in the wide open spaces of Chancery Lane.'

'Chancery Lane? Did you say Chancery Lane?'

'Well, it was just' – Haverford hadn't really meant his son-in-law any further harm – 'a figure of speech.'

'How did you know he kissed her in Chancery Lane? Is that where the "Dolce Vita" is?'

'Yes. That's why I said it. I just imagined that might have been where he kissed her. If he'd ever dared to do anything quite so flagrant.'

'Isn't that near the *Informer* office?'

'Near his office too.'

'You don't mean to say you actually *saw* them?'

'Now, Molly Coddle. I told you. It was a pure guess. Just something I happened to say. That's all.'

'I don't believe you.'

She turned her attention to her book. There was a long silence. Curled up and sucking her thumb, Jacqueline appeared to be asleep. Two dragonflies were now skimming the pool.

'How does it come about,' Haverford said, 'that you and I are so entirely different?'

'Please, I don't want to talk about it any more.'

'You see, I don't think it matters whether you believe me or not. What matters is that you should understand me, even understand old Hughie too, comprehend our weakness. Not be forever ferreting out the truth like some merciless inspector of police. The truth is probably the least important thing about us.'

She didn't answer him and he knew that she felt no sympathy for what he had said.

'I'd like you to understand me some time. Particularly as I'm thinking of making a bit of a change in my way of life. What would you feel, tell me honestly Molly Coddle, if I decided to get married again?'

She looked up at him unbelieving, and said, 'Anyone in particular?'

'Well, it'd have to be an old girlfriend. We might not be able to put on much of a show now, but at least we'd have our memories. And someone, well, self-supporting or, even better, Haverford-supporting. Come on now, let's have a bit of this truth-telling you're so famous for. Wouldn't it be a relief not to have to take me on any more holidays?'

'Who on earth' – Molly looked at her father – 'are you thinking of marrying?'

'What do you think of Nancy Leadbetter?'

'But' – Molly was amazed – 'she didn't even remember you.'

'Always one for a joke, old Nancy,' her father smiled back at her. 'We used to understand each other pretty well, and no doubt we shall again. We were once happy, you know. I'm sorry not to see you happy. Is that my fault, would you say?'

'Please. I'm perfectly all right.'

'Or is there something in what old Don Marco said? Do Englishwomen want a husband who'd care enough to kill for them?'

'Is that the subject of your "Jottings"?'

'Yes, as a matter of fact. I'm writing a few extra so I'll have a store to fall back on, if I go back to England.'

'If you say that sort of thing, you're going to get smothered in letters from outraged women in England.'

Haverford knew she was right. Covens of women, he told himself, from Battersea to Birkenhead, would write furiously to the *Informer* demanding his head on a platter, and without a second wife with a spot of cash to her name he couldn't afford to lose his job. He went back into the house to compose a more neutral final paragraph. But Molly closed her book and sat staring into the water, thinking of what her father had said. Then she picked up Jacqueline as the one sure thing in an uncertain world but the child struggled in her arms, as children will, anxious to be free.

Hugh found it hard to believe that the effect of a single postcard, which never reached its destination, could be so long lasting. His acts of contrition appeared unavailing and the fact that his knowledge of Mrs Tobias stopped short at the edge of her designer wardrobe seemed not to mitigate his offence but to fuel his wife's quiet outrage. As he and Molly now had little to say to each other, he spent more time with the older children and discovered an unexpected sympathizer in Henrietta, who was always prepared to widen the gap between her parents. Samantha, a middle child, who had the least of her father's attention, now found him seeking her out and asking her questions about her school, which half-flattered, half-embarrassed her. In return she sat on his lap, even though she felt too old for it, disturbed his hair and told him how young he looked, cheering him up considerably and acting a role which Mrs Tobias might have filled had their relationship not terminated at lunchtimes. So, unexpectedly, the effect of the matrimonial quarrel was to turn Hugh to the company of his children, and they enjoyed their holiday more because of it.

'Sometimes,' Henrietta said, 'I just don't understand her

at all. You know what I found her doing the other morning?
Packing.'

'What?'

'Well, taking her suitcase down ready to pack.'

'She isn't going anywhere, is she?'

'It seems she was thinking of it, Dad.'

'Thinking of what?'

'Clearing off.'

'You mean leaving us?'

'It's happened to all my friends' parents. They've practically
all split up.'

Hugh's feelings were mixed. A sudden sense of freedom
alternated with the fear of an uncertain future. A new worry
assailed him: would he feel bound, on the strength of all those
lunches, to become the second husband of Mrs Tobias? Away
from home, sitting in the sun outside the restaurant in the Piazza
del Campo with two attentive daughters, watching the people go
by and the pigeons wheeling through the air like a squadron of
crack pilots, he was detached about the future.

'But she *didn't* pack up and go, did she?'

'Not this time. She probably stayed for the sake of Jacky.'

'Jacky!' Samantha said with feeling. 'That's all she thinks
about.'

'And Gamps.'

'What do you mean? Why should she stay with me because of
Haverford?'

'Oh, because he's longing for you two to divorce.' Henrietta
had unusual worldly wisdom for a girl of fifteen. 'And she doesn't
want to give him the satisfaction of seeing it happen.'

Hugh considered his situation and came to the conclusion that
it was unsatisfactory. He wasn't in a position to enjoy the company
of either his wife or Mrs Tobias. Indeed he seemed to have
enjoyed the company of very few women. Unusually, he felt
envious of old Haverford who, approaching death, was able to
look down a long line of mistresses; some of them he might have

forgotten and some might have forgotten him, but at least they had been there and might, with luck, be remembered. And when Hugh could no longer put on his socks with ease what would he have to remember? A string of not entirely successful divorce cases and a long line of lunches.

'It seems to us,' Samantha said, 'that Mum's been different lately.'

'Quite, quite different.'

'In what way?'

'Well. She's not being very nice to you, for instance.' Hugh had bought his daughters a number of small china objects and decorative pencils to take back to their schoolfriends. He had also bought them each a man's shirt, to stop them pinching his, and stood Henrietta a white wine and Samantha an orange Fanta. He didn't put their sympathetic attitude to him down to cupboard love, however. Henrietta's wide eyes and serious expression seemed to show serious concern.

'It's crossed our minds,' Henrietta said, 'that she might have found someone else.'

'Why ever should you think that?'

'She never seems to want to be with *us*,' Samantha reminded her father.

'She actually goes off *alone* to Mondano,' Henrietta whispered, as though it were the most serious crime on the indictment.

'She makes a lot of phone calls, too.'

'And she doesn't care about me going out now.' Henrietta said this with severe disapproval.

'I thought you'd appreciate that.' Hugh was puzzled.

'It's as if,' Henrietta explained, 'she just didn't care about any of us any more.'

'And *why* do you think that is?' Samantha summed up triumphantly.

'She must have found a boyfriend.'

In all the years since he had met his wife Hugh had never felt jealous. Now, in spite of all that had occurred over his ill-advised postcard, he felt an entirely new sensation, a stab of anger at the idea that Molly might be deceiving him.

'Hullo there! Long time no see.' It was Ken Corduroy, with his handbag strapped to his wrist. 'Don't mind if I do.' He sat down at their table and the girls looked at him with narrowed eyes; he was, after all, their number one suspect. 'Everything's going smoothly at "La Felicità" now?'

'No further trouble with the water, if that's what you mean.' And Hugh bought Ken a *gin e Schweppes*.

'Now that's over, it's best forgotten.'

'I suppose so.'

'You might let your wife know that.'

In the sunshine, having got outside most of a bottle of white wine from San Gimignano (Michelangelo's favourite tipple, his father-in-law had told him) Hugh seemed to hear and see with unusual sharpness. Ken Corduroy's face was very near him; he could see the open pores in the man's suntanned skin, the grey curls and the fleck of shaving soap which lingered behind his ear. He also saw a smile which seemed to suppress anger.

'I expect she knows.'

'Well, then. I think she's making a mistake.'

'What?'

'Taking people to deal with the Water Board. Getting mixed up in other people's business. After all, you've only been here a couple of weeks, haven't you?'

'That's all.'

'It takes years to get to know the ropes round here. Years of experience. There are ways and ways, let me tell you, of dealing with Italian *burocrazia*. You can't just blunder into it. Spoils things for those of us chaps who've got to live here all the time, you know. She might have thought of that.'

'I don't think I know what you're talking about.'

The children looked at the two men who might be about to quarrel, they thought, over their mother.

'I think she'll understand,' Mr Corduroy said, 'if you give her the message.'

They got back to the villa in a good mood and had been singing 'Green Grow the Rushes' in the car as they used to do when the children were much younger. Hugh spread out his propitiatory gifts of white wine, Dolcelatte cheese and Baci chocolates on the kitchen table. He had even bought Italian cigars for Haverford and a small police car with a wailing siren for Jacqueline. Henrietta produced a bunch of richly smelling carnations her father had bought for her to give her mother. Molly looked at all these things without smiling and, when she was alone with her husband, said, 'Did you *have* to kiss that Tobias woman in Chancery Lane?'

'Who told you that?'

'And why on earth did you wait to do it until my father was coming along the street? Were you afraid I might not get to know?'

Hugh could think of nothing to do but slam out of the room and sit by the pool with the two-day-old *Telegraph* he had found in Siena. Molly stayed in the kitchen and started to look through the packet of photographs he had brought home developed. There were a number of pictures of the children behind plates of spaghetti and Coke bottles on the terrace, one of Haverford in an armchair looking rakish and several, blurred and uninteresting, of the landscape. And then she saw the picture which the waiter had insisted on taking on their first visit to the Piazza del Campo. There was Jacqueline holding a child-sized silk banner and old Haverford staring at the passing girls; there was Hugh smiling quizzically into the camera and there she was, looking as though she wished no one was taking her photograph. Then she held the picture closer to her eyes to study a man who was sitting alone at a table behind them; he was wearing a red shirt and sat with a glass and a folded newspaper in front of him. It seemed that these were the colours of the clothes he often wore because she was as sure as she could have been of anything that it was the same man who had been sitting on the further side of the pool in the picture that had been sent to her before she ever saw the house. And then she made an even more daring assumption. As Giovanna came in with a basket full of clean laundry she held the photograph under her eyes.

'*È il Signor Kettering, Giovanna?*'

'*Sì, Signora,*' the maid had to admit, '*è il padrone.*'

So Buck Kettering had been alive and well and sitting in Siena on the day the water vanished. His subsequent movements were still a matter for speculation.

CHAPTER SEVENTEEN

'You're curious about Buck?' asked Nancy Leadbetter. 'Well, I can tell you. I've known him, of course, since he was quite a lad.'

It was half-way through their holiday and the weather had changed. In small, hardly noticeable ways there was a hint that it might be time to start thinking about autumn. The mornings were as hot as ever, but sometimes there were clouds in the afternoon and a wind rustled the trees and the long grass on the other side of the swimming-pool. It flapped at the shops and the cafés in Mondano and made them roll up their awnings. The sunflowers in the fields had faded, gone brown: their stalks collapsed and they were ready for harvesting. There were also new smells, like faraway bonfires. Jacqueline, following Giovanna round devotedly, had learned to say *buon giorno* and count to four in Italian. Haverford, sitting at the table in the garden, with the wind lifting his 'Jottings', looked out across the hills and dreamt of a winter with Nancy beside the log fires and among the art works in the Villa Baderini. He would ring for a man to bring him a glass of champagne before lunch, and avoid having to go out in the icy rain at the World's End to flog an armful of review copies for the price of a dinner with some pick-up from the Nell Gwyn pub he didn't even fancy. And then, as though in answer to his unspoken prayers, Nancy Leadbetter invited them all to dinner.

The change in the weather had brought her, it seemed, a change of mind. When she telephoned she had not only grasped the fact that they were the Ketterings' tenants who had had some sort of trouble with the house, but the figure of Haverford seemed to have cleared the mists of memory. 'Your father and I were old chums, of course, more years ago than a girl cares to remember. Why don't you bring him with you, if you could bear to? It won't be a big party. I've done my duty by the British colony for this year. Probably just us and Tosti Castelnuovo. You know the Prince, don't you?'

'No,' Molly admitted on the telephone. 'I'm afraid we've never met.'

'Then it'll be fun for you' – Nancy reverted to her old disconnected ways – 'to get together again.'

So they sat in the dining-room at the villa where the high chimney-piece, carved in stone with the Baderini escutcheon and a Cardinal's hat, stretched up to the ceiling, and the fireplace seemed to Molly to be about the size of Hugh's old bed-sit. Part of Arnold's collection of modern art hung in little pools of light on the walls and, in the shadows at the distant end of the room, a huge Calder mobile creaked and clanked in the draught when a high door was opened. Prince Castelnuovo turned out to be over eighty; he had a cautious expression and a small, tortoise-like head jutting almost straight out from his collar-bone. He wore a dark blue cashmere scarf over his shoulders and spoke English almost without an accent.

'There are no spiders in this house, are there?' the Prince had asked Molly when they sat together for a drink before dinner. 'Have you stayed here? Tell me quite honestly if you have ever seen spiders.'

'I see you two are getting along,' Nancy had said, 'remembering old times.'

'No. We're the ones who're remembering old times,' Haverford had called from the sofa where he had been sitting with Nancy. The sight of a man so clearly much older than himself had cheered him up considerably, as had the fact that his hostess now seemed to remember him without difficulty. 'Who *is* that old boy exactly?' he whispered to her on their way into the dining-room and, 'Do you expect him to live through dinner?'

'Don't be naughty,' Nancy smiled at him. 'Tosti was always a great help to Arnold.'

It was when they were arranged round the dinner table, a little raft of people in the ocean of a room, and the sallow manservant in white gloves was handing round dishes of iced soup, that Nancy turned to Hugh on her left and offered to satisfy his curiosity on the subject of Buck.

'Buck?' Hugh looked, for a moment, blank.

'Well, of course,' – Molly, on the other side of the table, had pricked up her ears – 'You can't help wondering about someone whose house you are in.' Hugh drank his soup, conscious of the fact that, from the moment his father-in-law had mentioned a kiss in Chancery Lane, it was impossible for him to say the right thing.

'You have a house here?' the Prince said very slowly.

'No. We've leased the Ketterings'.' Molly wished to deal with him quickly so that she could listen to Nancy.

'I sincerely hope your house' – Prince Tosti's voice was tremulous and had a note of fear in it – 'is spider-*free*.'

'Buck Kettering,' Nancy told them, 'came to work for my husband when he was about eighteen. I don't know what he was: tea-boy, runner, general dogsbody. But very willing. There wasn't anything you couldn't ask him to do. Arnold took a liking to the boy, promoted him. He had an area of the property business to look after. Arnold gave all the young boys an area, a "Fiefdom" he used to call it. Well, Kettering's area was around Buckland Terrace in the East End of London. Whitechapel, I think. He collected the rents. Managed the properties. My husband always said he managed them beautifully.'

'Tremendously good fellow, your husband.' Haverford had become bored with the turn the conversation was taking and wanted to guide it to some more interesting subject, such as himself. 'I always thought, Nancy, that Arnold had a great deal in common with the late Lord Nelson. He knew when to turn a blind eye.'

'So that's how young Kettering got the name Buckland. After his area, you see. When he came to us we all knew him as Terence. I think of him as Terry still.'

Molly was listening, astonished. It was as though all her ideas had been turned upside down once more. She had thought a lot about the name Buckland but never dreamt that Kettering might have been called after a street in London where he collected the rents. She looked at Nancy who sat huge and motionless in her high-backed, carved chair at the head of the table and seemed pleased by the effect that her story was having on at least one of her listeners. In her shapeless, filmy red dress and with her dyed, copper-coloured hair their hostess looked like an old fortune-teller on the end of Brighton Pier.

'Well, he got promoted in the business and Terry became absolutely fascinated with Arnold's collection. He went to night school and actually took some sort of a degree, I think, in the history of art. He must have worked hard at it because I imagine he left school when he was about fifteen. But he had a real feeling and better taste than I had, quite frankly. He got so good, Arnold used to send him abroad to buy stuff for him. He came back with some marvellous bargains.'

'Clever old him.' Haverford was still hoping for a change of subject. 'The world is divided between those who can create art and those who can make money out of it. In my own small way, of course, I've always been one of the creators.'

'But how' – Molly felt that if only she could keep the old woman going she would hear the sentence which would allow her to understand everything about Buckland Kettering – 'how did he come to get the house here and . . .'

'Marry Sandra? Is that what you want to know?' Nancy seemed only too ready to gratify her curiosity, but before she went on she leant forward and tinkled a silver bell, which summoned the man in white gloves to remove the soup plates and bring on the bollito misto. 'Well, I'll tell you. When Arnold bought this place we used to have Terry out to stay, part holiday and part to report on the business. And it was then he began to look at the *old* pictures. He'd spend days, weeks sometimes, in Florence and Siena. He was bowled over by them. He wouldn't speak about it. I remember he used to say, it's secret. They have to be enjoyed in secret. He never took anyone with him: always went to the churches and the galleries alone. Well, he had a bit of money by then, thanks to Arnold, and so he bought "La Felicità" when it was pretty well a ruin with cows and horses living on the ground floor and chickens upstairs. And he did it up. So then he looked round for a wife.

'And found Sandra,' Molly asked, 'in a sweet shop in Siena?' Hugh looked at his wife and wondered why she had bothered to find out all these things.

'You've got it. Have you met Sandra?'

'Not yet. We've spoken on the phone, of course. She sounded –'

'Common?'

'I wasn't going to say that.'

'That's what she is, though, dead common. Nothing particularly wrong with that. I'm common.'

'Most uncommon, I'd've said, Nancy.' Haverford rose gallantly to the occasion.

'Nonsense. I'm common as dirt, always have been. It's a funny thing, Arnold's father was a little tailor in Whitechapel but he was never in the least bit common and Terry was the lad from Buckland Terrace and he wasn't common either. You know, the way he's done up "La Felicità". Nothing common about that, is there? I mean, no cocktail cabinets or tanks of tropical fish like a successful East Ender would flaunt at you.'

And so many art books on the shelves, Molly thought, and all the paperbacks stuck up in the loft. And yet T. Buckland Kettering felt deeply about the pictures in them, something she had always known.

'I was staying with Andrew Spratling at Porto Ercole,' the

Prince piped up in a small, precise voice as though he were adding some useful information to what Nancy had told them, 'and I awoke at about two in the morning. I couldn't get back to sleep so I turned on the light to read and what should I see but a large spider hanging from the ceiling by means of a string produced from its own body! I did not hesitate. I got out of bed stealthily and dressed as quietly as possible so as not to disturb the insect. I packed all my clothes and shut my case; the spider was still hanging there as I tiptoed out of the room. It seemed to me that its awful little eyes were upon me. I went down the stairs and let myself out of the front door. Then I walked to the hotel where luckily there was a porter on duty and a vacant room. Early the next morning I returned to my own home in Milano. I shall not stay there again. I become nervous of spiders and of *omosessuali*, and at Andrew Spratling's house one finds both.'

If that old fool were to pass away in the night, Haverford thought, it'd be a merciful release. He's had his four score years. How much more can he expect?

'Well,' Nancy Leadbetter turned to Molly and asked, in the silence that followed, 'have I satisfied your curiosity about the Ketterings?'

'Except for one thing.'

'Oh, and what's that?'

'What sort of connection Sandra Kettering has with the Water Board.'

Nancy said nothing but looked at her guests' empty plates, stretched out a plump arm and rang her silver bell. Then she looked at the old Prince and said, 'We mustn't bore you with local gossip, Tosti. Tell us all you know about Jack Gerontius and the Arnaldo woman. Is she liable to get *all* his money?'

'Who'd've thought it?'

'Who'd have thought what?'

'All those years ago. When Arnold was buying this place and he sent you out to look at it. I'd taken off for Siena, do you remember, allegedly to do my book *Oscar Wilde and the Soul of Socialism*, but really so we could meet.'

'And did we?'

'What?'

'Meet.'

'You don't remember that room I had behind the hospital, and the wine that tasted of sulphur and ox blood?'

'I remember coming here,' Nancy said, 'when there was no furniture and the mess old Baderini had left it in. I remember the cold and the stone floors . . .'

Sitting beside her on a sofa after dinner, Haverford was enormously encouraged. He remembered the bright chilly day in December when they had bought a picnic, lit pine branches in the fireplace and made a bed of their overcoats on the floor of the room they were now in, and Nancy had been perfectly willing to oblige him. He remembered her long, white legs, her red hair and easily provoked laughter. On the sofa opposite them, Prince Tosti Castelnuovo was asking Hugh if he were, by any chance, related to some Pargeters who lived outside Tunbridge Wells and were obscurely connected with the Greek Royal Family and thus to Tosti's deceased wife. 'We must be sort of cousins,' he told Hugh sadly. 'Everyone I meet is related. My poor wife once spent a weekend with your Tunbridge Wells relations. She said it was an appalling experience. They took no precautions whatever against insects.'

Molly stirred her coffee and thought over all that Nancy Leadbetter had told her. She watched her father blow out the blue flame which was singeing the coffee beans floating on his large glass of Sambuca. She couldn't hear what he was saying to their hostess.

'You obliged me just over there, before you had a single carpet down.'

'This place is too big for me now,' Nancy told him. 'I rattle around in it like a pea in a drum,'

'Too big' – Haverford took a swig of his hot, sticky drink – 'for a person alone.'

'You could certainly say that.'

'But for two people . . .'

'It never seemed too big when Arnold was here.'

'I think Arnold would have liked it.'

'What would Arnold have liked?'

'Us being together. He always liked you being with artists. Artists need you, Nancy. Arnold knew that. You cheered us up considerably. I believe you even did something for my prose.'

'There's one thing I wish you'd make clear to your daughter . . .'

'I was born with a perfect ear, of course. But during my marriage to the mother of my child . . . Well, hardly a child any more. You see her sitting over there? Looks as though she's got all the cares of the world on her shoulders.'

'I told her about Buck Kettering. I really can't tell her any more.'

'During my marriage to her mother my prose style became somewhat doleful. Long sentences. Marriage to Molly's mother was a pretty long sentence in itself!' Haverford laughed. After drinking his way through dinner, his mind staggered from one subject to another.

'Arnold brought Buck up in the business. Then Buck carried some things on as Arnold would have liked. That was all it amounted to. I don't think women should take too much of an interest in a business. Arnold didn't think so either. He would have turned in his grave at some of the things Sandra's been doing. Arnold believed in the family, but he thought the man should run the business.'

'You wouldn't expect me to do that, I hope.' Haverford was tired of this incessant talk of the Ketterings. He wandered, a little unsteadily, to the drinks tray under a grey and yellow still life, lemons on a plate. He sloshed out more sticky Sambuca. 'You wouldn't expect me to run any business?'

'Hardly,' Nancy called out to him. 'From what I remember you could never add up a bill.'

'Order what you like, that's my motto, but never add up the bill!' Haverford tried to light his drink but the match went out between his shaking fingers. The hell with it; he drank and refilled his glass, conscious of his daughter watching him as her mother would have been watching him, with disapproval. He closed his eyes and remembered the young Nancy, her sweater pulled up under her armpits, her clothes scattered, her white body lined up on the overcoats with bigger breasts than he had actually bargained for, but a comfort, he had told himself, in the cold weather. It was a picture he would have to keep continually in his mind during his future encounters with the greatly increased Nancy Leadbetter. There were still years, perhaps many years, for them to enjoy. She had told him she was lonely, that she was tired of rattling about alone in this huge villa where the gardens had been planned by a Cardinal. No time like the present, he thought, for popping the fatal question. He refilled his glass and returned to sit by Nancy on the sofa.

'So there's no reason for any of you to concern yourself,' Nancy said, 'with Buck's business.'

'Of course not. I'll be happy to leave that entirely to him, when the time comes.'

'When the time comes?' She looked at him, he thought, nervously. Well, it was a bit late for Nancy Leadbetter to start acting like a virgin.

'Hasn't the time come for us to go on where we left off?'

'Where we did what?'

'"How sad and bad and mad it was"' – Haverford fell back on a quotation. '"But then, how it was sweet!"'

'I do seem to remember,' Nancy said carefully, 'coming here with you when the house was empty.'

'You said you were all alone now,' Haverford began in a heartfelt whisper, anxious that Molly shouldn't overhear him. 'Of course I'm lonely too, although I hardly "rattle round" my little flat at the World's End. What I so much want to do with my life is . . .' But what he wanted to do immediately was to answer a sudden, peremptory call of nature. His proposal speech was to be succinct but the answer might be long and hesitant. This was no moment to risk incontinence, an ever-present threat to Haverford. He thrust one hand deep into his trouser pocket, crossed the room with a curious half-running, half-limping gait and crashed out of the door.

Once in the marble-paved passage he was uncertain as to which way to bolt and dared not waste time by returning to the sitting-room to ask. He saw a pair of glass doors which opened on to the terraced garden, ran and wrenched them open. There was moonlight by now, with black shadows cast by clipped yew hedges with niches in them for sculptures. In front of him was a balustrade with an opening on to a broad, pebbled staircase which led to other terraces and the pool. Haverford ran across the grass, steadied himself by leaning with one hand against a statue, unzipped himself, stood looking up at the moon, and experienced an enormous relief. He remembered a story about Sibelius, whom some admirer had seen standing in a darkened garden and approached with reverence, thinking that the master was evolving another *Finlandia*, only to find him contentedly watering the lawn. Haverford felt he had at least this in common with the composer Sibelius, they both loved peeing in the open air. However he was probably more drunk than Sibelius and he leant heavily against his supporting statue. It was a Giacometti figure, a lanky and desiccated pin woman, a pride of Arnold's collection but not carrying the weight to support an intoxicated Haverford Downs. Furthermore its concrete base had become cracked and somewhat powdery over the years. The result was the collapse of Haverford in the anorexic arms of a spindly statue, a sensation as far removed from sinking into the welcoming vastness of Nancy Leadbetter as could well be imagined.

When he had picked himself up, Haverford also did his best to pick up the statue. This was not an easy task, although it was a great deal thinner than he was, it was also considerably taller. For some while in that moonlit garden Haverford Downs gave the appearance of a man dancing with a skeleton. At last he had it upright and although it tottered a little on its broken foot he was able to withdraw cautiously without it toppling to the ground.

He didn't immediately return to the house. The night air had made him dizzy and he wanted to recover. His trousers were a little splashed and he wanted to give them time to dry. He also reconsidered his approach to Nancy. Perhaps it was a mistake to pop the question so suddenly after dinner with his daughter sitting almost within earshot. He would do it on paper, where he was always at his best. He would write her a letter, funny, charming, self-deprecating, but offering Nancy a few more years of laughter such as they had known when the world was a better place and no one took life so ridiculously seriously. 'We are old enough now, surely,' he sketched out a few sentences, 'to be quite irresponsible. Shall we do our best to be problem grandparents, senile delinquents? Shall we concentrate on shocking our children; they are, after all, so delightfully shockable?' As he walked up and down the grass terrace, designed by that Baderini who was described as Cardinal for the Office of Corruption at the court of Pope Urban VIII, Haverford heard the wail of a police siren and thought that the place was really getting more like New York every day. So he decided merely to say to Nancy that he had something of the greatest importance to tell her and that she would hear from him soon. He lit one of the Italian cigars that Hugh had bought him, took another turn up and down the terrace, made sure the Giacometti was still precariously upright, and went back into the house.

As he did so, he heard a car arriving with a screech of tyres in the drive on the other side of the villa, a bell rang and, as he went through the tall, glass doors, he heard distant and excited Italian voices. He appeared in the drawing-room and all its occupants rose to their feet.

Molly saw her father come in with a cigar in his hand and his zip still half undone. 'I have something of the greatest importance to tell you . . .' he said, but was interrupted by four frowning *carabinieri* pushing through the door behind him, followed by the protesting manservant in white gloves. Molly looked at Nancy Leadbetter as the law arrived and saw, on her face, an expression of terror.

CHAPTER EIGHTEEN

There were so many parties in that week. Even the grey and usually dour town of Mondano-in-Chianti had a party. Jacqueline had a sleep in the afternoon so that they could all go to it.

'What's this party for?' Samantha asked as they struggled down a seemingly endless line of cars parked on both sides of the narrow road, among a moving stream of tourists and local inhabitants, lit by the headlights of cursing drivers trying to get in or the tail-lights of cursing drivers trying to get out, where a fragment of a twelfth-century wall, the crumbling remains of a fourteenth-century castle, were floodlit. From the square came the hugely amplified sound of a group from Florence pounding electric guitars and intoning 'Bimini, Rimini, Bim, Bim, Bim', a number which had won *nulles pointes* for Italy in the Eurovision Song Contest.

'For?' Haverford was panting as he struggled to keep up with them. 'I have no doubt it's some religious festival. Probably the feast of the blessed Santa Margherita of Mondano.'

'Who was she?'

'A person' – Haverford looked at his daughter who was walking beside him – 'who died of curiosity. Like the cat.'

Their group was separated for a moment, and lit by the red brake-lights of another backing car. Police whistles shrilled in the darkness. 'Bimini, Rimini, Bim, Bim, Bim,' they could hear the group baying. When they were walking together again, Molly warned the children, 'You shouldn't believe everything your grandfather says.'

'A married woman who lived in perfect obscurity in Roman times. She happened to be a Christian. No one would have worried unduly about that but she couldn't resist asking questions. At great personal inconvenience she sought out the governor of the province and asked him what he thought would happen to his immortal soul. She intruded on a minor sort of general in his tent to ask him if he had considered the text "Blessed are the peacemakers". Then she travelled to Rome; she threw a letter at the feet of the Emperor asking him if he had considered his position with regard to the doctrine of original sin. In the end they arranged for her to meet a lion and a wolf in the public arena. She might even have been let off that if she hadn't asked her judges whether they thought the conception of Jupiter was in any way immaculate. She was canonized by Pope John Paul I, so there's hope for you yet, Saint Molly Coddle . . .'

'I like wolves,' said Jacqueline from her father's shoulders. And then a firework zipped into the purple sky, exploded with a crack that silenced the guitar players and fell in a shower of silver balls and sharp detonations. In spite of all Haverford said the town festival appeared to have no religious significance. The Virgin remained imprisoned in the stuffy church and wasn't taken out for an airing. Don Marco was preceded by no procession of candle-carrying choir-boys, nor did he wear lace. He was in his usual soup-stained cassock, standing beside what seemed to be a Bring and Buy stall in aid of the Partito Comunista d'Italia. Strings of brightly coloured sweets hung like jewels beneath naked electric light bulbs. After the fireworks Samantha, Henrietta and Hugh tried their hands at shooting the pips out of alien playing-cards. Molly led Jacqueline to a long table under the walls where her father sat drinking Chianti Crocetto out of a paper cup and viewing the passing scene through watery blue eyes.

'What was the point of all those lies about Saint Margherita?' She accepted a cup of mineral water and gave Jacqueline a sip.

'Not lies. A myth of my own devising.'

'I've got a subject,' Molly told him, 'for one of your precious "Jottings". And there's nothing mythical about it.'

'Is it something unbelievably sexy about homemade cannelloni?'

'I can give you a scoop. Wouldn't you like to expose the water racket in the Tuscan hills, the unacceptable face of free enterprise among the well-heeled ex-pats? That sort of thing'd be meat and drink to the readers of the *Informer*.'

'Investigate the water? I wouldn't know where to begin.'

'Don't worry. I think I can tell you all you need to know.' A final firework, which had been hard to light, went off with a cannonade which echoed round the walls and died away along the road to Siena.

'Perhaps,' Haverford said, 'I don't need to know anything.'

'Oh, I'm sure you do. It's much better to know things, isn't it?'

'That's a proposition, Molly Coddle, on which you and I might agree to differ.' Jacqueline had slid off her mother's knees to embrace a swarthy Italian four-year-old in satin shorts and a bow-tie. This scene, which brought sighs of ecstasy and delighted laughter from the extended family seated around them, seemed to Haverford only fit for the most revolting type of postcard.

'Water's like gold in these here hills. Everyone tells you that.' Molly went on relentlessly, 'Don't you think Arnold Leadbetter tried to cash in on it?'

'Old Arnold, who was always careful to turn a blind eye?'

'Not when he saw a chance of making money. All he needed were friends in the Water Board who could turn off the supply on request. Then the desperate holidaymakers could be expected to pay through the nose to get their water back again. I'm not sure how far the business extended. I wouldn't be surprised if it went all through Tuscany.'

'Arnold may have cut a few corners in his life.' Haverford called for a refill of his paper cup. 'But you seem to forget; he's been called by the Great Property Developer in the Skies.'

'And Nancy's taken over the racket.'

'You heard her, didn't you? She doesn't think women should be concerned with business.'

'I'm sure she doesn't. So she left it all in the capable hands of Arnold's right-hand man, T. Buckland Kettering. But, I'm sure' – Molly seemed anxious to absolve Buck from as much guilt as possible – 'Sandra Kettering had a great deal to do with running the affair. She's got no old-fashioned ideas about a woman's place being in the bedroom. She's the operator who gets a letter from someone called Claudio, with a list of profits from the *Idraulica*.' She had once thought it was a love letter but nothing in Sandra Kettering's story as she now told it had much to do with love. 'Sandra and this Claudio seem to have planned to get Buck Kettering out of the business.'

'How on earth do you know all this?'

'I guessed some of it; most of it seems pretty obvious. You saw Nancy's face when the police arrived.'

'Anyone foolish enough to keep a spindly tin statue wired to the police station in just the place a chap has to lean when he wants to pump ship' – Haverford had taken to this nautical way of putting it in recent years, perhaps when he saw himself as a grizzled ship's Captain, weathered by the storms of life – 'Anyone foolish enough to do that is in for a very nasty surprise.'

'I don't think she was surprised by the police. I think she'd been expecting them for a long time.'

'It was all explained to them.'

'Nothing was explained, really.'

'And anyway, what was all that about a letter?'

'It came for Sandra Kettering.'

'Then how do you know what was in it?'

'I steamed it open.'

The music started on a child's roundabout in the square. Her two elder sisters took Jacqueline off to ride in a bright submarine. Haverford looked at his daughter. He was profoundly shocked.

'You open other people's letters?'

'It's necessary sometimes. To expose crime.'

'My God, what have I done?' Haverford was prepared to take at least part of the blame. 'Spawned a member of M.I.5?'

'I don't know exactly who else is in the racket but I suspect Ken Corduroy, expert in patios and pool equipment. The Baronessa Dulcibene fits into it all somehow but I'm not quite sure where. I shall find out, of course. And Signor Fixit, he must have known what was going on . . .'

'Just assuming for the sake of argument' – Haverford fumbled in his pocket and found money to buy another refill for his paper cup – 'that there is the slightest truth in all this. What, for heaven's sake' – and here Haverford saw his reblossoming friendship with Nancy Leadbetter withering on the bough – 'are you going to do about it?'

'It's you that's got the column in the paper.'

'Then what are you asking me to do to poor old Nancy?'

'Expose her.'

'I did that once on the floor of the very room we were sitting in, about thirty years ago.'

'I should have known it was hopeless trying to interest you in anything that wasn't to do with sex.'

'Yes, I suppose it is.' Haverford looked at his daughter for a long time, smiling, as though she had paid him a compliment. She looked back with blue eyes which were like his, but clearer and less merciful.

'You're a puritan, Molly Coddle,' he said, 'such a puritan.'

'Because I object to being cheated?'

'Everyone has to be cheated in this life, from time to time. Otherwise you'll never get any fun. Every time you take on a new girl you have to bargain for being conned in the end, lied to, robbed a little and finally dumped. On the whole the good times make it worth while. How will you ever enjoy a dinner if you spend the entire meal wondering if you're going to be charged twice for vegetables?'

She had heard this before and now lost patience with it. 'You make absolutely no distinction between good and evil!'

'The denial of pleasure is evil. Coming between an old man and his last chance of happiness is clearly evil.' The group were playing, 'Bimini, Rimini' again, inappropriate music when Haverford should have been accompanied by the sighing of violins. 'You don't think I've got any hope of ending my days in the Villa Baderini if either of us calls Nancy a criminal?'

'She's exploiting all of us. I thought you called yourself a Socialist.'

'But you don't! You believe in entrepreneurial initiative and the free market economy. Even if, and it's a simply enormous "if" because most of what you say seems to be pure guesswork, but suppose there's a grain of truth in it, what have Arnold and Nancy done but take advantage of the laws of supply and demand?'

'You mean they can cut off the supply and then make their demands.' He smiled at that: his daughter, he thought, sometimes showed a glimmer of his talent for constructing a sentence.

'Of course I'm a Socialist,' he told her, 'but until we've got the red flag flying, Molly Coddle, we have to live with the rat race.'

'You're obviously quite used to living with the rats.' She got up then, and looking at him it seemed to her that he had suddenly shrunk, so that his shirt and suit were several sizes too big for him.

'Molly Coddle! Remember my age won't you? Don't you want to see me settled?' He called after her, but she went on walking away from him in the direction of the children's roundabout, where Henrietta and Samantha were in conversation with two Italian boys, and as she approached she saw the Baronessa with Jacqueline reaching up trustingly to hold her wrinkled, beringed hand.

'Time for bed.' 'Oh, can't we stay a little longer, honestly?' 'Come on, we're never allowed to do anything.' 'I will drive them home to you safely: you can rely on me.' The Baronessa was looking grey-haired and dependable. 'I am, after all, four times a grandmother.' In the end Molly took Jacqueline and left the other children to be brought home by Vittoria Dulcibene. After she had finished with her father she didn't want to spoil anyone else's pleasure in that evening.

Dear old Nancy, old thing,

[Haverford sat up in his bedroom writing after the Baronessa had brought Henrietta and Samantha home and the house was deeply silent.]

No one's perfect and perhaps you and I are less perfect than most people. I have to confess that I haven't been much of a success, either as a husband or as a father. My daughter, who I hoped would grow up like you, understanding the weaknesses of mankind, has turned out to be a puritan. Of my first marriage, little need be said except that I seem to have spent the long years it lasted apologizing for everything from my jokes, my political and artistic beliefs, to some occasional forgetfulness about the condition of my flies. It is strange how often I left them half open when I consider how infrequently my late wife called upon my undoubted talents in that direction. I have, I'm ashamed to say, written stuff that was unworthy of my talents (I cannot think of some unsigned articles on 'Great Men of Letters' I wrote for Kiddie's Encyclopaedia *without blushing. My piece on the divine Oscar, for instance, mostly hinted that he fell foul of the law in some obscure way at the end of his life, perhaps for non-payment of rates). How impossibly boring we should all be if we had nothing to look back on but a life of unbroken honesty. Many of my best 'Jottings' have been con tricks, worthy, perhaps, of your beloved Arnold at his most inspired.*

Speaking of Arnold, I would like you to know that I entirely understand and indeed respect the position in which he left you. Property may be theft, perhaps old Proudhon was right, but there is so much else that makes the world go round. Every time we make love we may be stealing

someone's affections and one can't keep alive without
purloining the hen's eggs or slices of the cow's rump. Even
Will Shakespeare pinched his plots from Plutarch and
Holinshed, and who can say how many of my 'Jottings',
praised for their originality, may not have been acquired by
stealth from Oscar, or G. K. Chesterton, or even, and I
confess this to my shame, from the other chap, name now
forgotten, who writes in the Sunday paper. All this is to
assure you, Nancy, that there is no risk of me being a
puritan on the subject of property, or, come to that, on
the subject of theft.

Now I know, perhaps the world knows, that dear old
Arnold had to cut a few corners when building up his
property empire. How else can a fellow start off with
nothing but a demob suit and end up with some of the
best Braques and Picassos in private hands?

I am quite prepared to turn a blind eye on Arnold's
activities in view of his magnificent contribution to the Arts.
After all, Michelangelo was wise enough not to ask the Pope
exactly how he came by every penny needed for the ceiling
of the Sistine Chapel. And as it was with property, so it may
well have been with water. Who am I to complain?
Particularly as I'm sure dear old Arnold would have liked
some of the profits of that enterprise too to be spent on the
Arts, for instance, in allowing an old master of English
prose the time to polish off the few remaining 'Jottings' he
may have tucked away inside of him.

I hope by now, my dear old thing, you will have got the
drift of this letter. My daughter Molly has suggested I
devote one of my 'Jottings' to the mysterious arrival and
disappearance of water in Tuscan holiday homes. I shall
not do so. I am quite sure that she wouldn't indulge in
any such exposure herself if she knew that it would hurt
one of the family. Of course I have looked on you as a
dear member of my family for years but why don't we, as

*they say, make it legal? Some, as William Butler Yeats
wrote, 'loved the pilgrim soul in you'. Others may love the
beauty of your house and the rich hospitality of your
surroundings. Speaking for myself, I love it all, so what
do you say, old thing? Shall we give it a whirl? I await
your reply in breathless anticipation.*

    Yours till the Chianti runs out,

                           Haverford

He was pleased with this communication, which seemed to him
to convey its message clearly without being painfully explicit. He
put it in an envelope and decided to ask Don Marco to take him
round to deliver it in the morning. Then he climbed into bed and
thought of waking up in one of the huge four-posters in the Villa
Baderini as the Tuscan sunrise slowly lit up a long, almond-eyed
Modigliani nude on the wall. Later, he fell into a deep, innocent
and dreamless sleep.

Molly woke at four. Half a moon shed a white light on the
world outside the bedroom window and a mosquito, whining,
failed to wake up Hugh. It's time, she told herself to get your
thoughts in order.

She was convinced that she had been right about the water
shortage; but, even as she explained it to her father, it seemed
trivial and only a small part of the mystery which, she liked to
think, surrounded the Ketterings and 'La Felicità'. Her meth-
odical mind began to list things still unexplained: who had left
suddenly on their arrival; what did the list in the Piero della
Francesca book mean, and who had taken it; why and in what
circumstances did Signor Fixit die: and was Buck Kettering in
fact *lost and gone forever?* He had been in Siena on the day the
water ran out and nobody, not even his child, seemed to have seen
him since. She thought of all she now knew about Buck. He was
tough, a hard man who collected rents and probably evicted
tenants for Arnold Leadbetter, with enough charm to get on in the

Leadbetter empire and enough of a soul to become obsessed with the paintings she loved the most. In Italy he must have deliberately changed and taken on a new personality. The old Buck, who took his name from a terrace of houses, whom she could imagine out with the boys boasting of his business and sexual triumphs over a round of whiskies in some Mayfair bar near to the Leadbetter office, had vanished and given way to the more aloof, cultured and knowledgeable *padrone* of 'La Felicità'. All the old Kettering had been hidden away like the love stories and thrillers in the attic. What remained was the man whose books and furniture were in such impeccable taste, who wished to organize the lives of his tenants so they should fit in exactly with what he felt to be the pure spirit of his place. None of the young rent collectors he had laughed with, she thought, would be invited to candlelit dinners on the terrace as the sad strains of *Turandot* cried out into the Tuscan night. The voice of the new Buck, she was convinced, was to be heard in the letters, firmly, aloofly, but with an occasional half smile and a flicker of irony, setting out the rules of the house. They were Buck's letters, although Sandra might have put her initial on them. But she no sooner admitted that to herself than she thought why? Why had he withdrawn and let Sandra send the letters; why had he let her run the business and conduct the dubious relations with the Water Board when he, as Arnold's right-hand man, must have known every detail of such dealings. How on earth was it, she thought, that Sandra Kettering had succeeded in obliterating all traces of her husband?

Half an hour before Molly had been in a deep sleep. Now, she was lying wide-eyed and alert. She heard, as she had once before, the sound of someone moving quietly and continuously in the house. The door that opened slowly, the footstep which lingered on one stair before daring another move were unmistakable. Her awareness communicated itself to her husband and he woke up. 'What's the matter. Can't you sleep?'

'I can hear something,' Molly whispered.

'What sort of a something?' Hugh whispered back.

'Somebody downstairs.' There was a small but audible scraping sound, furniture being moved, perhaps, across a stone floor.

'I can't hear anything,' Hugh whispered hopefully.

'There *is* somebody.'

'Do you want me to go and look?'

'No.'

'Well, that's all right, then.' He turned his back, pulling the bedclothes round his shoulders.

'You don't want to go, do you?'

'Considering there's nobody, it seems unnecessary.'

She heard another sound, a drawer shutting perhaps, or a cupboard. 'I'm going.'

'Do you really want me to come?' But as she had gone he settled back to sleep and left her to it.

The sounds came from below them, so she went down the stone staircase as quietly as she could manage and stood facing the door of the big drawing-room. She looked at it a long time because there was a strip of light at the foot of the grey double doors; whoever their visitor might be, he was making himself thoroughly at home. Then she stepped forward and turned the handle as quietly as any intruder might have done.

There was only one light in the room, and that was on a writing-table at the end nearest the door. A slim figure in jeans, with blonde hair, was standing with its back to Molly, going through an odd collection of bits of paper from the drawer which had been pulled out and set on the table. Before she discovered who it was Molly became aware of other shapes, inert figures in sleeping-bags or covered in blankets, in pairs or alone. They lay along the floor or on the raised platform with the piano at the other end. There may have been seven or eight shapes in all, dossed down like casualties in a hastily converted hospital behind the lines. In the quietness of the night the army of young people had billeted themselves on Molly.

Then the girl at the writing-table turned and she saw that it was Chrissie Kettering. Molly stepped forward to greet her as warmly as though she had been one of her own children.

Third Week

CHAPTER NINETEEN

'We knew that if we asked you wouldn't let them come' was how Henrietta explained it.

She and Samantha had come on as the advance party, driven home by the Baronessa. Before they went to bed they had unlocked the front door, leaving the citadel of 'La Felicità' defenceless. The invaders had stayed dancing in the square and come later on bulging out of a Fiat. They had let themselves in and spread out on the floor for the night because they had gone off Nancy Leadbetter's where the servants were 'really unfriendly'. Samantha and Henrietta had been proud to offer them hospitality. 'You're not going to turn them away, are you?'

No, it seemed that Molly wasn't going to turn them away. She remembered, with some pleasure, the exchange between herself and Hugh when she had come back to bed. 'No one there?' he'd asked. 'Only about eight people in sleeping-bags, all over the floor of the big drawing-room.' 'Well, that's all right then.' He was relieved that things between them had so far lightened that she could make a joke and went back to sleep.

Now some of the liveliest of the young people were at breakfast on the terrace, spooning up melon, tearing off chunks of hard bread to smother with Oxford marmalade. Two of them were closeted, it seemed for eternity, in the bathroom; others were still asleep on the floor downstairs. Giovanna went around the house with her broom, clucking and hissing with disapproval as though she wanted nothing so much as to be able to sweep all the new arrivals into the black plastic bags which she drove in, after her work each day, to be tipped on to the communal rubbish dump in Mondano. Haverford kept out of their way, knowing that, as an old man, he was likely to be ignored and Hugh, whose muttered protests at the turn of events had been ignored by his wife, went out to the pool with Jacqueline. There he was disturbed to find a sixteen-year-old Italian girl lying on her back, her hairy armpits exposed, and her bare nipples pointing at the cloudless sky. He gave her a tentative and ignored '*buon giorno*', then concentrated on teaching Jacqueline to swim. Only Molly fussed around the visitors, pouring out coffee and offering them peaches.

'It must be very hard to keep away from your house,' she said understandingly to Chrissie Kettering.

'It's kind of you to have us. Henrietta said you wouldn't mind at all. Oh, and by the way, I brought you some nougat.'

'That's very kind of you. How long did you plan to stay?' Molly was determined to sound friendly but she did wonder.

'Not long, I think. Some people are going to take off for Dubrovnik tomorrow, by train.'

Molly wondered at this child's capacity for adventure. At the age of forty, renting a villa in Chiantishire seemed a sufficient challenge.

'Which of you exactly?'

'All of us meant to but some of us have lost our passports.'

'So they won't go?'

'Oh yes' – Chrissie spoke with the confidence of youth – 'we'll all get there.'

'What were you looking for last night?' Molly had decided it was time to ask the question.

'Looking for?' Chrissie's large brown eyes seemed entirely innocent.

'Yes. In the table drawer. I thought you were looking for something.'

'Oh, in *there*,' the girl suddenly remembered. 'My reading-list for the holidays. Miles and miles of Jane Austen and D. H.

Lawrence. And the dates for next term. I think they must have got sent here. Mama's forgetful about things sometimes.' I'm sure your Mama, Molly thought to herself, never forgets anything. She asked, 'Did you find what you were looking for?'

'No luck. It's very annoying.' It must be, Molly thought, particularly if what you were sent to find was a letter signed 'Claudio'.

'Well, if they turn up, we'll let you know. Not, I suppose, that you're going to read much Jane Austen on the train ride to Dubrovnik.'

'That's very kind of you, Mrs Pargeter.' She had excellent manners, covering a toughness of character and the aloof, faintly superior smile which might have been taught her by her father. Chrissie might also grow into someone who could combine rent-collecting in the East End of London with knowing all about Piero della Francesca.

'No trouble at all. I know it must be hard not to be here for your holidays. What did you do in the evenings?' Molly remembered something Signor Fixit had told her. 'Musical comedies in the big drawing-room? It sounds enormous fun.'

'Not musical comedies, Mrs Pargeter,' Chrissie corrected her. 'Charades.'

Stifling in his bedroom where he had been taking refuge from the young people, Haverford ventured out at last to the table by the pool. There he was reminded that he had never liked page-boys with hairy armpits and he was relieved from the painful task of staring at a blank page by meeting Hugh who was watching Jacqueline jump repeatedly off the diving-board in her rubber ring. His son-in-law had the air of a man who was looking forward keenly to the end of the holiday. His gloom only deepened when Haverford pulled up a chair beside him.

'Alien corn this is for you, isn't it, old chap?' Haverford was at his most dangerous when he showed sympathy.

'I have really no idea what you're talking about.'

'Alien corn and you're standing in it in tears. Sick for home.'

'Not a bit of it. I'm thoroughly enjoying the break and I hope you are too.'

'You have all the reckless gaiety of an old lag enjoying a stretch in Wormwood Scrubs.'

'Why did you do it?' Hugh turned a stricken face on his father-in-law.

'Why did I do what?'

'You know perfectly well.'

'You sound exactly like your late, unlamented mother-in-law. Accusing.'

'You've just pretty well broken up our marriage. That's all.'

'How on earth have I done that?'

'Telling Molly you saw me' – Hugh had difficulty finishing the sentence, but in the end he brought out – 'kissing Mrs Tobias in Chancery Lane.'

Haverford turned his head up to the sun and laughed for so long he had to mop his eyes with a red and white spotted handkerchief. By this time the laughter was not entirely convincing. 'And is that,' he asked when he recovered himself, 'what's going to break up your marriage?'

'You may find it very funny. No doubt everyone laughed at marriages breaking up in the "swinging sixties". I happen to take mine a little more seriously.'

'Do you really?'

'I suppose I've got a sense of responsibility.'

'Poor old you. I hope you get better soon.'

'That is the sort of remark,' Hugh said with dignity, 'that may seem frightfully amusing to the pinko anarchists who read the *Informer*. It seems absolutely pointless to a person trying to bring up a family.'

'Nonsense. You're not trying to bring them up. Henry and Sam are bringing themselves up with the aid of their gallant band of over-privileged hobos scattered around the terrace and snogging in the bathroom. Even Jack the Lad doesn't find your gloomy poolside presence particularly instructive.'

'And I suppose you were such a rip-roaring success as a father?'

'Not at all,' Haverford said truthfully. 'As a father I've been a dismal failure.'

'So you admit it.'

'Oh yes. I have lost my daughter's love. I have no reason to expect that I shall ever regain it.'

Hugh said nothing, his victory being more complete than he could ever have expected.

'All the same', the old man grinned, 'Molly and I have things in common.'

'I can't think of any.'

'Oh yes. You'd be surprised.'

'What sort of things?'

'We both have, somewhere deep down in us, a sneaking respect for excess.'

'You're talking about Molly?' Hugh was astonished.

'Remember her love for great works of art. Remember, too, that she had a mother who deliberately crashed cars. And her father never exactly did things by halves. That's why she finds it so intolerable that your activities with the fair Tobias should be confined to a chaste kiss in Chancery Lane.'

'Which you told her about,' Hugh gloomily repeated the charge.

'I also told her it probably meant absolutely nothing. Of course that only added fuel to the flames. Listen, shall I tell you a song that might find a path to the sad heart of Hughie when sick for home?'

'I wish to God you'd stop quoting things.'

'Forgive me. We literary hacks are always capering on in borrowed clothing.'

'And I'm in no mood,' Hugh told him firmly, 'for a "Jotting".'

'Then let me tell you loud and clear how to win back my daughter's love and respect and get the whole Pargeter family grinning from ear to ear.'

'I wish I knew.'

'Tell Molly that you've been having a rip-roaring affair all the year, not only with the fair divorceé but with the girl on the switchboard and, oh, I don't know, a lady estate agent from Fulham. Then, take my daughter to bed and tell her you'd rather roger her than the whole lot put together. Will you tell her that?'

'Do you think I'm mad?'

'No. I'm afraid not,' Haverford affected extreme disappointment. 'Incurably sane. If you like . . .'

'What?'

'I'll tell her for you. I'll say you just made me a full confession. Would that be a help?'

'Please.' Hugh looked desperately at his father-in-law, and gave a cry from the heart. 'Please don't try to help me any more.'

That night they played charades. In fact it seemed like one charade to Molly, for the importance of the evening lay when she guessed far more than the word involved.

They sat in the long downstairs drawing-room, which they never used, with table-lamps on the floor flooding the platform with the piano on it. The first team of visitors had done a word, easy to guess and not particularly entertaining to watch, so that even Jacqueline had got bored, slid off her mother's lap and mingled with the actors. Only Haverford, in an excellent mood and easily pleased, had clapped loudly and shouted 'bravo' and '*bis*'. And then it was the turn of the second team led by Chrissie Kettering. There was a considerable delay before their charade began, for the make-up and costumes were elaborate. The audience waited for a long time in the darkness, hearing the sounds of consultations and giggling outside the door, the clatter of props being assembled and the banging of cupboard doors throughout the house as clothes were pulled out, tried on, rejected or finally put on for the show. Then they heard the deafening tones of a ghetto-blaster and Chrissie Kettering appeared wearing a tight-fitting black dress from Hyper Hyper, Doc Marten's shoes by Ken. Market, shiny red lipstick and black liquid eye-liner. Her blonde hair was woven into a palm tree, and tied at the top with a red ribbon. (The sources of this get-up were revealed to Molly next morning by Henrietta in tones of awe and wonder.) 'Welcome,' Chrissie shouted at the audience, 'to the Muckrakers Club!'

Then the stage seemed to be full of visitors wearing jeans or cut-off shorts, topped with leather jackets, T-shirts from Boy and basketball caps. They were smoking Gitanes, calling for Budweisers and asking for more 'hip hop' and 'trouble funk' music. Neither Samantha nor Henrietta, although part of Chrissie Kettering's team, had appeared as yet. As the dancing grew wilder and the ghetto-blaster mounted in a crescendo, Jacqueline returned to her mother's knee and watched entranced.

Over the yelping of the music certain dialogue was audible. The group seemed to be discussing someone who was due to arrive, known to them as 'Far-out Fay, the Queen of the Squeakies', a girl who was said to be 'hard-core trendy', and whose 'street cred., you know what I mean?' was of the best. Before the arrival of this paragon, however, Molly was surprised to see herself come nervously but determinedly into the Muckrakers Club inquiring for her daughter. She was played by Henrietta, who had borrowed one of Molly's Laura Ashley dresses and a pair of her sensible moccasins from Harvey Nichols. She had stuffed a cushion into the top of the dress to simulate her mother's ample bosom and wore one of the house's straw hats, together with Molly's worried expression.

'I have come here' – 'Henrietta!' Molly blurted out – 'to look for my daughter. Goodness only knows what she may be up to. Something quite unsuitable, I'm sure. Drinking Budweiser beer! Scoring weed and bonking in the toilets, I shouldn't be at all surprised.' Each of these suggestions was greeted with hilarious and mocking laughter from the Muckrakers.

'It's you, Molly Coddle,' Haverford crowed with delight. 'She's got you to a T.'

'Steady on.' Hugh was doing his best to be loyal. 'Is that meant to be Mum?'

'Bonking in the toilets.' Haverford was still laughing. 'It's a good line that!'

'Hang about,' the Muckrakers warned the stage Molly. 'Who do you think you're insulting?' 'Nothing dodgy going on here' and 'You're well out of line.' 'She must be drunk,' one of them thought. 'That's right,' another agreed. 'She's blowing chunks all over us.'

'I really do take exception . . .' Hugh started, but Molly was watching Chrissie Kettering who had moved to the centre of the stage. 'Be quiet,' she told her husband. 'They're doing it very well.'

'Here comes the Queen of the Squeakies herself!' Chrissie announced like a ringmaster. 'The one and only Far-out Fay!'

At which Samantha appeared, her small, heart-shaped face smeared with eye-liner and fuchsia pink lipstick. She was wearing tight black bicycling shorts and a gingham top which exposed her shoulders and stopped short of her slender midriff. She began to dance in a parody of the erotic movements that would suit her in five or six years time and to draw luxuriously on an unlit cigarette.

'Good heavens,' shrieked Henrietta, the stage Molly, 'whoever's that?'

'That, madam,' Chrissie said coldly, 'is your daughter.'

At which the distracted mother appeared to faint dead away.

'That's the first syllable,' Henrietta said, as she rose to her feet and joined the general rush off the stage.

Her father said, 'I do hope it's not all going to be like this.'

'"Have you heard the argument?"' – Haverford couldn't resist quoting – '"Is there no offence in't?"'

'The first syllable,' Molly said. 'Has anyone got any ideas?' She had an idea herself but only about the charade.

'No, no. "They do but jest"' – Haverford went on with his quotation – '"poison in jest; no offence i' the world."'

*

The next scene concerned shopping. All sorts of tins, packets of cereals, pots of jam, marmalade and bags of pasta were stacked on the piano. One of the Italian boys acted the part of lame Lucca, skipping round his shelves and saying *poi* whilst other visitors became the shop's regular habitués, sitting on chairs and being greatly entertained, as Molly – once more played by Henrietta, with the Laura Ashley dress flapping like a tent on her slim body – tried to buy unheard-of English luxuries such as Ribena and Bovril.

Then Chrissie appeared wearing white trousers and the jacket and tie Hugh brought out and, crowned with a panama hat and smoking one of Haverford's thin cigars, she walked with the jaunty strut affected by the late Fosdyke. 'My dear lady,' she said, 'are you in any sort of trouble? If you are, all I can advise you to do is to forget your worries and rely on old Signor Fixit to fix it.'

'Really?' Henrietta-Molly gushed. 'I say, what an enormous relief!'

'I thought it might be.'

'You seem to be the answer to a housewife's prayer.'

'That is exactly what I am! I'm old Bill Fosdyke. The Santa Claus of Chiantishire. Just give me your shopping-list.' He took it from her. 'Now, what's your most urgent need?'

'Two groovy Italian boys to stop my daughters getting bored on holiday.'

'I think I know just where to put my hands on them.' Signor Fixit went behind the piano and brought out two English boys who, doing their best to look Italian, danced seductively in front of Molly and gave her a chorus of 'Bimini, Rimini, Bim, Bim, Bim.'

'I can be absolutely relied on to get you anything at a price,' Chrissie-Fixit said. 'You want the Mona Lisa. I can get you the Mona Lisa. You want acid, speed, coke, horseradish sauce, 501 black or white Levis, anything under the sun, licit or illicit, Bill Fosdyke's the name and Fixing is the game. Lucca! A packet of

your very best fish-fingers for the Signora!' The end of the scene
had been somewhat under-rehearsed and slid into the confused
discovery of various articles from about the house, plates, books,
pictures and, finally, a paper crown from the attic as Henrietta-
Molly was chosen Shopping Queen of Mondano to general ac-
claim.

'I'm not sure it's in the best of taste,' Hugh worried. 'Making
fun of somebody who's dead.'

'Fosdyke wouldn't have minded,' Haverford told him. 'The
old boy had a sense of humour; greatly admired my "Jottings".
Well done!' He was clapping Chrissie Kettering. 'Pity you
couldn't manage the squint. And they got your carefully controlled panic around the shops to a T, Molly Coddle.'

Molly was silent, thinking about the scene that had just been
played. Her thoughts were interrupted at last by Chrissie Kettering announcing, 'Third syllable!'

The third scene was more like a French farce. Neither of the
Pargeter daughters took part in it. A wooden-legged couch was
wheeled on to the stage, to represent a bed in which Chrissie lay
with an English boy, apparently her husband. Under the bed her
Italian lover lay concealed. The wife told the husband that she
could hear burglars downstairs and when he went off to investigate the lover climbed in with her and their kisses were
interrupted with repeated 'oohs' and 'ahs'. When the husband
returned, the wife, covering her lover with a sheet, told him to
look under the bed from which she was sure she could hear
noises. As he searched fruitlessly the roles were reversed. Now
the wife and the lover were in bed with the husband on the floor
under it. At the end of this simple and perfunctorily acted event
Chrissie jumped out of bed and said, 'And now we're doing the
whole word.'

It was at that moment that the lights went out.

'What have you done now?' Hugh shouted, unnerved. Molly
tried to remember the various electrical combinations which, her
letters of instruction had told her, would end in black-out. 'You

must have been using the hair-drier without disconnecting the refrigerator!' she called into the darkness. But Henrietta, somewhere quite close, answered, 'Do be quiet! It's a stage effect.' Then they heard *Turandot* playing and one candle was lit on a table on the stage, then two and then three candles, and the scene was of the Pargeters having dinner on the terrace. They were all acted. An English boy played Haverford as though he were at least a hundred years old, reminiscing about a girlfriend he had known in Chelsea and singing Beatle's songs like old music hall ditties. The Italian girl who had been sunning her armpits at the pool had on a bib and beat a spoon on a plate, as though she were Jacqueline. The family talked in a somewhat banal way about the splendours and miseries of a holiday at 'La Felicità' and then began to suspect that they were not alone on the terrace. They picked up the candles and discovered, one by one, the rest of the cast in blankets and sleeping-bags dozing at their feet. When the lights came up the performers sprang to life, dancing and singing and playing the ghetto-blasters. The boy playing Haverford and the girl who had portrayed Jacqueline pouted in a particularly smouldering way as they gyrated round each other.

'Bonk!' Haverford speculated. 'What sort of a word has its first syllable, "bonk"?'

'The second scene was two syllables.' Hugh was puzzled. 'Shopping was it?'

'And what about the whole thing?'

'Dinner-time? Hitchhikers . . .?'

'*Turandot?*'

'You're all cold,' Henrietta said. 'You're absolutely icy.'

'What was the last syllable? Bed?'

'Husband?'

'Lover?'

'Do you give up?'

'Give us a clue.'

'Well, what did they say in the last syllable?'

'"Ooh." Chrissie kept saying "Ooh"!'

'"Ooh" and "ah".'

'Felicità,' Molly said as though she had never been in the slightest doubt about it.

'However do you work that out?'

'Far-out Fay. The first syllable was Fay.'

'That was me,' Samantha said proudly, her face still ghostly with skull-like shadow for eyes and pale, painted lips. 'The Queen of the Squeakies.'

'All right' Chrissie agreed. 'What was next?'

'Licit. Didn't he say, "I can get you anything licit or illicit"?'

'That's not fair.'

'Oh yes, it is. You only have to mention the word once.'

'Mum, you are absolutely *brilliant*!'

'Pure mathematics.' Haverford was put out by his daughter guessing the word while he had been mystified. 'She's always had a calculator for a head.'

'Fay-licit-ah,' Molly told them. 'Now do you think you could all start tidying up. The whole house is an absolute shambles. Really, Chrissie, I don't know what your mother would say if she saw it.'

'Mother?' said Chrissie. 'She'd probably just laugh. Although she might have thought we went a bit far tonight. They're quite easily shocked, you know. The Italians.'

'Anyway, go and tidy up. Then we'll have a drink in the kitchen.'

'A bottle of Chianti Crocetto' – Haverford was quite cheered up – 'to calm us all down after the entertainment!' They all started to carry bottles, plates, tables and costumes upstairs and to tidy the big drawing-room. Molly walked outside into the moonlight, past the well head and the courtyard and on to the grass beside the track. She walked some way, smelling the wild mint and fennel, and then looked up at the stars and thought about another possible answer she had found in the knowing, cruel charade the children had acted.

It was Chrissie Kettering's line as she walked into the shop as Signor Fixit that Molly remembered. 'I'm old Bill Fosdyke,' she had said. 'The Santa Claus of Chiantishire.'

Long ago, it now seemed almost a life-time ago, she had stood in one of the children's bedrooms and the dead man, she must get used to thinking of him as dead, had said, 'I'm not Kettering, or anywhere near it. The name's Fosdyke. William Fosdyke.' So he was known to the family at 'La Felicità' as Bill – another 'B.' perhaps, even the 'B.' referred to in the cryptic note which had disappeared from Kenneth Clark's book on Piero, the 'B.' who needed to be *lost and gone forever*. And Bill was certainly gone, more definitely, more irretrievably than Buck, who might be only awaiting his moment to return from any part of the world in which he might have been hiding himself.

The list hadn't been signed. It had been typed on the Ketterings' machine but might have been composed by either Buck or Sandra. And would the woman who had started life in a chocolate shop in Siena write notes to herself in English? Molly, perhaps in her eagerness to convict Sandra, had avoided that consideration. And then she thought of her family's arrival at 'La Felicità'. Who had they disturbed and had someone, perhaps two people, been staying in the house, keeping it supplied and leaving quietly by the back road when the Pargeters arrived much earlier than expected? She remembered the feeling of someone watching her from the shadows of the terrace and the key forgotten in the lock.

She walked back into the house and climbed past the tidiers and furniture removers to the first floor. In the kitchen Haverford was acting the host, pouring out glasses of wine and Diet Coke. Hugh was feeding Jacqueline a biscuit. Molly went past them and into the big bedroom she shared with her husband.

She locked the door and pulled the suitcase down from the top of the wardrobe. The zip was undone, which didn't surprise her as all the young people had been in there looking for dressing-up clothes, and the letter to Sandra from Claudio gone. The mystery of the vanishing water was no longer what concerned her.

She stood looking at her clothes and Hugh's and then she remembered something else. The first sight she had had of the wardrobe with two white garments, a man's shirt and a woman's skirt dangling from coat-hangers. And even when they all arrived at the house, she was sure the wardrobe hadn't been entirely empty. She pushed her clothes along the rail and found what she had been looking for, squashed against the wood.

The shirt was plain white, but had initials embroidered in blue on the breast-pocket. The letters were B.A.F. She couldn't tell if the A. was the first letter of a name, or if it had merely been inserted to separate two letters which might otherwise have looked ridiculous.

CHAPTER TWENTY

The next morning the visitors packed up as efficiently as an army on the move and left. Chrissie said goodbye and thanked her hostess as politely as she might have been taught to do when she was a little girl leaving a party. 'Thank you for having us, Mrs Pargeter. We had a *smashing* time.'

'Goodbye, Chrissie. Oh, and please come and see us in London. I know the girls would love to see you.' Molly looked at the brown-armed, self-confident girl who had unwittingly told her so much in the charades. What had happened, what might be about to happen, would be hard for Chrissie Kettering. She felt a curious longing to keep her with her and to look after her. 'Do stay with us a little longer, if you'd like to.'

'No, really. I must go with my friends. But it's very kind of you.' At which Molly put her hands on the girl's shoulders and kissed her cheek, as though asking forgiveness for whatever she intended to do. Then Chrissie broke away and ran out to the old, overloaded car in which the front seat was being kept for her as the undoubted leader. 'Thanks again,' she shouted. 'Send you a postcard,' and slammed the car door shut.

'They're marching away, Molly Coddle. Off to lie by someone else's pool and take the mickey out of someone else's parents. They're leaving us behind. Unless Henry and Sam have gone off as camp-followers. Did you search their baggage?'

Haverford was sitting on the terrace finishing his breakfast. Molly sat opposite him and poured herself a cup of cool coffee.

The house, in which her own children were still asleep, was empty and silent.

'That girl Chrissie,' Haverford said, 'looks remarkably like her mother.'

'Really?' Molly tried not to sound over-interested. 'Have you ever met her mother?'

'Not been formally introduced but I have an idea she was the woman I saw with the Baronessa at old Fosdyke's funeral. I mean she looked like the daughter, only spread out a bit, of course. I suppose it would be natural for her to go to the funeral.'

'I suppose it would. Who else was there?'

'Only me and the priest. A few undertaker's men, of course.'

'Poor old Bill Fosdyke . . .' Molly used the name she had only just learned.

'Oh, yes. I heard that. They called him "Bill".'

'Didn't you?'

'Oh, no. I called him Fosdyke. But then I came from a vanished age.'

'You had dinner with him?'

'Steak and kidney pie and apple crumble. It was an extraordinary occasion.'

'Why extraordinary?'

'Can't do it, Molly.' Haverford shook his head.

'What do you mean?'

'A chap has got to respect the secrets of the confessional. Especially when I must have been one of the last people Fosdyke ever spoke to.'

'What on earth are you talking about? The confessional?'

'Fosdyke, in a manner of speaking, unburdened his soul to me.'

'But you're hardly a priest, are you?'

'I have not,' Haverford admitted, 'taken Holy Orders, although I think I might well have enjoyed the Papacy had it come to me some time in the fifteenth century. I think I could have managed the public appearances with dignity and the private parties would have been a joy. I can't pretend that my dinner with Fosdyke had any great religious significance. But he told me something in the strictest confidence.'

'Oh, well then, that's that, isn't it?' Molly, who knew her father better than anyone, got up to go.

'Hang on a minute. Why do you ask?'

Molly sat down again. She knew that he couldn't resist sharing a secret.

'I was just thinking. No one's really *explained* his death, have they?'

'And of course you want to explain it. You want to explain everything.'

'Don't worry. I'm not asking you to put it in one of your articles.'

'I suppose he might not have minded you knowing, as one of my immediate family.' Haverford took a swig of coffee and lit the last of the cigars Hugh had given him. He lay back in his chair, blowing smoke and twiddling the white book of matches in his fingers. He was enjoying the moment. 'It was the usual sort of problem. Fosdyke told me he'd fallen for some woman. He came to me, I suppose, as an expert on the subject.'

'A woman. Who was she?'

'Don't ask me, Molly Coddle. Fosdyke didn't seem to think her name should be mentioned in the Mess. I got the feeling, though, that the involvement was pretty serious. He asked me if he should take on some immense new responsibility.'

'I can guess what you told him.'

'Well, you know me, Molly. Always ready to take on anything except responsibility. Responsibility is a passion-killer like tights and dirty bra straps and . . .'

'Where did you get those matches?' Molly interrupted him. She had heard that particular speech many times before.

'These?' Haverford looked at the small white book between his fingers.

'Urbino.' Molly took them from him. She had recognized the

picture of the Ducal Palace on the flap from one of the many guide-books in the house. It was the end and aim of the Piero della Francesca trail.

'Oh, yes, of course. Didn't tell you. I slipped away for a dirty weekend with Miss Hairy Armpits from the side of the pool.'

'I just wondered . . .' Molly lifted the flap and saw the name of the concern it had been printed for: MOTEL VALLOMBROSA, URBINO and a telephone number.

'What a super 'tec you are. Shall I get you a magnifying glass and a little deerstalker hat for Christmas?'

'I was only curious.'

'And you get curiouser and curiouser.'

'When you picked them up. I mean none of us had been there and . . .'

'Lay off, Guvnor,' Haverford lifted his hands in surrender. 'You got me bang to rights. I half-inched them.'

'You what?'

'Pinched them. And I can even remember when.'

'Really?' Now Molly also remembered.

'That party in the smart flat, where we saw the Palio. I got a light from that distinctly fanciable old school chum of yours, Rosie Fortinbras. I remember getting home and finding I'd slipped them into my pocket. Perhaps she'd been to Urbino.'

'Oh yes' – Molly remembered that also – 'she'd been on the trail.'

'Well, then, any more little mysteries you want solved, my dear Watson?'

Molly said she'd better go and see if the children were showing any sign of life and she forgot to give her father back his matches.

Haverford sat on alone until the sallow manservant from the Villa Baderini arrived on a motor bike to deliver a letter to the Signor Downs of 'La Felicità'.

My dear old friend, [it started].
Memory plays odd tricks on us. I suppose we blot out things we

*may have enjoyed a darn sight too much as well as those too
horrible to remember. Since I got yours and read it carefully (well,
old dear, your handwriting does look like a spider who's been on a
binge for about forty years. I held it up to a mirror, tried it upside
down, but at last I made sense of most of it) . . . Reading your
three-volume scribble made it all come back to me. We had our
moments undoubtedly, and someone ought to put one of those
tablets on the floor in front of the fireplace:* NANCY
LEADBETTER FELL HERE, AND DIDN'T GET UP FOR SOME
TIME!

*Now I know writing comes as naturally to you as p****g up
a lamp-post does to a blind mongrel, but I do most heartily
welcome your decision not to write about our local water
problems in your paper. As a woman, and out of respect for
my late husband's wishes, I know very little about business
matters, and I'd like to know less, but us ex-pats have to work
our a****s off to keep the Italian bureaucracy sweet, and I
know full well that you wouldn't want to make life difficult
for us, would you, old dear? Arnold was always very careful to
keep any mention of his business dealings out of the papers.
'Once you let them know how you make your money,' he
always said, 'they'll start taking it off you.' Little as I know,
or indeed, care to know about business, that has always been
my motto too. So far as your daughter is concerned, she
seemed a sweet girl although I suppose she could do with losing
a little weight. Well who's talking? I can hear you say, you old
devil. You know, I look on you and her as family. She wouldn't
want to hurt her family's feelings, would she now?*

*Well, that's enough about business, which to be quite frank with
you, I don't understand anyway. It seems we've got a lot more
than business to talk about. So why don't you come over at your
soonest, and then we can chat? I'll keep something cool for you
(and perhaps something warm too, for the sake of old times).*

Best as ever,

Nancy L.

Haverford read this letter twice over with great satisfaction. Give him a pen and a sheet of notepaper, he thought, and he could always work the oracle. Dear old Nancy, of course she remembered! What a sweet old thing she was, with her innocent habit of writing rude words with asterisks. He folded the letter carefully and put it into the breast-pocket of his shirt. When he went down to the table by the pool he was whistling a little tune. After all, it wasn't too bad to have seen seventy-eight summers and still be absolutely irresistible to women.

On her way back from shopping Molly stopped by the square tower of the thirteenth-century church near Mondano's walls and parked the car. She walked across the road and into the gates of the cemetery. Although she had not been at the funeral she found the newest dug grave easily. She stood looking down on it and on the fresh roses which filled the gleaming brass vase, and heard an Italian voice calling her, 'Signora Pargeter.' It was the priest, his cassock flapping on a bright, windy morning, threading his way through the grass towards her far more nippily than Haverford would have managed it, although they must, she thought, have been of an age. 'Signora Pargeter. It is I. Don Marco.'

'*Lei conosco bene. Lei in casa mia, "La Felicità."*'

'Please, Signora. Your father likes to try to speak Italian to me. I try to speak English to him. Now shall we use that language together?'

'That'll be very nice.' Molly felt suddenly foolish standing by Signor Fixit's grave, as though she'd been caught out spying on someone. 'Do you want to talk to me here?'

'In my house perhaps. We can speak in *privato*.'

So they left the remains of Fosdyke and walked across the road and through the old church, restored in the eighteenth century, which had barley-sugar pillars and theatrical red curtains backlit by the sun. God the Father was painted on the ceiling as a cross old man with a walking-stick. Don Marco led her past the altar and out across the smallest of courtyards to his house and into a dark, airless living-room that smelled of furniture polish and onions. She allowed the priest to pour her a minute glass of grappa and they sat together at a table with a green baize cloth like a couple about to enjoy a hand of whist.

'Signora Pargeter. I am anxious about your father.'

'I gave up being anxious about him years ago.'

'He is known in your country, is he not, as a great writer?'

'Well, hardly.'

'*Non ho capito.*'

'He is known as a writer. In a newspaper.'

'Karl Marx has said that poets are different from the rest of us. There must be other rules for them.'

'I'm sure my father would agree with that.'

'I am anxious, you see, if Signor Downs is able to understand the sanctity of marriage.'

'I very much doubt it.'

'He speaks of his life with your mother now dead and he speaks of it lightly. An unhappy marriage is a cross to bear. Did your father bear it patiently?'

'Not in the least.'

'That is my opinion. He has now asked me to celebrate his marriage to the Signora Leadbetter.'

So now Molly understood why there would be no mention of the water scandal in the 'Jottings'.

'They are both old people. They must set an example of growing old with grace and resignation.'

'I don't think' – Molly was doing her best to answer truthfully –'either of them will be much of an example of that.'

'Surely they do not marry for' – Don Marco drained his grappa as though to give himself strength and whispered in a low voice which Molly found unexpectedly thrilling – '*sessualità?*'

'You mean sex?' What she felt like saying was 'You want to bet?' She contented herself with 'I don't think you should exclude the possibility.'

'On the other hand' – the priest refilled their glasses with further minute quantities – 'Signora Leadbetter is good to Mondano-in-Chianti. She finances our fiesta and provides the fireworks. She contributes generously to the Partito Comunista. I would not like to offend Signora Leadbetter.'

'I understand.'

'On the other hand, I am afraid Signor Downs doesn't understand us completely.'

'He doesn't completely understand a lot of things.'

'The people are Communists here you see. This means they are very old fashioned in their opinions. We are conservatives. We are not like Signor Downs, who is always talking of free love and other new ideas. We believe in family life and the sacrament of *matrimonio*. In your opinion, Signora Pargeter, is your father a fit person to take part in this ceremony? I speak as a priest, you understand.'

'And I' – Molly finished her grappa and looked at him equally earnestly – 'speak as his daughter.'

'That is why I ask.'

'Don Marco, you have said marriage is a cross we have to bear.'

'Sometimes' – he nodded his grey and celibate old head – 'a heavy, heavy cross. *Pieno di sofferenza.*'

'My father,' Molly said with feeling, 'is my cross.'

'*Davvero?*' Don Marco raised his shaggy eyebrows.

'Sometimes the weight of it is almost unbearable.'

'Signora?'

'If we were to return to England and leave him here, safely married to a lady who can afford to give the village fireworks, I must tell you, in all honesty, that it would be a great weight off my mind. I think we should encourage it.'

There was a long silence between them and the slow dawn of a mutual understanding.

'Signor Downs is a member of my church, he tells me, although he has lapsed a little. I think that he may understand the sacrament of marriage very well, after a short period of instruction.'

'We're only here for another week,' Molly told him, 'so perhaps it should be as short as possible.'

The priest appeared friendly, so she decided to ask him another favour, a scrap of information. 'I saw that there were fresh flowers on Bill Fosdyke's grave. I wonder if you know who put them there.'

Don Marco shook his head then and said, '*Non capisco,*' although the sentence seemed no more difficult than others he had understood with ease.

As she drove away from the church, Molly was smiling. She had, she thought, solved the mystery of the district water supply and she had no further plans for using her knowledge. The solution was, for her, an end in itself.

Her inquiries, at any rate, seemed to have led to one desirable but quite unexpected result: her father kept in comfort in his last years far away from her and her family. Whatever else happened, that was, as Haverford wouldn't have been able to resist saying, a consummation devoutly to be wished. Perhaps, now that he knew that she knew, the water would no longer be stolen and people like the Pargeters and the Greensleeves no longer robbed. She could only hope so. But she had other matters to attend to and another quest to go on. She was determined that the holiday shouldn't end before all her questions had been answered. It had been cloudy that morning and there had been a pattering of rain on the windscreen of the car. It was hotter again now and the sun was shining, but autumn was near. Before it came she was determined that someone else should know all that she had found out.

Molly's last call was for wine. She drove into the courtyard of the Castello Crocetto, got out of the car and pulled the bell rope which usually summoned the old man in pyjamas. Nothing happened and she stood for a while looking out between the cypress trees over the hills and the track that led to 'La Felicità'. Then a shutter high up in the wall was pushed open and the Baronessa looked out. 'Come up, why don't you?' she called. 'I seem to have been left alone in the world.' A heavy key, which might, if misdirected, have stunned her, fell at her feet. 'That is for the *porta principale*.'

'I'm sorry it's such a slog!' The hall of the Castle was dusty and there were lighter squares on the plaster of the walls from which pictures had been removed. As Molly climbed what seemed an endless stone staircase, going up to and above a spreading chandelier that looked well past its days of being lit, she thought that whatever part the Dulcibenes might have had in Sandra's business – and she had remembered that half her rent had to be paid into the Barone's account – it could not have been large or enormously profitable. And then she heard the call from above her and looked up to see the grey-haired Baronessa leaning over the balustrade with sunlight streaming through an open door behind her. 'See! We have retreated back to the nursery. We have become children again.'

'I didn't mean to disturb you. I only called in for wine.'

'For wine? I thought you had come to ask more questions.' The Baronessa led her into a small, bright sitting-room in which every available space was crowded with silver-framed photographs of the extended Dulcibene and Baderini families. Behind her were tall windows, balconies loaded with pots of geraniums and an aerial view of olive groves, woods and white ploughed fields which seemed to stretch as far as Siena.

'I think,' Molly said, 'that most of my questions have been answered. One way or another.'

'How delightful! Then it has been a successful holiday?'

'Let's say, it's been interesting.'

'Well, that's the best we can hope for, isn't it? Holidays can be terribly dull occasions. That is my husband.' Molly was looking at a painting, hung over the fireplace, of a bald-headed man in a yellow sweater patting the head of a labrador retriever. She had last seen him, she remembered, dancing with Rosie Fortinbras at Nancy's barbecue. 'he is travelling now. He doesn't like to come here, now we have had to sell so much of the land and the castle is not as he remembers it. So he is away trying to sell our wine abroad. It's such good wine, so pure. But the French will mix it up with something not so good of their own, and a lot of Algerian rubbish, and call it Beaujolais. What can one do?'

What you can do, Molly thought, is to retreat to the nursery and make the best of things with your good friend, Sandra Kettering. 'I hear,' she said, 'you went to Bill Fosdyke's funeral?'

'Oh yes,' the Baronessa had a cigarette in her mouth and was grinding the little wheel of her gold lighter which, as usual, produced no answering flame. 'Signor Fixit. He was quite a character.'

'Nancy Leadbetter didn't like him much.'

'Nancy has some strange ideas. She doesn't like everyone.'

'But she likes Buck. Buck was her husband's discovery.'

'Oh, yes. She liked Buck. As I think I told you, you would find him very charming.'

'No doubt I'll find that out. When I meet him.'

The Baronessa abandoned her lighter and found a box of kitchen matches under a pile of books. When she had the pleasure of blowing smoke out of her nostrils she said, 'You expect to meet him, then?'

'Well, yes. Shouldn't I meet my landlord?'

'I think you may find some difficulty. Even his wife and his daughter can't find him.'

'I know. I'm sorry about that,' Molly said. 'But I may have more luck.'

The Baronessa, who had greeted her smiling, looked hostile and yet anxious, as though she had said far more than she intended. She found an alabaster ashtray on the mantelpiece and ground out the cigarette she had lit with so much trouble. 'Married life is not particularly easy for any of us. I'm sure you understand that, Mrs Pargeter.'

'My father, in an article he wrote, suggested that it might be easier in Italy.'

'Oh, really. And why is that?'

'Italian women, he thinks, like husbands who can be violently jealous. Wasn't it your husband's ancestor who locked his wife up in this castle because she'd danced twice with another man?'

'That's an old story. And it may not even be true. Didn't you come here to buy our wine? If you will come with me, I will find the keys.'

So they went down to the clean white-washed cellars and Molly bought six bottles of the unchemicated, unpolluted Chianti that had not yet been adulterated by the French, and the Baronessa, smiling again now, took her money and saw her out to her car.

'If you find Buck,' she said, 'you will send him my love, I'm sure.'

'I will remember to do that,' Molly told her, 'when I meet him.'

'Oh, and tell him to come and collect his terrible dog.'

After Molly had gone, Vittoria Dulcibene climbed back into her eyrie under the castle roof. She stood on the high, geranium-filled balcony and watched as Molly's car crawled across the hillside and down the dusty trail and then she turned back into the old nursery and made a telephone call to Rome.

The telephone rang again in the *piano nobile* and Sandra Kettering's high heels clicked across the marble-paved hallway. She greeted her friend Vittoria Dulcibene and then fell quiet, receiving information. Someone, it was now clear, knew where Buck Kettering was to be found and was on her way to visit him. Well, did Sandra want to know where her husband had hidden himself away, or did she not? Sandra undoubtedly did, and who was going to find him? An Englishwoman, it seemed, and like all the English she delighted in secrets. And then the Baronessa began to suggest how Buck might be found – by means of a small military operation like those she had planned when she was a schoolgirl, bicycling off to meet her friends in the hills behind San Pietro when the Germans were there to be fought. It would be best if some friends could go with Mrs Pargeter and watch carefully where she went to meet him. But when she knew where Buck had taken refuge, what did Sandra intend to do about him?

'*Sono affari miei*,' Sandra said. 'That's my business.'

CHAPTER
TWENTY-ONE

Hugh felt that he was behaving rather well. He had been greatly misunderstood in the matter of a postcard but he hadn't complained unduly. Much had happened during the holiday in which he had taken no part, and some of it he hadn't fully understood. He had been content to watch his youngest daughter swim under the water like a fish, to drive to the shops when he was asked to, even to remain calm when the house was invaded by an army of young people who emptied his refrigerator and managed to dispose of a dozen bottles of his Chianti. A man he had scarcely known had died. They had made some friends, it seemed, and been invited to the Villa Baderini. There had been trouble with the water, now happily over. In all of these events he had played his part patiently and well. Why was it then that he felt that his wife was involved in a secret life which excluded him? He watched her and wondered if the children's wild suppositions could possibly be true. Could Molly be planning to leave him? He rejected the idea as he couldn't conceive of anyone loving his wife more than he loved her himself, which was certainly, at that time, not enough to spur him into any sort of violent action.

'I want to go off alone,' Molly said. She was unpacking her shopping on the kitchen table and, in a desultory manner, Hugh was helping her put things away. He stood clasping a tin of peeled tomatoes and said, 'With anyone?'

'Don't be ridiculous. I'm not like you. I don't write postcards.'

'Am I ever going to hear the last of that?'

'Probably not.'

'Then what do you mean?'

'I'll only be away for a night. Something like that. I'd be back the day after.'

Hugh put the tomatoes in the cupboard. He felt a pang of disappointment, as though a door to a new life had been closed. He said, 'Where do you want to go?'

'On the trip I've always planned to take. The Piero trail. Across the Mountains of the Moon to Urbino.'

'Is it all that far?'

'Too far to go there and back in a day.' She knew all about it. 'And it will take time to see the pictures. The children would only feel carsick and Jacky would hate it.'

'All right. We'll stay here then.'

'Yes,' was all she said.

'I wish you'd tell me exactly what's going on.'

'I just want to see some pictures, that's all. Is there anything very mysterious about that?'

'Your father,' he told her, and she gave a small sigh as at an unwelcome subject, 'thinks I ought to tell you that I've had passionate affairs with all sorts of people, including Mrs Tobias. He thinks that'd interest you enormously. Would it?'

'Not at all!'

'Why not?'

'I shouldn't believe it. Anyway, who's Mrs Tobias?'

'Oh, for heaven's sake!'

'Oh, yes. I remember. The one you can't wait to get back to.'

'Look' – he had behaved well, he told himself again, and he felt himself put upon, deprived in some way of his rights – 'don't you want me to come and see these pictures with you?'

'No.'

'Why not?'

'Because you don't really want to.'

It was true but he deserved a cause for complaint and thought of one. 'We'll be stuck here, without a car.'

'Only for a night.' The shopping was all unpacked. 'You're not going to starve.'

'And when you get back, what's going to happen?'

'I suppose we'll go home. Anyway, I'll have seen the pictures.'

'Well, go then. If you're going. As soon as possible.' He went to the door, glad to have something to feel resentful about, a pretext to match her anger about the postcard.

'Yes,' she said. 'That's what I mean to do.'

Henrietta was in her room, trying on the gingham top one of the girls had left behind. Her mother came into the room and sat on her bed. 'I want to go off,' she said, 'on a trip.'

Henrietta, excited, stopped pouting in front of the mirror. 'Who is it? You can tell *me*.'

'It's no one. I want to see some pictures.'

'Honestly?' Her daughter didn't seem to believe her. 'Does Dad know?'

'Yes.'

'Is he terribly upset?'

'I don't think so.'

'Mum.' Her daughter came and sat beside her on on the bed. 'I mean, I can understand, you know. Sometimes, well, most of the time I suppose, Dad's not that exciting.'

'Don't be silly, darling. I'm coming back.'

'Oh. Well, that's all right then.' Did she detect a note of disappointment in her daughter's voice? Molly hoped not and, putting her arms round her, hugged her unexpectedly. 'Chrissie Kettering' – Henrietta released herself tactfully after a decent interval – 'liked you very much. She's clever, isn't she?'

'Very clever.'

'She wants to come and see us in London.'

'I hope she will. Things can't be too easy for her. And I hope that I don't make them any more difficult.' Molly got up, walked to the window and pushed it open. There was a deafening sound of insects and the faraway barking of Manrico.

'Difficult for Chrissie?' Henrietta didn't understand. 'Mum, why ever should you?'

Molly didn't explain. The telephone in the hall was ringing and she went down to answer it.

'Mrs Pargeter? This is Nicholas Tapscott here. Enjoying yourself, are you? Been seeing some marvellous pictures?' The voice on the telephone was particularly friendly.

'No. Absolutely nothing. But I was planning to go to Urbino tomorrow. The Piero della Francesca trail.'

'The pregnant Madonna at Monterchi. "The Resurrection" at Sansepolcro. And then over the hills for the great "Flagellation". What a coincidence!'

'What is?'

'Connie and I are going on exactly the same trip. So long since we did the Ducal Palace. At least we can remind ourselves of how the big boys did it. He knew a thing or two, did old Raphael. We thought of going tomorrow, back the next day, and then perhaps you and your old man would come to dinner . . .'

'Well, that's very kind, but . . .'

'Taking the family are you? To Urbino.'

'No. No, I was going by myself.'

'Then why don't you snitch a lift with Connie and me. No point in trailing over there in two cars is there? I mean we won't force ourselves on you. Toddle off on your own, by all means, to absorb the works of Art.'

In the end Molly agreed. She could leave the family the car and so be free of some of the guilt she felt in leaving them. No doubt the Tapscotts would leave her alone for what she had to do, which included looking at the pictures.

'Be round at "La Felicità" at eight o'clock,' Nicholas Tapscott promised. 'Then we can do "The Resurrection" before lunch.'

That night Molly packed a small bag to be ready for the morning. She put in the book of matches from the Motel

Vallombrosa and thought of its source, her old friend Rosie Fortinbras. Rosie had done the trail too, but she must have done it in the other direction from Urbino back to Arezzo, before they met in the apartment on the Piazza del Campo. Rosie had, perhaps, no more than hinted that she had seen Buck but Molly knew her well enough to be sure that visiting motels was not her style, unless she had been to such an unlikely refuge for a very special reason. And was not Rosie, on her own evidence, the only Brit that Buck could trust?

And if Buck had been there, her faith in her journey was so far beyond reason, why should he not be there still waiting for her to expound, as all the detectives in all the stories she had read did in the last chapter, the brilliance of her deductions. Before she zipped up her bag she put in it, beside the book of matches, the photograph of Buck taken by the waiter by chance when the Pargeter family were having a drink in Siena during the first week of their holiday.

CHAPTER
TWENTY-TWO

'The frescos in Arezzo are the centre of Piero's career and have been considered his chief claim to immortality,' her father had said when she told him where she was going.

'You've been reading Kenneth Clark.' She remembered the essay.

'It's one of the best books here.'

'You didn't find anything in it?' she asked him.

'Of course. It's packed with good things. His discussion of the enigma of "The Flagellation" . . .'

'No. I mean, did you find a sheet of paper in it, a sort of shopping-list?' Was that, perhaps, the explanation for its disappearance. Had Haverford merely removed the clue from the book and lost it?

'A shopping-list?'

'Yes, in a way.'

'And it's gone.'

'Yes.'

'Is that inconvenient for you?'

'Not really. I can remember it very well. And I don't think I'll need it any more.'

'Well, that's all right then, isn't it?'

Nicholas Tapscott had telephoned to suggest they start at 7.45. 'We might just knock off the frescos before breakfast.' He and his wife collected Molly in a car which was as white, elderly and dusty as the Tapscotts themselves. They arrived in

Arezzo, as Nicholas said, 'dead on schedule', well before nine o'clock.

Although she had done her best to prepare herself for Arezzo, Molly still had difficulty in making out the story. Things were not made easier by the fact that the frescos were only illuminated when someone put money into a machine, and so were often plunged into sudden darkness, like Hugh's old bedsitter when the meter ran out. In many places the paint had faded, leaving naked stretches of wall, blotting out half a battle, the legs of a torturer or a woman's face. Then, as the lights came on and the walls were lit up with sky blue and stone grey, the green of grapes and olives, the pale red of wine held up to the light, she saw the round, invariably handsome, always unsmiling faces, with eyelids that seemed heavy as stone, looking down with perpetual detachment and even, in the case of the women, a kind of contempt.

It was only after a while that it became clear that these aloof people were engaged in some long and obscure drama, a plot that covered centuries and continents and included virgins and emperors, dying warriors and men in tall hats with the faces of remorseless judges.

There had been a Mass in progress when they came into the church, and she and the Tapscotts had sat obediently and respectfully at the back, although Italian families and German visitors strolled and chatted in the aisles, children ran across the empty stretches of stone floor and braver tourists approached as near as they dared to the priest and the altar to peer up at the frescos, then lost in the shadows. Now the service was over and they walked freely into the choir. Nicholas and Connie Tapscott lifted the telephones that described the paintings in a variety of languages and then lounged by them as though they were chatting to old friends from England.

Standing looking upwards, her guide-book open in her hand, Molly did her best to follow 'The Story of the True Cross', born of a branch of the tree from which Eve took the apple, planted in

dead Adam's mouth and cut down to decorate the palace in which
Solomon received the Queen of Sheba. The lights went out and
when they came on again the Emperor Constantine was sleeping
in his tent before battle, seeing the vision which would turn the
Roman Empire to the True Faith. Then she saw the Cross lost
and a latter-day Judas was shut up in a dry well until he told
where it lay buried. A waterless well, she thought, a place of
terror even in the days when Piero painted.

Then she moved towards the battle in which the Emperor of
the East savagely punished the King of Persia for setting a cock
at his left hand and calling it the Holy Ghost, a painting which
Vasari had described as an 'almost incredible scene of wounded
and fallen dead'. Molly was staring at a man on his knees. Over
him stood an assailant with a white helmet the shape of a coolie's
hat and of a peculiarly Mongolian cast of countenance. The
kneeling man, sturdy with hooded eyes, resigned but holding his
defenceless hand out against the sword, made her think, as she
did always now, of Buck Kettering. It was a face she was to find
often in the pictures she saw that day.

'Things they are always on the look-out for in the Consular
Service are chaps who go "bush". Got to like the country where
they're posted better than their own. Can be a ghastly embarrassment in spots like Tahiti or Fiji. Get a whole intake of perfectly straightforward chaps from the U.K. and they start going
round wearing long cotton skirts or sticking hibiscus flowers
behind their ears. Fellow I know went bush in Riyadh and
beheaded his wife. It's so darn easy to do. I have to admit I went
bush in Florence.'

'Not ten o'clock yet, and we've done Arezzo.' They were
drinking cappuccinos under an umbrella outside the San Francesca church and Connie Tapscott looked at her watch with deep
satisfaction. 'It won't take us long to knock off the pregnant
Madonna.'

'It all got to me. Pictures. Churches. Driving down the Arno in the early morning. Well, they called me back to the U.K. and they said, "Look here, Tapscott. We hear you're going bush in Florence. Only one thing for it. We're going to transfer you to Toronto." "Bugger that for a lark!" I said. So I took early retirement.'

'We both decided,' Connie Tapscott told Molly, 'to devote our lives to Art.'

'I've got to respect old Piero,' Nicholas said, 'because he could do it, and I can't. Although I very much doubt if he could hold down a job in the Consular Service.'

'He went blind,' Molly said.

'Well, there you are then. Whoever heard of a blind Consul? Come on, girls, Let's get our skates on.'

In the minute chapel at Monterchi, in a field off the main road, there is only one painting on the wall behind the altar. Two angels hold back curtains to reveal a young woman with heavy eyelids, unsmiling, solid and beautiful. She is so far gone in pregnancy that her dress, of the same blue as the sky, will not fasten. One hand is on her hip and with the other she touches her swollen stomach with delicate fingers. The picture is brown, pale pink, blue and green – the colours of the earth, the sky and the olive trees. Molly stood in front of it, elated by the excitement of her mission. The memory of her last pregnancy, when she was carrying Jacqueline, flooded back to her; the feeling of strength and purpose which she hadn't known again until she set out on the trail to find Buck Kettering.

'I think Nicholas is keen to hit the road,' Connie Tapscott sidled up to her and whispered. 'I know he wants to get to Sansepolcro before there's any risk of them closing "The Resurrection".'

'All right, girls. Had enough of the preggy lady? And shall we be pushing on?'

They pushed on at a great rate, past tobacco fields, through an industrial zone, and roared through narrow streets to come to a halt with a screaming of brakes in front of the Palazzo Comunale in Sansepolcro. Nicholas Tapscott bought the entrance tickets and took them at a brisk walk that seemed about to break into a loping trot, past lesser paintings and straight to 'The Resurrection'. There, he said with the complacency of a conjuror producing the flags of all the nations from a wine glass: 'Now you can see what all the fuss was about.'

'What fuss, Nicholas?' Connie gave him the feedline.

'All the trouble that girl had, back in the chapel at Monterchi.'

It was the trouble, which Molly had never had, of producing a man. And the man in question, with eyes that could never be forgotten, had one heavy, naked foot planted firmly on the edge of the grave from which he emerged strongly, solemnly, holding a banner. And behind him, of course, were the hills of Tuscany, pale and waterless with white trees, a castle and few clouds, pink with the dawn in the sky.

'That geezer,' Nicholas Tapscott said, pointing to one of the sleeping soldiers in front of the tomb, 'has got no blooming legs! I mean, look at him. He's anatomically impossible. Piero got away with it. But if I'd made a similar sort of nonsense in my job, I'd've been drummed out of the Consular Service. Rum do, isn't it, Art?'

'That's what Nicholas and I feel about Art,' his wife said. 'We never seem to quite get the hang of the rules.'

'Do pay your whack, Mrs Pargeter. If that would make you feel better?'

'Nicholas and I discussed it last night,' Connie said, 'and we thought you'd rather we went Dutch on this spree.'

'Spoils the party doesn't it, if you feel under any sort of obligation?'

Molly quite agreed and said that was exactly what she had expected. They were having lunch in a somewhat dark hotel, decorated with pictures of pale, bloodstained saints and the sullen heads of wild boars. Nicholas ordered large plates of pasta, slowly followed by unidentifiable chops disguised in thick tomato sauce.

'Always stoke up well,' he advised Molly, 'when you're out. Grey Tart calls for stamina.' She thought he was describing some particularly lugubrious pudding but then he said, 'Great visual Art calls for stamina,' and she knew that she had misheard him. 'Once knew a chap who tried to do the Uffizi on a ham sandwich. Fainted dead away in front of the Botticellis. That's not the way to do Grey Tart. Now we've got to get you to "The Flagellation" before the Ducal Palace shuts.'

'The point is' – Connie tucked in to the large ice-cream she and her husband later ordered *come dolce* and Molly wondered why with such an intake of Art and sustaining lunches, the Tapscotts remained so stringy – 'what sort of place would you like for dinner in Urbino?'

'I know where you can get fish. And boiled potatoes. Get a lot of stamina out of a boiled potato,' Nicholas told her.

'I'd rather like to wander round a little by myself this evening,' Molly was firm.

'Well, yes, of course. We'd respect your privacy.'

'I'll write down the name of this fish place. If you'd like to go there on your own?'

'I hope you don't think I'm being rude.'

'Course not. That was one lesson you had to learn in the Consular Service. If people come to you, you do your level best to help them. But if they don't come, for heaven's sake don't pry. People can get very funny, you know, if you start prying into their business. They seem to resent it much more here than they do in the U.K. It must be the hot weather.'

'It's sometimes irresistible, isn't it, Mrs Pargeter, to pry just a little? Other people's lives do seem so terribly interesting.' Connie smiled at her in a way Molly found suggestive.

'My wife is of a more prying disposition' – the ex-consul dug his spoon into his ice-cream – 'because her mother was a continental. On the whole, U.K. citizens don't pry.'

After Sansepolcro they drove out of Tuscany and into Umbria.

The road snaked to a dizzy height and Molly saw, marked on the map she was holding, ALPE DELLA LUNA – the Mountains of the Moon, as Buck Kettering called it. Her guide drove the heavy car with considerable élan and, no doubt strengthened by his ample lunch, he hurled it into the hairpin bends and wrenched it away from the ever-approaching precipice. 'Nicholas got his training in tanks,' Connie shouted back at their passenger. So they drove through the high pass between Umbria and the Marche and down the valley towards Sant'Angelo in Vado, through a new sort of country whose signposts pointed up towards ski-lifts and the scattered houses looked like Swiss chalets. It all seemed far from the gentle hills around 'La Felicità'. Then they were out of the mountains and driving towards the sea, across a plain that seemed endless. Molly's faith in her mission began to drain away. Buck may have met Rosie Fortinbras in Urbino but why should he have stayed to await her arrival? And if she ever reached him what, after all, could she say except, 'I have come from your house to tell you that I now know what happened.' Had she, Molly began to wonder, entirely exaggerated the importance of the truth. Now she had it, what, after all, was she to do with it?

With one hand on his hip, almost in the same attitude as the pregnant Madonna, the young Lord of Urbino stands, barefoot and serene, between two evil counsellors. What are they plotting, discussing, arguing about? What terrible and irrevocable decisions they may have come to, no one can tell. What is certain is that they are far too involved in their own concerns to notice the act of cruelty which is casually, almost elegantly, taking place at the remote end of the building. Christ is standing, an impassive, white figure against a white column. The arms of the flagellators are raised gracefully. Pontius Pilate in a hat with a long peak is watching with detachment. It was the picture Molly had in her mind all the holiday and the one that she had come so far to see. All the books she had read told her that its importance lay in its effect on what the architecture of the Ducal Palace was going to be, on the perfect balance of its forms and its special harmony. Molly was interested, far more interested, in the mysterious involvement of groups of people in their own awful concerns. They can be together, she thought, by the same walls, on the same floor and know nothing of each other's lives. They can commit terrible acts quietly, casually, at the other end of a room and nobody seems to notice. Of the things she felt she had to do that day, looking at the picture was the most exciting and the most alarming. She shivered a little as she stood before it, and the Tapscotts hurried away to 'knock off the Raphaels, before the place closes'. She stood on alone, in front of the picture, half expecting Buck Kettering to step out of the shadows and explain it to her. She stood for a long time but nobody came and she decided to go on to the final stage of her journey.

The Palace built by Federico di Montefeltro at Urbino – a house the size of a city which shines like marble – made Molly, as she walked down its wide, shallow staircase and round the peaceful courtyard, feel almost regal. Something of the ham actor in her father came out in her and she felt well qualified to command servants and detect conspirators. She came out into the hard afternoon sunset and her servants, the Tapscotts, were standing by their car, the long day's Art done and already thinking of dinner.

'Stunning pictures,' Nicholas said.

'Are they? I only saw one.'

'Well, Mrs Pargeter. That's your privilege. On this trip, we want you to do absolutely your own thing.'

They had chosen a characterless hotel by the station. Their rooms adjoined and Molly could hear the indistinguishable bark and murmur of Tapscott conversation as she dialled 'La Felicità'.

'Hello, Mum,' Henrietta said. 'Having a good time?'

'Oh yes. We've seen most of the Pieros.'

'Lucky you,' Henrietta said, without envy.

'Everything all right?'

'Absolutely. Gamps has been invited to dinner and to stay the night tomorrow with Mrs Leadbetter. We think it's absolutely disgusting. And we've got a surprise for you when you get back.'

'What is it?'

'It wouldn't be a surprise if we told you that. Do you want to speak to Dad?'

'Not really.'

'Well, goodbye, Mum.'

'I love you.' Molly didn't say that sort of thing often. She put down the telephone. Then she left the hotel and didn't let the Tapscotts know where she was going.

CHAPTER
TWENTY-THREE

After such a long time of waiting and speculation, Molly was in
no great hurry to end her mission in failure or success. She had
looked up the Motel Vallombrosa in the phone book in her hotel
bedroom and, picking up a plan of the city from the concierge,
decided to walk through the streets to her destination on the road
out to Rimini. So she entered the walls under a grey sky, with a
wind shaking the dry tops of the cypress trees, and the sound of
thunder trundling around the countryside. She walked, climbed
steps and made her way, her plan in her hand to guide her, down
narrow passages, between dark buildings from which came the
sounds of blaring television sets, dogs barking and family
quarrels.

She emerged into a square blazing with lights, with cars hooting
their slow way through thick crowds of wandering sightseers.
Café tables under tall arches were filled, policemen were blowing
whistles, and standing in front of a tobacconist's she saw the
Tapscotts choosing postcards. She turned down a narrow side
street and walked for a while past dustbins and the backs of
restaurants. Then she climbed more steps, and walked down more
dark streets, in one of which she surprised a girl who seemed to
be younger than Henrietta kissing passionately and hurried on.
She walked in bravely through the bead curtain of a bar and
ordered a glass of white wine.

The uncertainties she had felt, the fear of failure, the illogical
disappointment at not finding Buck Kettering in the Ducal Palace,

had given way now to a quiet confidence in her mission. She stood at the zinc bar and drank the wine as though she had always been used to travelling alone. Then she paid, said *buona sera*, and went on her way.

She was half way across the town when she emerged into the Piazza Duca Federico, in front of the palace built by a man who would fight for whoever paid him, who took many prisoners for the sake of ransom and killed comparatively few. On one side of the square there was a café, where a crowd who looked like English and American students doing holiday courses on the history of art sat, and she saw the Tapscotts again, looking for an empty table. She retreated into the dark streets once more.

Leaving the walls again she walked through a dusty belt of trees and out on to the via Giuseppe di Vittorio. Cars behind flashed their lights and accelerated past. She walked on undeterred. In about half a mile she was rewarded. A headlight momentarily illuminated a board on which a busty woman and a muscular man were depicted sitting beside a swimming-pool in front of an apparently palatial building. MOTEL VALLOMBROSA ... she read; the other letters had unaccountably faded: A 500 METRI. In due course she found a gap in a scrawny hedge and was walking down an unweeded gravel drive towards the address on her book of matches. Then she came to a brackish pool in which floated a Coca-Cola bottle and a sheet of newspaper blown there by the wind. Beside it were a couple of rusty chairs and behind it a desolate erection in cracked concrete. Half a dozen cars with foreign number-plates were parked on the gravel.

The reception area of the Motel Vallombrosa was no more cheerful. There was a bar with three stools covered in torn plastic leopard-skin lined up in front of the espresso machine, and a few bottles and some dolls dressed as Italian peasants. A couple of plants wilted, the dry earth in their pots fertilized with cigarette ends; there was a bench covered in black plastic, also torn, and a coffee table on which the copies of *Oggi* and *Cronaca Vera* were yellowing with age. Molly went up to the reception desk which was attended, at that moment, by no one at all.

Behind the counter hung a calendar, not torn off for two months, showing a discontented girl wearing a black suspender belt and sitting on a motor car tyre. There were two rows of hooks, most of which had keys hanging from them, and a framed picture of the Virgin Mary on a cloud. On the counter against which Molly leant was the top of a tin of sweets filled with cigarette ends and an annoucement that the establishment took American Express. What it didn't seem particularly keen to take were customers. She stood and heard nothing but the wind stirring the branches outside and the distant sound of traffic. The storm had moved away, it seemed, to water other and more fortunate areas.

Then Molly looked down at the desk behind the counter. There was an old cash-book, a couple of biro pens, a German passport and a pocket calculator. Then she saw a list, she supposed of room numbers, some of which had names beside them. With no one to observe her she picked it up and started to read the names. KOENIG was the only K, and there was no sign of Kettering. Then she went through it again and saw, opposite 31 and written in faded biro, perhaps long before the other entries, T.B. ARNOLD. Her reaction was immediate. She moved behind the desk, took key 31 off the hook and went quickly through a glass door and up a concrete staircase. She was no longer speculating but felt certain that Buck Kettering was using, for whatever reason in this unlikely retreat, his first initials, and the name of his benefactor, Arnold Leadbetter. She went down an uncarpeted corridor and, without bothering to see if she had been noticed, unlocked the flimsy, plywood door of room number 31.

The place, she saw when she switched on the single, unshaded overhead light, was as unwelcoming as a prison cell and as austere as quarters in a monastery. The three-quarter sized bed had no pillow. The shower behind a torn curtain ran directly into a hole in the ground. In the cupboard she found three shirts and a pair of linen trousers hanging on wire hangers, and a locked suitcase, the most expensive-looking article in the room. Beside the bed was a book fit to take its place on the shelves in 'La Felicità': an illustrated copy of the memoirs of Benvenuto Cellini. And leaning up against the mirror on the dressing-table, beside a half-empty bottle of Italian brandy, was a picture postcard which relieved Molly of further doubts. It was 'La Flagellazione' from the Palazzo Ducale in Urbino. She looked in the drawers of this rickety piece of furniture and found nothing but underwear, socks, some neatly folded handkerchiefs and an insect spray. She sat on an upright chair facing the door and waited.

She was as clear in her mind, as detached as though she had taken some drug which made the heat, the tiredness, the pain of her period recede or seem to belong to someone else with whom she wasn't particularly concerned. She was as excited as she had always been when the great detective summons the suspects to the library and starts, slowly and logically, to reveal the truth until the moment when the guilty party, the least probable suspect, starts from a leather armchair shouting, 'Damn you, you'll never prove it!' She waited almost motionless and for a long time.

Then she heard footsteps in the corridor and voices. There was a conversation in Italian about a key; two men were talking. The door was unlocked and Buck Kettering stood looking at her. '*Bene, grazie,*' he said to some unseen motel attendant. Then he shut the door behind him.

CHAPTER TWENTY-FOUR

'Mr Kettering. You are Mr Kettering, aren't you?'

She had stood up when he came into the room, an act of recognition for the man she had thought about so often and pursued so relentlessly. And now he was there, between her and the door, standing solidly and barring her escape. Whatever she had in mind, she now had no alternative but to go through with it.

'I've got a photograph of you outside the café in Siena. Giovanna said it was you.' She called her evidence quickly, before he could deny his name. 'I'm Molly Pargeter. You know, I've taken your house.'

He stood silently, watching her. He was unshaven with the heavy-lidded eyes she had seen in so many paintings and his reddish-brown hair was brushed back without a parting. He was wearing his red shirt, linen trousers and a pair of leather sandals. He stood with his feet apart, as though waiting for an attack. The room seemed colder and she felt what she had not bargained for, real danger, and not the secondhand fear of detective stories. It was as though she had climbed to the top of a mountain and the only way down was dark and precipitous.

'Did she send you?'

'She?'

'My wife. Did she send you?' His voice was low and husky, still with traces of an East London accent mixed with the sounds of the Italian he had become used to speaking.

'Of course not.' She did her best to smile and got no response.

'I don't even know your wife. The only person I met at "La Felicità" was Bill Fosdyke.'

He looked at her, still without moving, as though the name meant nothing to him. 'Why did you come here?'

To tell him that she knew. That was the reason and some time, very soon, she would have to do it. But not yet. Not when he was standing so imperturbably between her and the door to the outside world, her life with Hugh and the children, and the Tapscotts who seemed ordinary now.

'I came,' she tried to say casually, as though they had just met at a party, 'to see the pictures. You suggested that, didn't you? In one of the letters. I wanted to see the Pieros. Particularly that picture.' She looked towards the postcard of 'The Flagellation'. His eyes also flickered towards it for a moment and then returned to the business of watching her.

'No pictures in this dump,' he told her. 'It's not exactly an art gallery.'

'I came here to see you. I thought I should tell you what I've discovered.'

'What've you discovered, Mrs Pargeter?'

'About Bill Fosdyke.' After so long she couldn't help herself and had to say it. 'About how he died.' It was as though she had been forced to blurt out something obscene.

'They say he got drunk and fell into an empty swimming-pool. That's what I heard.'

'Yes,' she told him. 'I heard that too.' Then there was a silence. She couldn't, for the moment, go on with the shockingly intimate business of accusing him.

Then he said, 'And how did you know where to find me?'

'Rosie Fortinbras.' She was compelled to be honest.

'Rosie told you?' He frowned.

'No, she didn't tell me. But I guessed she came here to see you.'

'She's an old friend.'

'An old friend of mine too.' That seemed to reassure him. He began to smile at her and she knew it was the smile that had launched a thousand dangerous deals when he ran the dark side of Arnold Leadbetter's business.

'I'm not too keen on my wife finding out where I am. Not just at present.'

'I guessed that.'

'There's plenty of reasons for a man not being too keen on his wife finding out where he is.'

'I'm sure there are.'

'To be perfectly honest with you . . .' And that, she thought, was how the crookedest dealing started, with a smile and a protest of honesty. 'I'm not staying here under my own name. That's sad, isn't it? Sad when I tell you what I think of my house and my children. And my wife. What I still think of my wife. But that's how bad things have got between me and Sandra. And it's no use trying to hide it.'

'I know you're calling yourself Arnold. After your old boss.'

'Did Rosie tell you that too?'

'Yes.' She lied, not wanting to alarm him by her powers of deduction, hoping that he would move away from the door, and wondering, if he did so, if she could leave him, her task unfinished and the truth untold. And then, to her considerable surprise, he offered her a drink. 'Take a glass of brandy, Mrs Pargeter?'

'Thank you.'

He disappeared behind the shower curtain and she heard his voice. 'You like the Pieros, then?' Her way of escape was open but she had to answer him.

'I'm not sure "like" is the right word.'

'And that one . . .' He came out from behind the curtain carrying two tumblers. He nodded at the postcard as he half filled them with Stock brandy. 'Undoubtedly the world's greatest small picture?'

'I'm not sure I understand it.'

'Oh, what don't you understand?'

It seemed extraordinary to her that they should be standing

together, in that bedroom, discussing a work of art. 'I don't know exactly what's going on.'

'You surprise me, Mrs Pargeter.' He had become more cheerful since he had, it seemed, decided to use his charm to disarm her. 'I thought you understood everything. Do sit down. You're quite safe. It's not *gran confort* but we don't have bugs in the furniture.'

He handed her a glass tumbler and she sat bolt upright on a fragile chair with a black plastic seat. He sat on the end of the bed and appeared to be laughing at her. He lifted his glass and said, 'Here's to marriage. Your's going all right, I sincerely hope?'

'Yes,' she said, impatient at his way of deflecting her purpose. 'Yes, of course.'

'You didn't come here with your husband?'

'I came alone. I came to see you.'

'Drink up, Mrs Pargeter. Then perhaps we can find out why.' Molly did as she was told. Then he thought of something which seemed to come as a relief to him. 'Don't tell me you've had some trouble with the water at "La Felicità"?' She was no more than a complaining tenant, such as he'd been accustomed to deal with all his life.

'Well, of course we have.' Molly was impatient; the brandy gave her courage and the words poured out of her. 'That must have been a bit of mistaken enthusiasm considering how deeply your family are all involved in the water business. I'm sure it wasn't meant to happen, any more than the pool was meant to be drained at the house Bill Fosdyke was looking after. That Claudio doesn't seem to be very efficient. He even gets letters delivered to the wrong people. The water business is all over. I didn't come all this way to complain about that.'

'Then why . . .?'

'My father wrote an article about Italian women.'

'Is that what you came to tell me?'

'He says,' she went on doggedly, 'that they like their husbands to be ridiculously jealous. Mrs Kettering, that is, Sandra, she's Italian, isn't she? I wonder how she felt when you found out about her and Bill Fosdyke.' The names, so familiar to her, had gone round and round in her head, changing places, during the past three weeks. 'He was quite a handsome sort of man, I suppose, If you didn't mind the squint. And tremendously anxious to oblige. No wonder you wanted him *lost and gone forever*.'

He was looking at her, unsmiling now; the coldness had returned. 'What did I want?' he asked, hardly above a whisper.

'Just what you wrote in your list left behind in the Kenneth Clark book on Piero. At least it was there until you came back and removed it.'

'Go on,' he said, no louder than before. So she began, methodically, to inflict his own story upon him.

'I'm sure you called on Fosdyke at that house to warn him off Sandra. I suppose you got into a fight. Two men fighting over a woman. When he fell in that way it may have been an accident. Really, I know no more about it except that you killed him.' She had said it now, the great obscenity. She caught her breath as he stood up and took a step towards her; a man, she had now realized, who was capable of killing.

'You know nothing of the sort!'

'Then why are you hiding?' She could not stop herself arguing with him. 'It's not just to get away from your wife.'

He looked at her for a long time, apparently considering the weapons he might use against her. Then he said, 'What do you expect, Mrs Pargeter? Do you expect money?'

She felt the flush rising to her neck and she looked at the dusty point of her sensible white shoe. 'Of course not!'

'I'm only staying here while certain things are being arranged. I'll be getting money in a day or two now.'

'Don't be ridiculous!' She had become brave enough to rebuke him. And he looked at her, apparently unable to understand her refusal of cash so easily earned.

'Then what have you come for?' She could scarcely believe

that she saw his eyes flicker towards the awful, hard, pillowless, three-quarter-sized motel bed.

'Nothing,' she said. 'I want nothing. Truthfully.'

All his manoeuvring was over. He stood quite still, the tumbler of brandy in his hand, his strong feet in sandals planted on the ground, and seemed to look out at nothing. He was the boy from Whitechapel, prepared to do anything to bring off a deal, but he was also Buck Kettering who had been struck speechless by the paintings he saw in Italy, who had made his house beautiful, who had lived in it like the king of a small country until his throne had been usurped and he was left an exile in an appalling motel. And there she had come, to flog him with her knowledge.

'I believe I can understand what you felt, if that's any sort of comfort to you.'

She knew that, having failed to make any sort of a deal with her, he had no idea what to do next.

'We'll be back in England in a couple of days,' she told him. 'You've got nothing to worry about as far as I'm concerned.'

'Nothing.' She couldn't tell if it were a statement or a question.

'I haven't told anyone about this visit. And I shan't. The friends I'm with know nothing about it.'

'Friends?' He looked at her with mistrust.

'Only some people' – she did her best to sound reassuring – 'who drove me over to see the paintings.' She finished her drink, feeling a shot of sweet fluid at the back of her throat and a dizziness when she stood up.

'You're leaving?' He seemed, then, to fear being alone.

'Yes. You won't see me again. Whatever secrets you have are perfectly safe with me.'

'Whatever secrets . . .' he repeated. 'How can I let you go?'

'Easily. I haven't come to make trouble.'

'I still don't understand. What have you come to make?'

'Sure. Goodbye, Mr Kettering.'

She walked past him then and went to open the door. She felt his eyes burning, heavy-lidded behind her but when she turned back to look at him he was again sitting on the end of the bed and seemed unable to move. She thought, he'll sit there for a long time, too tired to take the next step, quite uncertain of what the next step should be.

'I can find my own way out.'

He smiled at her faintly and let her go.

As she left the Motel Vallombrosa and walked beside the road which led out of the town, she was surprised to see, coming towards her under the trees, the pale figures of her guides, the Tapscotts.

'Great Scot,' Nicholas greeted her, 'there you are!'

'We looked everywhere for you. In some of the restaurants.'

'Why?' Molly was worried about news of the children. 'Nothing's happened?'

'Oh, absolutely nothing. Then we decided to do a tour outside the walls.'

'Not madly picturesque out here, is it? You might as well be in Basingstoke.'

'There's really no point in Italy,' Connie said, 'when it's not being picturesque.'

'Did you find somewhere decent for dinner?'

'I just walked and looked at things. I didn't really bother about dinner.'

'So it's back to the hotel then. Shall we wander?'

Molly allowed the Tapscotts to lead her back through the town. Connie said, 'Nicholas thinks there's no need to rush madly in the morning. We've done all we came for. Do you want to see anything else?'

'Nothing,' Molly told her. 'Nothing else at all.'

They parted in the hotel. As she undressed, Molly heard, through the thin wall between their adjoining rooms, Nicholas telephoning, although she could make out no words.

The ringing had echoed again in the marble-halled Roman flat. When she picked up the telephone Sandra Kettering learnt that her husband had gone to ground in a grotty motel called Vallombrosa and might still be there the next day if she wished to see him. Mrs Kettering, who had no intention of ever seeing her husband again, was grateful for the information and thanked the Tapscotts warmly. They had acted, she said, like true friends. Later she made further telephone calls and other arrangements for someone to visit Buck Kettering.

Molly fell into a deep and dreamless sleep as soon as her head touched the pillow. She was exhausted as though by an act of love.

CHAPTER
TWENTY-FIVE

The storm which had been threatening, summoning up its forces, bumping and trundling about the sky all the previous day, burst over Tuscany in the afternoon, washing dusty terraces, replenishing wells and making families abandon wet swimming-towels and saturated lilos by the side of pools to take refuge indoors, play Scrabble and think of England. Headaches were cured, wet lizards slid under stones and unexpected holes were found in the roof of 'La Felicità'.

Rain didn't fall in Urbino. There Molly woke late, feeling unusually well and rested. She bathed and dressed slowly and, when Mrs Tapscott knocked at her door, asked if they could do some shopping before they started home. Walking through the streets their roles were reversed. It was Molly who, apparently released from all anxiety, chattered endlessly. The Tapscotts were frequently silent and Nicholas no longer looked at his watch, nor did he make sure that they kept up to schedule. As they walked round the walls a police car went wailing past them, followed by an ambulance driven at speed. At last they got started and Nicholas thought that they might as well have another lunch in Sansepolcro. 'With any luck, we'll get back too late to paint. Won't have to discover our complete lack of hidden talent until tomorrow.'

Late that afternoon Nancy's chauffeur arrived to take Haverford to the Villa Baderini for dinner and to stay the night.

He splashed out to the car, wearing his panama hat at a rakish angle and carrying a small suitcase. 'My respects to Molly Coddle when she gets back to the family circle,' he shouted at Hugh, 'and I hope to relieve her of all responsibility for my continued existence.'

When he arrived at the Villa the door was opened unbidden by the sallow manservant, who had clearly heard the car crunching the gravel, and Haverford was swallowed in the shadows. The curtains flapped at the tall windows; outside the cypresses bent in the wind and the swimming-pool was lashed into a miniature storm at sea. Climbing the staircase under the domed and painted ceiling, with a man in white gloves carrying his suitcase in front of him, Haverford felt that he was entering into his inheritance at last. There was no sign of Nancy in the silent house and when he was shown into his room he asked in his phrase-book Italian, '*Dov'è la camera della Signora Leadbetter?*'

'*La Signora sta dormendo.*'

'*Si. Capito. Ma dov'è sua camera da letto? Dov'è?*' he repeated, when the man seemed reluctant to come out with the information.

'*A destra,*' the man said finally, waving a hand in its general direction. '*In fondo al corridoio.*' He then left Haverford with a token bow and an expression of deep contempt.

Not in the least put off by his reception Haverford arrived in the drawing-room in the very best of spirits. He had bathed in the marble, gold-tapped tub adjoining his room and anointed himself with a liberal selection of the colognes and after-shave lotions there displayed. He had enjoyed a siesta under the silken canopy of a four-poster bed topped with the Baderini escutcheon and awoken to switch on the lights, one fixed on the end of a huge candle in the hands of the Baroque statue of a Cardinal, another gently illuminating the cream and rose coloured flesh of a pair of Marie Laurencin girls over the fireplace. He wondered why anyone possessed of the wealth contained in the house should bother herself with a small business concerning the water supply, but told himself that the rich keep rich by concerning themselves in small businesses and, in any event, he had always preferred to treat the process by which money is made as being too tedious for his attention. He dressed himself with considerable care in his off-white suit and a mauve shirt with a pink bow-tie. He sprinkled a drop or two more of the eau-de-Cologne on the pink summit of his head, combed what was left of his hair and considered, as he glanced in a gilded and cherub-festooned mirror, that he hardly looked a day over sixty.

After all these preparations he was not best pleased to find Prince Tosti Castelnuovo occupying a minute corner of the sofa and reading *Country Life*. However, he said *buona sera* in as pleasant a manner as possible and requested a *gin e Schweppes* from the manservant.

The Prince, who apparently remembered the dramatic outcome of Haverford's last visit, said, 'Shall you be staying long?'

'Just possibly,' Haverford told him, 'the rest of my life.' Conscious of having, in his resentment at the presence of another guest, rather overstated his position, he retreated to the window and looked out at the rain pounding down on the old garden and the modern sculpture, 'I mean that I would like to stay here and complete my life's work, a tribute to the Socialism of Oscar Wilde.'

'Oscar Wilde?' The Prince's small head was pushed forward and quivering; his tortoise eyes blinked in alarm. 'You knew Oscar Wilde?'

'Well, scarcely. I was born about ten years after the divine Oscar went out to dine in Paradise. I suppose' – he looked at the ancient Prince who was gripping *Country Life* as though it were a link to the world of sanity – 'you and the great man might have overlapped. Just.'

'You say he was divine?'

'Can you think of anyone in history you would rather have join us at the dinner table tonight?'

'Oscar Wilde!' The Prince whispered, as though he had just

noticed, dangling over his head, a particularly large and un-common spider. '*Omosessuale!*'

'Well, yes.' Haverford plunged himself on the sofa beside the other guest, stretched out his legs and took a swig of his gin and tonic. 'I think he's been out of the closet for about ninety years. Like Michelangelo, Walt Whitman, Proust and Verlaine. You're not going to hold that against Oscar? He wanted to bring beauty to every class of society. He was one of nature's Socialists.'

'*Omosessuale*,' the Prince repeated in an even more sibilant whisper. He clearly didn't regard whatever sort of Socialism Oscar Wilde may have professed as any mitigation. To his amusement Haverford saw the old Prince press himself even more closely against the arm of the sofa as though to put the greatest possible distance between himself and the highly perfumed old writer. 'And who is Whitman?' Tosti asked, as though the poet were some particularly undesirable guest Nancy Leadbetter might have asked to dinner.

'All writers' – Haverford sounded extremely reasonable – 'must have a pronounced feminine side to their natures. I myself have always been drawn to woman as the insolent urchin, the daring little tomboy. Of course, I'm also deeply appreciative of the more voluptuous charms of our hostess tonight.'

'You are *omosessuale?*' The cracked voice was hardly audible. Before Haverford could further clarify the situation, however, the great doors swung open and, to the Prince's obvious relief, Nancy was among them.

Molly was glad to be back. 'La Felicità', on that evening of the storm, had never felt more like her loved and natural home, nor had it, even when they first arrived and found it so miraculously well-stocked with fruit and groceries, provided so warm a welcome. Her journey back with the Tapscotts was largely silent. They had used up all of their conversation on the way out, so she was glad to leave them ('We might have had a bit of a chance if that bloke Raphael hadn't done it all so blooming well, Mrs Pargeter') and squelch through the rain to the front door. And as she climbed up the stone staircase and met her family the house seemed to live entirely up to its name. She even heard a sound which had been absent from their lives for a long time. Hugh was singing. It was a number which had been popular when they first met. She wondered as she climbed the stairs if it had been her absence which had brought about such unusual happiness.

She stood at the kitchen doorway and saw them all engrossed in piling wood, collected from the garden and the neighbouring scrub on to the fireplace. For a moment they didn't notice her. Then Jacqueline saw her and ran towards her. She picked her youngest child up to hug her and the others turned to bombard her with information. They were going to use the grill for the first time. They had bought enormous steaks in Mondano and they were having baked potatoes. Gamps was off with his girlfriend and it would be just them. Jacqueline could stay up, couldn't she? The storm had been tremendously exciting. At one point in the afternoon, all the sky at the back of the house had been white with lightning. Only Hugh stood silent by the fireplace, looking at her as though he had never seen her before.

He had thought of her while she had been away as the Molly he knew all too well; the big, untidy woman with fair, untidy hair, given to uncontrollable flushes. She was a woman who seemed seldom relaxed, who lurched at life, screwing herself up for a series of attacks only some of which were successful and many of which were inspired by panic. She was a wife who caused him guilt and had not, for a long time now, brought him pleasure. The fact that she had received no pleasure from him hadn't made him feel less inadequate. But now as he looked at her she seemed to be a different person entirely. The rain had flattened her fair hair and her cotton dress was wet, clinging to her like a dress in a painting. Her size, so calmly and contentedly was she standing with her youngest child in her arms, made her seem not clumsy but beautiful. The smile on her face was one of fulfilment. He felt something he hadn't experienced for so long he barely recognized it. He desired his wife.

'What would you like?' He moved towards the cold white wine, open on the table.

'I think I'd like a swim.'

'Of course you would.'

Molly swam up and down the pool ten times as the rain splashed around her, the thunder still rumbled in the distance and there was an occasional lightning flash. Each length she swam made her feel more contented.

At dinner Haverford seemed unable to keep off the subject which made Prince Tosti most nervous.

'All artists need a patron,' he told Nancy as he helped himself liberally to wine. 'Patronage is as old as art itself. Even Shakespeare.'

'Shakespeare?' the Prince repeated fearfully.

'What would Shakespeare have been without the kind hospitality provided by his long-time boyfriend, the Earl of Southampton?'

'*Omosessuale*,' the old man whispered in despair, looking up at a corner of the painted ceiling.

'Patronage is not a favour conferred on a genius, it is his birthright. Where would Tchaikovsky have been without the Von Meck woman?'

'Tchaikovsky.' Tosti Castelnuovo could be seen to wince.

'Or Haydn without Prince Esterhazy?'

'*Omo* – ' Tosti began fearfully, but Haverford cheerfully set his mind at rest. 'Not to worry. I've never heard it suggested that old papa Haydn was a poofter!'

'Where's your daughter tonight?' Nancy was getting tired of this discussion of people she had never met.

'At home, I think. She's been to Urbino.'

'She has?' Nancy put her hand over her glass to stop her servant pouring wine and became attentive. 'Why Urbino?'

'To see the pictures.'

'Oh. Is that all?'

'After all, he was one of the world's greatest patrons.'

Nancy frowned. 'I don't understand.'

'The old soldier of fortune.'

'Who your daughter went to see?'

'I am speaking, my darling dear, of Duke Federico di Montefeltro, who built his palace at Urbino to give support and comfort to Raphael and Piero della Francesca. Just as Nancy Leadbetter gives her hospitality to Haverford Downs, the Master of the Jotting.' Haverford was smiling at his hostess but he didn't appear to be joking.

When they went to the drawing-room for coffee Haverford hoped the old Prince would soon deprive them of his company but he stuck like a limpet to his refuge at the end of the sofa. At last Nancy yawned, got up and went to the door. Haverford followed her and whispered, 'I'm coming too.'

'Not now.' She put a hand on his arm, as he thought, affectionately. 'We mustn't upset Tosti.'

Why ever not? Haverford thought that he didn't mind if Tosti was reduced to a state of senile lunacy by the great love affair that was about to be renewed. However he nodded tactfully, whispered 'I know the way' to the figure of the retreating Nancy and went and sat opposite the other guest, discoursing eloquently on the divine Oscar's particular brand of Socialism which would free us all from the sordid necessity of living for others. The old Prince stared at him with growing panic until Haverford felt that it was his turn to yawn and go up to his bedroom.

'About that postcard . . .'

'For heaven's sake, what does that matter?'

The bedroom roof at 'La Felicità' had sprung unexpected leaks, water dripped regularly into a bucket on the stone floor. In a corner it sounded a high, more frequent note in a tin bowl. Molly found this was exciting, as though they were camping out.

She said, 'People have more serious things to worry about, I suppose, than postcards.'

'I felt you'd been away for a long time. Not just last night, but as though you'd taken this whole holiday on your own. I must say' – he was undressing carefully, avoiding the drips – 'I've felt a bit left out.'

'Have you? I've been so busy. It's all over now.'

He sat on the edge of the bed and looked up at her. She was standing in front of the long speckled mirror, an arm raised to brush her hair. He was unusually moved again by her beauty, the placid and fulfilled look of one of the Three Graces, an appearance she seemed to have discovered so recently.

He asked her, as he never did at home, 'Have you been happy?'

'I don't know about that. But not bored, not ever bored. I've loved the house, you know. And I've found out about a lot of things we never seem to meet at home.'

'What sort of things?'

'Lost souls. I suppose you could call them that,' she said in a quiet, matter of fact way, as though they were discussing plans for their journey back.

'You mean you found that in the pictures you saw?'

'Oh yes. In those too.'

That night they made love with an absorbed intensity they had never experienced before, even when their children were conceived.

Alone in his bedroom at the Villa Baderini, Haverford let an hour pass, and then a little longer, to be sure that the whole household was at rest. Then he went to the bathroom, renewed the fading cologne on his scalp and slapped his pink cheeks with after-shave. He found a tin of talcum powder, *Pour les Hommes*, and dusted himself liberally. To get himself into the right mood he thought steadfastly of certain young female page-boys and fearless tomboys he had known well. Then he tightened his dressing-gown cord, switched out his light and tiptoed out into the corridor. He turned right and went to what he thought was its extremity, before gently turning a handle and pushing open a door.

The room he entered seemed larger, grander even than his own. In the darkness he could just make out the swagged curtains of a huge four-poster bed and hear light and regular breathing. Haverford undid his dressing-gown, slipped it off and dropped it on to the floor. He advanced until his knees were touching the side of the bed and then he said, as clearly and as lovingly as possible, 'My dear darling. Shall we go on exactly where we left off?' He pulled back the covers and did his best to hop into bed. Then a light was switched on and he found himself staring into the terrified eyes of Prince Tosti Castelnuovo, who sat bolt upright with his old hands clutching a blanket about him. The sleeping villa was awoken with a scream of terror, as though the Prince had just seen the largest and most malignant spider in the world.

The Return

CHAPTER
TWENTY-SIX

The next day the sun returned, but it was a weaker sun with much of its feverish heat lost in a blue sky flecked with clouds. The wind still stirred the olive trees, exposing the silvery underside of their leaves, and shook the cypresses a little. The extremes of August were over and it was September weather, time to begin to think of returning to the cities, the end of school holidays, when Chiantishire was left to the Italians and those Brits who would spend the winter drinking, quarrelling, grumbling at the inadequate central heating and sometimes emerging with the sunshine to say, 'It makes it all worth while, being able to lunch out in December.' The richer Italians began to trickle back to their radiators and fur coats and games of bridge in apartments in Florence or Milan.

But on her last day in 'La Felicità', Molly found it still warm enough to sit out in her nightdress on the terrace at breakfast-time. In the house Giovanna ironed the final wash and the children began the interesting process of packing their suitcases, which they calculated would take them the entire day. Molly watched as Don Marco's little car came clattering down the track and her father got out of it carrying his suitcase. She watched an inaudible parting between Haverford and the priest, with many handshakes, smiles and promises. Then her father joined her on the terrace.

'Would it be too much,' he asked as he sat down, his voice full of suffering, 'to ask for a small cup of coffee and perhaps a roll?'

As she served him breakfast Molly asked, 'How's the wedding?'

'You heard about that?' Haverford gave the small, brave smile of a man who had told himself he could meet with triumph and disaster and treat those two impostors just the same.

'The priest told me. By the way, when did you become a Catholic?'

'Lapsed. I became a lapsed Catholic.' And he had to admit, 'One man in his time plays many parts. I somehow fancied the idea of a church wedding in Mondano, perfectly possible as I'm a widower. All that was yesterday. Things move rapidly in this part of the world.'

'Whatever happened?' She sat down beside him. He buttered a roll and added marmalade, bit into it as though it were the last square meal he expected to receive.

'Nancy sent me home without breakfast this morning. She said I'd better get back to you, Molly Coddle. She seemed to think I needed constant supervision.'

'Whatever' – Molly didn't seem unduly put out – 'did you do this time?'

'I lost my way.'

'That doesn't surprise me.'

'I lost my way and strayed into the wrong bedroom.' Haverford couldn't suppress the beginning of a chuckle. 'I tried to tuck up with that aristocratic old fart who's scared to death of poofs and spiders, to neither of which breed do I happen to belong. I gave him, I'm delighted to say, the shock of his declining years.'

'How did Nancy come into it?'

'Because of the screams.'

'Whose screams?'

'Old Prince Anti-Pooferini's. He wailed like a banshee and she rushed on stage and calmed him down, mopped his brow and poured *acqua minerale* down his old gizzard. Then she announced that they were getting married.'

Her father looked at her with watery blue eyes and crumbs down the front of his shirt. Against all her better instincts, and despite the fact that he smelt of stale eau-de-Cologne, she felt sorry for him.

'She said Arnold had always called her his Princess and now she was going to be one in real life. She's selling up round here and moving to Milan. He's got a town house there and a villa on Lake Como. It seems she's given up the water business, so I couldn't really put the screws on her.'

'The water business . . .' Molly seemed to be remembering the distant past. 'That was never important.'

'You thought it was once.'

'When I first found out about it.'

'Took a high moral tone with me, from what I remember.'

'There's no point in doing that with you.'

'I'm so glad you understand that at last.' Haverford looked at his daughter as though there was a possibility they might be friends. 'I'd hoped Nancy would be my patron. I could have done my book. I've always wanted to be between hard covers. Anyway, I always felt at my best in palaces. If you're not going to marry me, I told her, at least you could keep me as a sort of writer in residence.'

'What did she say to that?'

'She said I'd nearly given her precious Prince Tosti a heart-attack. Neither of them wanted to see me in the house at breakfast. Somewhere around dawn I rang Don Marco and he brought me back to you.'

'I see.' She drank her coffee. Jacqueline came out of the house and clambered on to her grandfather's knee, pleased to see him home.

'Poor old Molly Coddle. You're stuck with me for ever.'

'I always thought I would be.'

'Well, one thing's absolutely for sure.' Haverford seemed to cheer up. 'She's not going to get much of a rogering from that geriatric. And he flattered himself that I fancied him! The world, I tell you, Molly Coddle, is full of self-deceivers.'

*

After breakfast Hugh and Molly drove into Mondano together. He got the car filled up for their journey to Pisa airport the next morning and she went into Lucca's shop to buy the lunch. As the shopkeeper found her parmesan cheese and ravioli, she remembered Fosdyke, *lost and gone forever*, who had taken some pride in showing her where to get Oxford marmalade.

'Mrs Pargeter. I believe you're leaving us?' She turned round and found herself looking into the grey, slightly mocking eyes of the Baronessa Dulcibene.

'I'm afraid so. Back to London tomorrow.'

'And your trip to Urbino. Was that worth the detour?'

'I think so.'

'I'm so glad that it turned out to be a success. The dear old Tapscotts told us exactly where you went.'

Molly looked at the amused woman who was dressed so elegantly for shopping in Mondano. Suddenly, she wondered about the Tapscotts. Had they been only too anxious to take her wherever she wanted to go? Perhaps it didn't matter any longer.

'He has left me at last, the terrible Manrico.'

'The dog?'

'Oh, yes. Last night. He bit through his chain and he must have run off somewhere. To you perhaps?'

'No.' Molly shook her head. 'He didn't come to us. I remember I never heard him barking.'

'Quite honestly, Mrs Pargeter, we are extremely glad to see the back of him.'

That was the last conversation Molly had in Italy about the matters which had concerned her so much that summer. After lunch she and Hugh packed together and early next morning they all set off for Pisa airport. Giovanna spent the next two days cleaning and scrubbing and removing all traces of the Pargeter family from 'La Felicità'. Their lease was at an end and their temporary occupation over.

*

It was October and Molly was giving Jacqueline her tea in the kitchen of the house in Notting Hill Gate, baked beans on toast and bacon, of which she couldn't resist eating a good deal. Henrietta had her homework spread over the table and Samantha was stopping and starting her way through a Chopin mazurka on the piano in the living-room. Hugh was leaving his office in Chancery Lane to come home. That morning he had received, to his considerable relief, a letter from Mrs Tobias, telling him that she intended to marry a certain Charlie Slotover, a partner in her ex-husband's business, and, much to her regret, she felt that their lunching days were over.

'Mum,' said Henrietta. 'I know you'll say no to this.'

'You want to go to the Muckrakers Club?'

'I knew you'd stop me.'

'What is it? A party?'

'Chrissie Kettering's birthday.'

'Oh. Have you been seeing Chrissie lately?' To her surprise Molly found that she felt very little curiosity about the matter.

'No. A girl who goes to our school knows Chrissie. She told her to ask me. By the way, something awful's happened to her.'

'To the girl?'

'No, to Chrissie.'

'What?'

'About her father.'

And then time rolled backwards, to the sunlit kitchen in 'La Felicità', with the deafening sound of insects, the smell of wild mint and fennel, and the silver olive trees and purple hills beyond the windows. Molly held her breath for a moment and then said, 'What about her father?'

'He was killed in an accident. Some time ago. I think it was just before we came home.'

'An accident?'

'A lorry, I think it was. In somewhere called Urbino. Is that where you went? The driver didn't even stop, so Chrissie's not at all sure how it happened.'

Time stopped and Molly thought, what have I done? I found Buck Kettering. But who else did I lead to him? Who had wanted him found so that the death of her improbable lover, the untimely end of Signor Fixit, might be avenged. She paused with a fork full of Jacqueline's baked beans raised to her lips. 'I found you, Buck,' she said to herself. 'Did I kill you by finding you?' But the question, as she asked it, immediately sounded absurd, belonging to a crime of passion between strangers, far from her home, living in a house she would never see again. What was left to her was a new passion in her own life, a love affair with her husband which had been lit as a small fire, may be by a spark from a furnace.

Time stopped and then returned to London in the rain, to October, to homework and the children's tea. She ate the baked beans gratefully.

'Can I go, Mum?'

'Yes. Of course you can go.'

Molly was looking at the notice-board on the wall to which were attached lists of school dates, vital telephone numbers and some of the children's drawings. Pinned to it there was a postcard reproduction of 'The Flagellation' by Piero della Francesca, said, by some, to be undoubtedly the greatest small picture in the world.